JILTING JORY

*Compliments of
K. Lyn Smith*

K. LYN SMITH

Copyright © 2022 by K. Lyn Smith
All rights reserved. No part of this publication may be
reproduced, stored or transmitted in any form or by any means
without the prior written permission of the author.
The only exception is by a reviewer,
who may quote short excerpts in a review.

Jilting Jory is a work of fiction. Unless otherwise indicated,
names, characters, places and incidents are products of the
author's imagination, or are used fictitiously.
Any resemblance to actual events, locales or persons,
living or dead, is entirely coincidental.

ISBN: 978-1-7376579-2-7

"The heart has reasons
that the reason knows not of."

- Blaise Pascal

PROLOGUE

LONDON, 1812

Miss Anna Pepper listened for footsteps beyond the library door, biting her lip against a runaway smile. A small card lay on her father's desk, the words simple and yet so powerful they'd caused her stomach to drop: *For my beloved daughter on her birthday.*

Beloved. Had he actually used that word? She stared at the card some more, but there was no mistaking the letters that flowed in her father's bold script.

Hearing nothing but the chatter of a bird beyond the library's leaded window, she carefully opened the burgundy jeweler's box that lay beside the card. After nearly sixteen years of waiting for her father's notice, she was unsure what she would find inside, but the delicate locket stole her breath. An oval of smooth, green enamel wrapped in gold filigree, it beckoned to be released from its velvet cocoon. She settled instead for running a fingertip across the top, reveling in the lacy pattern of the wirework.

She couldn't recall ever receiving a gift from her father, much less one so fine. It was unlike any locket she'd seen before. Certainly her sister Margaret—despite her perfection in all things—had never received anything so lovely. Why, her father must have had it commissioned especially for her.

Tears burned the backs of her eyes as she pondered his sudden affection. Then, refusing to over-question this unexpected change, she slowly closed the box and replaced it on his desk. Her birthday was next week; there was time yet to practice her reaction. She peered around the door to ensure no one was in the hall before she hurried to her room with a skip in her step.

Anna's birthday arrived, and excitement bubbled in her chest as she approached her family in the breakfast room. She was pleased her great-aunt Catherine had come to visit, but her smile slipped when she saw her father had not joined them.

Rallying, she said brightly, "Good morning, Mama. Aunt Catherine, it's wonderful to see you." She circled the table and placed a kiss on her aunt's proffered cheek.

"My dear," Aunt Catherine said. "Sixteen agrees with you. Look how radiant you are."

Anna blushed at the praise. "Thank you, Aunt. Please say you'll join us on our outing to the shops today." She pressed her hands together. "Please, please, please?"

"Anna, it's not polite to beg," Margaret admonished with all the wisdom of her eighteen years.

"Your sister's right, of course," her mother said.

"Yes, Mama," Anna said, catching Aunt Catherine's wink. She moved to the sideboard to fill a plate, hesitating over the sliced pound cake as she felt her mother's eyes at her back. It was her birthday, though, and she felt daring. She forked a tiny piece onto her plate and ignored her mother's stare as a footman poured her chocolate.

"My dear, I'd be delighted to join you on your excursion," Aunt Catherine said. "We shall have a grand time. Perhaps we can enjoy ices at Gunter's after we've exhausted ourselves shopping."

Anna beamed, unable to contain her glee. Shopping, ices at Gunter's, a gift from her father. Could this day get any better?

"That would be lovely, don't you think, Mama? Mary Riverton says we must try the lavender ice."

Her mother's frown intensified, but after a moment's hesitation, she relented. "Yes, of course." Gunter's had been Aunt Catherine's suggestion, so she could hardly disagree. Few dared to disagree with Aunt Catherine.

Anna nibbled the corner of her lip then asked, "Do you think Papa would like to join us? For ices, that is?"

Her mother flinched in surprise. "You know your father is too busy for such diversions, and we'll have a much more pleasant outing without his grumbling about the expense."

"Yes, Mama." Anna ignored the familiar sting of disappointment. Her aunt gazed at her with something that looked like pity, and Anna straightened, pulling her shoulders back. They didn't know what she knew. They didn't know about his gift.

After breakfast, Anna passed the library, hesitating at the closed door. Her father could hardly give her the locket if he didn't see her, could he? Before she could change her mind, she lifted a hand and rapped quickly on the door.

"Enter," came his gruff command.

She hesitated then turned the knob. Her father's head was down, his gaze focused on the papers before him as she approached the desk. The burgundy jeweler's box was nowhere to be seen.

"Good morning, Papa—Father," she corrected. He'd always preferred formality from her. He looked up, clearly surprised to see her in his domain, and she offered a tentative smile.

"Yes? What is it?" he asked.

She swallowed. "We're going to Gunter's today, and Aunt Catherine is to join us." Why did her tongue always feel too thick for her mouth when she spoke to her father? "Would you like to accompany us?"

He turned back to the pages on his desk. "I've matters that require my attention. I haven't the time for frivolous pursuits."

Anna clenched her hands and blinked, waiting for the sting to ease from her eyes. "But—I thought—"

She stopped, confused. She'd thought . . . what? That he'd wish to join his *beloved daughter* on her birthday? The burning in her eyes intensified and she curtsied, anxious to leave before the tears fell in earnest.

―――

A FOOTMAN BALANCED A TOWERING stack of boxes as their party returned to the Pepper carriage. Anna had determined to enjoy the day despite the disappointing encounter with her father. He was often preoccupied with "matters" that required his attention, so his indifference was to be expected. She merely needed to be patient, a talent she'd yet to hone.

Of a certain, he'd present her with the locket that evening, perhaps with the family gathered 'round. Wouldn't Margaret be surprised? She put thoughts of her father from her mind and focused instead on the day's successes.

The weather had been fine, the shopkeepers accommodating. Nothing back home in Berkshire compared with the luxuries that could be found in London. They'd acquired several new bonnets and some lovely ribbons, and Aunt Catherine had insisted on buying Anna a new pair of slippers to celebrate her birthday.

In shop after shop, Anna had run her hands lovingly over bolts of fine silk and velvet, eager for her come-out so she might put up her hair and wear such elegant trappings.

"You must be patient," her mother said.

"But I'm ready to meet some eligible gentlemen now," Anna protested. "I don't see why I can't go with you and Margaret to the Haversham's supper next week."

"You know Mama won't bring you out until I marry," Margaret said.

"Then hurry your Mr. Claxton along," Anna grumbled.

"Never fear, sister. My plans in that direction are proceeding quite well."

"There will still be plenty of gentlemen left when you have your come-out," Aunt Catherine assured Anna, thumping her cane once for emphasis. "I dare say you'll have your pick of them like I did in my day. Why, I had three proposals within the first two weeks of my debut."

Anna sighed. "I would like to be so fortunate. How did you manage it, Aunt?"

"I will tell you a secret," Aunt Catherine said, leaning closer. "Confidence. And confidence, my dear, is naught but an illusion. The *appearance* of confidence far outpaces competence. Make them think you know what you're about, and no one will gainsay you."

"A handsome dowry doesn't hurt either," her mother added. "There's nothing that encourages a gentleman's affections more than money. And some strategic flirting."

"Pish," Aunt Catherine said. "Money merely gives you options, my dear. But you've much to recommend you, so you mustn't settle for anything less than love."

Anna's heart fluttered optimistically before she checked it. She didn't have anything special to recommend her, despite her aunt's words. She wasn't particularly accomplished or witty, although she looked forward to the day she could try her hand at flirting. She was vain enough to recognize her own beauty, but she suspected that once a gentleman came to know her—to truly know her—he'd find there wasn't much substance to her character. Why, her own father barely acknowledged her existence.

Then she recalled the jeweler's box and the card in her father's handsome script. *For my beloved daughter.* Perhaps he saw something worth his admiration after all.

———

ENERGY AND PIN MONEY SPENT, their contingent traveled to Berkley Square, where a waiter came to the carriage to take their orders. Several children played in the square beneath the watchful eye of a governess, and the sun cast its final warming rays of the day as Anna settled on a bench next to Margaret.

"Oh, look," Anna said, dipping a spoon into her lavender ice. "There's Mary Riverton and her mama." Her mother and aunt stilled, but Anna paid them no heed as she waved at Mary.

Anna's mother, for reasons she couldn't fathom, had always taken the Rivertons in dislike while

Anna found them perfectly enjoyable. She and Mary were of an age—indeed, their birthdays were only a week apart—and they shared common interests in fashion and the latest hairstyles.

Mary's father was a mysterious man who had been away making his fortune in America for as long as either of them could remember. Anna often reminded herself that while her own father may have been a disinterested parent, at least she knew what he looked like.

And yet, Mary's father often sent fanciful gifts, regardless of the distance, which was more than Anna could claim. She quickly chastised herself—her father had a gift for her now.

Mary towed her mother toward their bench. As the Rivertons approached, Anna noticed her own mother's lips pursing in an unattractive manner, causing white lines to fan at the corners. Surely, she would regret the wrinkles such a sour expression would cause. And her aunt, who had no ill liking for anyone, gazed down her thin nose at the Riverton pair.

Anna knew a moment of embarrassment for her family's poor manners, and she broadened her own smile to make up for their lack. Mary dropped her mother's arm and hurried forward with a dimpled grin. Clearly, she was near to bursting with news.

But as her friend neared, Anna's eyes widened. An oval of smooth, green enamel wrapped in gold filigree hung from a delicate chain about her neck. It was quite unlike any locket she'd ever seen before, save one.

Mary spoke as blood thundered in Anna's ears. "My father remembered my birthday," she said on a breathy whisper. "Just look what he's sent!" She lifted the locket for Anna to admire. "Isn't it the most beautiful thing you've ever seen? I think he must have had it commissioned especially for me."

―――

ANNA STARED AT THE EMPTY hearth in her bedchamber. It couldn't be true. Mary Riverton's father couldn't be ... No. It was a mistake. Mary's father was far away in America, and surely there must be two such lockets. But how odd ...

Determined to return her world to its proper axis, she ventured downstairs to find her father. Once he presented *his* locket, all would be right again. They would laugh over the coincidence of Mary Riverton receiving precisely the same necklace, although she wouldn't wish her father to feel poorly about purchasing such a common gift.

As she neared the drawing room, she heard the thump of Aunt Catherine's cane on the wool carpet, and her aunt's voice reached her from beyond the partially drawn double doors.

"Have you no shame, nephew?" Aunt Catherine asked. "A necklace?"

A footman stepped forward to admit Anna, and she dismissed him with a hurried wave of one hand while she listened without remorse. Surely her father would offer her aunt some explanation, a confused denial that would set things right again. But he was frustratingly silent, and her aunt continued.

"The gel's parading it before everyone, telling all and sundry of the wondrous gift her father has sent from America."

A sickening warmth flooded Anna's stomach, and she pressed a hand to her mouth.

"This is none of your concern, Aunt," her father replied. Glass clinked against glass, and she pictured him unstopping the decanter.

"I disagree, nephew. Have a care, or you'll bring disgrace upon our family. You have two perfectly fine daughters—proper daughters, I might add. You should direct your concerns in their direction and end this ridiculous association with the Riverton woman. It can serve no purpose."

Cold sweat beaded at Anna's hairline, and her hands began to shake. She pressed them together, but that only shifted the shaking to her legs. The blood rushing through her ears muffled their voices, and she shifted closer to the door. She heard her name, followed by a put-upon sigh from her father.

"The girl's a peagoose like her mother," he said. "A complete gudgeon with more hair than wit—"

"The *girl* turned sixteen today, in case you failed to notice." *Cane thump.* "She'll need to make her come-out once Margaret's wed. It won't reflect well on you if you neglect to see her settled comfortably."

"Fear not," her father said sharply. "The chit will be well dowered. What man in his right mind would willingly tie himself to such a creature without recompense?"

"I disagree, nephew." *Cane thump.* "She may lack polish, but she's young. She just needs to—"

"Anna?"

Anna jumped at the sound of her mother's voice behind her. She'd been so intent on the conversation in the drawing room that she'd not heard her approach.

"Mama," she said. Guilt warmed her face, but it was nothing to the sick churning in her stomach. "I'm not feeling well. I—I think I'll take supper in my room." And with that, she turned and fled, swiping angrily at her cheeks.

CHAPTER ONE

LONDON, 1819 – THE PRESENT

ANNA STARED INTO THE MIRROR above her vanity, searching for the doubts that bubbled and simmered within her. She was relieved to see only the smooth perfection of her skin. The serene expression of a bride on the eve of her wedding. All was as it should be, she told herself.

If she felt only vague enthusiasm for her upcoming nuptials, it was not cause for alarm. She may not have been brimming with joy, but at least she would be well turned out. Everyone would long remember how enchanting the bride appeared at her wedding breakfast, especially since the bride's ensemble would be superior to any worn the previous season by, well, anyone. That counted for something, didn't it?

Anna put a lid on her simmering doubts and tilted

her chin up. The appearance of confidence was key.

"The dress is lovely, Madame Deveaux," her mother said as the modiste adjusted one of Anna's sleeves. "As I knew it would be. You never disappoint."

Madame Deveaux nodded, accepting her due. "Miss Pepper, she is not as tall and willowy as one might wish, but the dress, it makes up for much."

Anna ignored the slight for there was no argument: the dress *was* stunning. Unlike Mary Riverton, who'd worn one of her attractive but unremarkable Sunday dresses for her own wedding, Anna would wear a gown created especially for the event.

Her mother had insisted that no expense be spared, and Madame had taken her at her word. Indeed, Mary Riverton had gasped on hearing of the pale rose silk that flowed beneath a pleated bodice and lace overskirt. Of the tiny cap sleeves and delicate embroidered flowers circling the hem. And Anna, shamefully, had taken perverse delight in flaunting her mother's extravagance.

But as magnificent as the dress was, the slippers were by far the best part. She lifted her hem and turned one foot from side to side to admire the exquisite creation. Crafted of ivory brocade with a dainty, gold-threaded vine, the slipper glinted and shimmered as she moved. They weren't the most sensible shoes—only the most intrepid dared to wear ivory in London's streets—but what lady wished to be sensible on her wedding day? And certainly, the delicate slippers eased the roiling in her stomach whenever she thought of her pending marriage.

"Of course, you must have Meg arrange your hair *à la Grecque*," her mother said. "That style always makes you appear taller."

"Yes, Mama."

"I think we must tuck some more flowers in your bonnet," her mother continued. "The ivory silk poke with the little velvet rabbit is so darling, but more flowers couldn't hurt. Lady Stinton's daughter wore pink roses when she married Burbridge, and everyone commented on what a lovely picture she made."

Anna agreed that roses would be a nice addition. She didn't believe in fairy tales, but that wasn't to say she couldn't look the part of a woodland nymph wreathed in flowers and vines.

Her mother gasped at Anna's reflection, eyes narrowing. "Is that a freckle?"

A freckle? Where? Anna leaned closer to the mirror, then wiped a spot from the glass.

"No, Mama. It was merely a spot on the glass."

Her mother sighed in relief, one hand pressed to her chest. "*Ach*, you gave me such a fright. You know gentlemen don't like freckles."

As Madame Deveaux and her assistant collected the tools of their trade, her mother leaned in.

"I told you Greenvale would come up to scratch, didn't I? All it needed was a little extra effort on your part. Pinch your cheeks, my dear. You're a trifle pale."

Her mother fussed with the ribbon at the back of Anna's dress while Anna pinched her cheeks. The door clicked as the modiste left, leaving just the two of them.

"It's just as well your pursuit of Mr. Corbyn didn't take," her mother continued. "And thank heavens you had the foresight to refuse Signor Rossi. Granted, his income rivals your own, but if you'd married him, you wouldn't be marrying a baron tomorrow." She shook her head as if she couldn't quite believe the words.

Anna winced as she normally did whenever her mother mentioned the Italian merchant. "Mama, I didn't *refuse* Signor Rossi," she reminded her as she leaned toward the mirror to tuck a stray curl into place. "I left him on the steps of Santa Maria. They are two different things, and I'm certain he, of all people, recognizes the distinction."

Her mother's face wrinkled in a thoughtful frown before she remembered to smooth her expression. "Well, the result was the same. We were fortunate he was too embarrassed to make much of a fuss over the matter, but I do wish you'd handled the situation with a little more grace. I was thoroughly enjoying Italy."

Her mother's Prussian heritage was showing in her slightly sibilant S's, her heightened accent the only sign of any lingering distress she may have felt over the unfortunate events with Signor Rossi. She clucked her tongue.

"I've always told you to follow your head rather than sentiment, but I suppose your impulsive nature will be Greenvale's problem now."

Following her head was precisely what had brought Anna to the position in which she now found herself. Her heart may not have leaped at the thought of marrying Greenvale, but her head had made up for the lack with logical arguments in favor of the match. Most of which she couldn't recall at the moment.

But she couldn't dispute that while Greenvale was not the most romantic of suitors, at least she'd not yearn for his affection, and that was reason enough to marry him. The ups and downs of unfulfilled hopes could be so very exhausting, after all.

Her mother tilted her head to one side then narrowed her eyes on Anna's reflection. "You're not having second thoughts about Greenvale, are you?"

"What? Of course not, Mama," Anna said, forcing her eyes to meet her mother's gaze. She waited a fraught second while her mother attempted to read her mind.

Satisfied with whatever she saw (or didn't see) there, her mother continued.

"Good. That's good. Your father, may God rest his soul, would have been pleased to finally have a title in the family. And while we were able to smooth over one jilted fiancé—and Rossi a papist, no less—don't imagine we can be so fortunate a second time. Even a face and fortune as lovely as yours can't overcome a scandal of that magnitude."

Her words heated Anna's skin. She swallowed and wondered what her mother would say if she knew the number was not *one* jilted fiancé, but two.

Although Anna didn't often allow it, she let her thoughts wander now to the boy she'd left standing by a stream in Cornwall, waiting for an elopement that never happened. Jory Tremayne.

An uncomfortable pressure built in her chest, and her eyes burned, which was precisely why she usually forced such thoughts aside. But she couldn't help wondering if he'd ever married, if he was happy now.

With his broad grin and easy temperament, eyes that sparkled like the sea beneath a summer sun and hair the color of wet sand, she was certain he must have found someone to take to wife. A plump, rosy-cheeked dairy maid, perhaps. A boy like that didn't remain unattached for long. Her confidence in the fact eased the unpleasant tightness, and she released a breath.

Her mother plucked at the seam of her dress, recalling Anna's thoughts from the past.

"You appear thicker about the middle. I was certain Madame Deveaux was going to have to let out your seams. Have you been eating Cook's pound cake again?"

"No, Mama," Anna replied. She looked into the mirror again but only saw the same trim figure from the day before. Short, yes, but trim. She turned to one side then the other. What did her mother see that she couldn't? Was the mirror faulty?

"You must make better choices so you don't go to fat," her mother continued. "You don't wish Greenvale to regret marrying a merchant's daughter. Just because you've caught the goose doesn't mean he's well and truly cooked."

Goose ... What? Anna wasn't sure what her mother meant by the odd metaphor, but she'd never been overly fond of goose. Nevertheless, she agreed. It was much easier than debating the matter.

"Yes, Mama."

She'd reached three and twenty this year, and as her mother frequently reminded her, spinsterhood loomed like the dark specter of death, beckoning with a skeletal finger. Thanks to her dowry and a hefty inheritance from Aunt Catherine, Anna had her pick of suitors, so putting an end to her unwedded state should have been a simple matter.

Not for the first time, she wished she'd been more successful in her efforts to secure Harry Corbyn the previous summer. A younger miss might have colored at the memory of how she'd shamelessly pursued the man, but she was long past the age—and humility—of blushes.

She'd not been overly concerned that he had no fortune or title as she had fortune enough for the both of them. No, Harry's appeal had been in his imminent departure. He'd recently sailed to Egypt for an extended excursion or expedition or some such. If one must have a husband, then a husband thousands of miles distant was surely the secret to, if not a perfect marriage, at least a tolerable one.

But Harry had been immune to both flirtation and fortune. So now, instead of an absent husband, Anna found herself stuck with Greenvale, who gave no indication of removing to distant lands anytime soon.

With her fortune to recommend her, she had no illusions about why, of all the ladies in London, Greenvale had chosen her. Certainly, he'd not proposed out of any degree of affection.

But what if, just possibly, they grew to love ... No. She forced the thought down. Allowing herself to hope for more would only make her miserable in the end.

She mentally cursed Jory Tremayne for causing her to feel sentimental.

"Heavens," her mother said. "You must remember to keep your smile about you. A frown like that will put Greenvale off for certain. A pleasant demeanor and some flirtation will go far toward managing a man like him. Now, let's get you out of that dress before it wrinkles."

―――

THAT EVENING, ANNA STUDIED LORD Greenvale across the broad expanse of the Pepper dining table and tried to picture him as a trussed and cooked fowl. The image escaped her.

He looked up and caught her staring. With a subtle motion he saluted her with his wine before turning back to the matron seated next to him.

"Will you take a wedding trip, Miss Pepper?" the gentleman beside her asked as he sliced a buttered parsnip.

Anna opened her mouth to respond, then snapped it closed when she realized she didn't have an answer. She was to be married tomorrow, and she didn't know where she would lay her head tomorrow night. Her heart skipped uncomfortably at the thought.

"Miss Pepper and I will travel to York," her fiancé said. "I thought to remain in London for the Season, but I've estate matters up north that can't be put off."

What? York!

No lady of her acquaintance took a wedding trip to York. Mary Riverton had toured the Continent. Paris or Rome, Brighton or Bath... any of those would have been better responses than *York*.

Anna took a long sip of wine to calm her stuttering heart. She swallowed then caught her mother's narrowed eyes from the head of the table. With deliberation, she replaced her glass on the damask cloth and touched a napkin to the corner of her mouth.

There was no need to panic. It was only a wedding trip. She was certain they would return to London once Greenvale concluded his business. Why, it was possible her presence in York wouldn't even be needed.

She'd speak to Greenvale about the matter, perhaps apply some strategic flirtation. It would be good to begin their marriage with clear expectations, and that included the expectation that she would not spend the London Season in York.

Then she brightened. York wasn't quite Egypt, but it was distant yet. Perhaps if Greenvale remained there, they could lead separate lives after all.

One more night, she reminded herself. She only had to quell her nerves for one more night, and tomorrow she would be a married lady. Certainly, she'd feel better once the deed was done.

But . . . York. Gads.

When the gentlemen joined the ladies in the drawing room, Anna maneuvered Greenvale to a quiet corner. Tall and angular, with dark brows slashing across a wide forehead, he towered above her petite stature. She took a tiny step back before planting her feet. *The appearance of confidence*, she reminded herself.

"Miss Pepper," he said. "I haven't told you how lovely you look this evening. Are you in readiness for our nuptials tomorrow?"

"Yes, of course," she assured him. She didn't miss that he still hadn't told her how lovely she looked, but she brushed that aside. There were more important matters to discuss.

She placed a soft hand on his sleeve and glanced at him through her lashes. He gazed back at her coolly, unaffected, so she curved her lips in a motion meant to draw out the dimple in her right cheek. When his expression softened, she continued. "I wished to inquire about your comments at supper, my lord. We're to journey to York?"

"Ah, yes. I've just learned of a problem with one of my estates, so I'm afraid we'll need to travel north. I hope that's acceptable?"

Anna tapped the corner of her mouth with one finger, drawing his eyes to her lips. "Well... I was thinking perhaps I should remain in London." At his silence, she added, "At least until your estate business is concluded and you're able to return. Then we could take a proper wedding trip."

She lifted her brows in an expression that was both hopeful and guileless. Wound a springy curl about her finger while she awaited his response.

Greenvale pressed his lips together. "Miss Pepper, I can't say how long my estate matters will keep me in York. Certainly, it will be better for us to travel there together."

She ground her teeth at his continued insistence on formality. They were to be *married*, but still he called her Miss Pepper. Unbidden, the memory of Jory Tremayne's rich, Cornish lilt wrapped about her given name sent a tingle clear to her feet. She wiggled her toes inside her slippers to dispel the sensation.

"I'm sure you know best," she said to Greenvale, "but... Lady Pilkerson's ball is next week, and Lady Rotherton's rout the following Thursday. Perhaps I should stay and... and represent the house of Greenvale." She thought that was a particularly inspired touch. "Here. In London." She gazed at him serenely, certain he would see the logic of such a sound argument.

"Miss Pepper," he said. "I don't think such a course would be a fitting start to our marriage. We'll travel to York tomorrow. Together." And with that, he bowed then left her frowning in the corner.

That was it? No discussion? No consideration of the very rational argument she'd made? Certainly it didn't bode well if her flirting talents were fated to be lost on her future husband.

CHAPTER TWO

~~~~

THE NEXT MORNING, ANNA WOKE early after a fitful night. She pulled aside the bed hangings to find a darkened room and fading cinders in the fireplace, an unprecedented event as she couldn't recall ever rising before the staff had tended the fire.

She peered at the clock on the mantle, squinting in the weak moonlight. Five o'clock. *In the morning.* Gads.

She placed bare feet on the cold floor and shivered. Reaching for a dark candle, she hurried to the hearth and held the wick to a lingering ember until it caught, then she pulled her dressing gown tight about her waist.

The warm, rumpled bed linens and plump, feathered pillows beckoned, but she knew she'd not find any more sleep.

Her dress hung on the front of the wardrobe, the

rose silk and pale lace glowing in the candlelight. Her heart picked up its pace again, although not in excited awe for the gown as one might expect. She closed her eyes and forced a slow breath through her nose.

One aborted wedding was regretful. Two, a trifle concerning. But three—three aborted weddings would be comical, in a bordering-on-hysterics sort of way. Three failed weddings were unconscionable. She was fairly certain Mary Riverton had only had the one, fully executed wedding.

She knew this, and yet she couldn't envision donning the rose silk, no matter how exquisite the gown was. Couldn't picture the precious vine-wrapped slippers treading the aisle of St. George's. Couldn't imagine pledging herself, body and soul, to Greenvale, much less traveling to York.

York. What on earth would she do in York?

And yet, if she didn't proceed with this wedding, she might as well take herself off to the moors, for no one would receive her if she jilted Greenvale. No amount of fortune would excuse such an action. Her life might as well be forfeit.

Very well then.

She sniffed and straightened then gave a sharp tug on the bell pull to summon her lady's maid. Now that she was resolved once again, she was anxious to have the matter done with.

Meg arrived with gratifying swiftness given the unholy hour of the morning.

"Miss Pepper?" she said with surprise and a curtsy. "Are you well?"

"Yes, of course," Anna replied. Although . . .

She swallowed. Was that a tickle in her throat? Perhaps she was coming down with something. The croup, perhaps, or a plague of some sort.

But no, she sighed. Such a happy occurrence would only delay the inevitable. Before she could begin fantasizing about a fatal carriage accident, she reined in her thoughts.

Meg bent to tend the fire and glanced at Anna over her shoulder. "Shall I have the kitchens send up breakfast, miss?"

Anna thought of Cook's pound cake, but she didn't think she could eat anything.

"No, just help me dress, Meg. I'm to be married today, you know." She tried to inject a note of eagerness into her voice, but she feared she only sounded feverish.

"You wish to dress? Now? But miss, it's barely five o'clock." Meg glanced at the still-dark window.

Anna frowned. She was to marry at ten—five hours still to go—so dressing now seemed a little silly, but she hoped focusing her attentions on the gown would settle her nerves. Perhaps seeing herself styled and shod would ease her anxiety.

She nodded firmly. "Yes, Meg. Please arrange my hair in the Greek style like we discussed."

"With the ivory ribbon?"

Anna nodded again then took a seat at her vanity while Meg heated the curling tongs. The familiar ritual had a calming effect on Anna's nerves, and she relaxed while Meg worked through sections of her hair.

As the maid began curling the right side, Anna asked, "Are you married, Meg?"

Meg's brows lifted as she looked at Anna in the mirror. "No, Miss Pepper."

"Betrothed?"

The maid blushed and ducked her head. "No."

"But you hope to be," Anna guessed.

"Yes, miss. To my Will, just as soon as he's saved enough."

"You love him then?"

Meg's blush deepened and she nodded, biting her lip. "Yes, miss. That I do."

Anna frowned at her reflection before she caught herself. She forced herself to relax and widened her eyes to smooth the wrinkles from her expression.

Surely Meg loved the *notion* of love, but what made her so confident in her feelings?

"How do you know it's love?" she asked.

"Miss?" Meg's confusion was evident as she stood motionless.

Anna awaited her answer until smoke began to curl up from the tongs.

"Meg!"

Meg dropped the tongs and released a curl. "Oh! Miss Pepper! I'm sorry." She waved a hand to cool the still-smoking spiral.

Anna leaned toward the mirror and inspected her hair. Fortunately, the curl was still intact. Wouldn't that be just the thing, to marry Greenvale with half her locks missing?

"Never mind," she said. "Just finish my hair and help me dress."

"Yes, Miss Pepper."

As Meg assisted her into a clean chemise and tightened her stays, Anna couldn't resist returning to her earlier line of questioning.

"How do you know you love your suitor?" she asked.

Meg was quiet while she helped her step into a petticoat and finally the rose silk dress. Then, adjusting the fall of the fabric, she shrugged. "I'm not sure, Miss Pepper. I can't explain it, but I just know. He's the one with whom I want to share my joys and my burdens. I wish for his happiness above my own."

Well, that was hardly specific. Anna frowned as she thought of Greenvale. She couldn't imagine sharing her joys with him, much less unburdening herself to him. And certainly, she didn't wish him to be miserable, but to place his happiness above her own? Hmm. Love seemed an unlikely outcome, so it was just as well that she had no expectations there.

She thought again of Jory Tremayne and his earnest declarations. They'd been the words of a dreamer, an idealist.

If he'd truly known her, he wouldn't have been so sure of his affections. Imagine how disappointed he would have been when his sentiment faded, as it surely would have.

It was his inevitable disappointment that had prompted her to desert him, although her chest tightened now as she thought of how he must have waited for her. Still, it was certainly better for him to suffer a single, minor disappointment than a lifetime of disillusionment. Marriage was to the death, after all.

She stood before the mirror and forced thoughts of what might have been aside. Admiring the line of her gown, she stepped into the vine-wrapped slippers. As she moved toward the bed, she felt the barest of wiggles in the heel of her left shoe. Leaning down, she removed the slipper and inspected it, finding a small place where the heel had loosened.

No. No, no, no. She shook her head. This would not do.

"Meg," she said, trying and failing to control the panic in her voice. "Look at this slipper. It appears the heel is coming loose."

Meg leaned closer and checked the shoe. "Yes, you're right, Miss Pepper. Perhaps we should change to another pair? What do you think of the yellow slippers with the little satin bows?"

Anna's eyes widened. Change to another pair? Had Meg lost her wits?

Her heart started its frantic pacing again. She closed her eyes, willing the organ to calm, but the shoe's imperfection shouted, commanding attention.

"No, Meg. It must be these slippers. There's nothing for it. We must visit the cobbler and have it repaired."

She was *not* changing her shoes, and she was *not* getting married with a loose heel.

"I can't get married with a loose heel," she said as much to herself as to Meg.

"Y—yes, Miss Pepper. I'll take it straight away."

"Bring my pelisse, Meg. I'm coming with you," Anna said, reaching for her bonnet.

She needed to move. To do something.

A visit to the cobbler to see to the slipper was a better distraction than pound cake. Her mother could only approve of her sensible choice.

ANNA EXCHANGED THE OFFENDING SHOES for a pair of cream moire slippers and marched down the stairs with Meg trailing behind.

Peters stared at her in confusion for a beat then rushed to open the door while Anna pulled on her gloves. She stopped short on the portico, and Meg squeaked as she skidded to a halt behind her.

Although the sun was beginning to tip the horizon, the only activity beyond the Peppers' door was that of vendors and sweeps beginning their day. While Anna had frequently returned late from a ball or some other event, she'd always been tucked into her bed by this hour, where she stayed until well after noon. She'd never seen London awaken. It boggled the mind.

"What time does the cobbler's shop open?" she asked Meg.

"I—I'm not certain, Miss Pepper. Should we send one of the footmen to inquire?"

Anna adjusted her reticule on her wrist. "No. We mustn't delay. I can't get married with a damaged slipper," she repeated. "We'll simply have to find a cobbler who's willing to complete the work now."

Meg nodded, and they set out for the shops two streets over.

The cobbler's establishment was, indeed, closed, but that didn't deter Anna. She knocked on the man's door, waited, then knocked some more. When the door remained stubbornly closed, she huffed a sigh and they moved further down the street.

She repeated this process twice more until, finally, she met with success.

An elderly man gazed at her in confusion from beyond the door of his shop. "I'm not open for another two hours," he said as he turned away.

"Wait!" Anna held a hand to stop the door from closing. "It's imperative that I have your services now. I'm to be married today, and a heel has come loose on my slipper."

She motioned to Meg to show the man the offending item. She knew how ridiculous she must sound, but she couldn't quiet her desperation. She simply could not join Greenvale in holy matrimony without these slippers. Why, to proceed with the event in anything other than these slippers was courting certain doom.

The man hesitated, his eyes narrowed on her and Meg, then he relented and pulled the door back to admit them. Grumbling, he took the slipper from Meg and set it on his work table.

As the man tended to her loose heel, Anna watched the street from the front window. The sky had begun to lighten, London unfolding its petals to the day. Across the way, a couple approached a coaching inn on the corner. Arm in arm, the lady giggled while the gentleman smiled fondly at her.

Anna smoothed the scowl from her face.

The lady pointed at a placard in front of the inn as they entered the building, and Anna leaned forward to read the sign. *Brighton Grand Sea Front: For Health and Pleasure.* Her scowl returned.

She turned and looked at the cobbler behind her. He hunched over her shoe as he worked to repair the little heel with a tiny hammer. Meg waited silently to one side, her back to Anna as she studied items for sale in a low case.

Anna returned her attention to the window. *She* should be going to Brighton. She should *not* be traveling to York.

In short, she should not be marrying Greenvale.

Her doubts rose full force to strangle her better sense. When she married Greenvale, there would be no going back. She would be his wife until she died. Or until he did.

What if she found she couldn't bear him?

What if he couldn't tolerate her?

What if someone better came along tomorrow, or the next day or the day after that?

She'd found over the years, to her great distress, that Jory Tremayne was the measuring stick by which all men were evaluated. What if Greenvale didn't measure up to Jory's light and warmth? What if he persisted in his formality, calling her Lady Greenvale for the rest of their days?

Her breathing quickened as panic threatened to choke her. The impulse to run was strong, but that was silly. Even a gudgeon with more hair than wit knew a lady didn't run. But she couldn't help thinking if she simply... disappeared... this suffocating anxiety would disappear as well.

Anna tried to calm her chaotic thoughts—truly, she did—but before she could stop herself, she'd opened the cobbler's door and escaped into the shadowed entry. Not daring to look behind her, Anna crossed the street to the coaching inn, her dark green pelisse fluttering in her non-running haste. She didn't stop until she was inside the inn, leaving Meg and the cobbler and her slipper behind her.

The tightness in her chest eased and she inhaled as deeply as her stays allowed.

Porters bustled about the inn with bags and trunks, and the couple she'd seen crossing the street now stood at a counter. The gentleman exchanged a coin for a ticket, and the pair moved on.

From the concealment of the inn, Anna chanced a glance at the street. Wagons and carts clattered past, oblivious of her distress. Across the street, Meg stood at the cobbler's door and looked left then right in confusion.

Behind her, the man at the counter cleared his throat. Anna pressed her lips and closed her eyes. What was she doing?

"Can I help you, miss?"

She turned and looked up at him. If only she could disappear...

"Miss?"

Anna approached the counter. The hands she held in front of her looked like her hands. The voice that came from her throat sounded like her voice. But she felt disembodied, like a spirit evicted from its mortal home, as she spoke to him.

"I'd like a ticket to Brighton," she said, eyes wide.

"I just sold the last ticket for Brighton," the man said without apology, thumbing through a sheaf of papers on the counter. "Next Brighton route is tomorrow."

Her spirit snapped back into her body, and Anna watched the happy couple exit to the stable yard behind the building.

"Where else can I go?" she asked, forcing the high pitch of panic from her words.

The man's brows lifted, but he consulted a sheet before him. "The stage to York hasn't left yet."

York?! She narrowed her eyes. "Where else?"

"I've seats left for Cornwall. But that stage leaves in"—he consulted a pocket watch—"three minutes."

Cornwall? Anna chewed her lip as she thought of Jory Tremayne yet again.

A vague sense of unease slithered through her, a feeling she strongly suspected might be guilt for her shabby treatment of him five years before. Guilt was not an emotion to which she was accustomed, but she couldn't ignore the itchy feeling of things left undone in Cornwall.

Anna wasn't overly superstitious—doomed slippers notwithstanding—but the stage schedule seemed a sign of some sort. Was she meant to travel to Cornwall then? To see for herself that Jory Tremayne was settled and happy?

The more she thought about it, the more she was convinced *he* was the reason she'd not been able to successfully complete a wedding. Jory Tremayne and her inconvenient guilt. But if she could satisfy herself that all was well with him, perhaps then she could shed this uncomfortable weight and move forward with her life. Surprisingly, the idea warmed her, dispelling her unease and soothing her panic.

"Miss?" the man behind the counter prompted.

"Does the Cornwall route stop in Newford?"

"Yes, miss. It's the last stop before Falmouth."

Decided on her course, Anna nodded. "The Cornwall route, then."

She was going to Cornwall.

Sarah Steward, her mother's childhood friend, lived outside Newford. She and her mother had visited Mrs. Steward that fateful summer five years before, and she was certain the lady would welcome Anna back to her home. She'd worry about how to explain her presence later, but for now, she had a stage to catch.

"Inside or out?" the man asked.

She looked at him in confusion. "Pardon?"

"Do you want to sit inside or out?" he enunciated slowly. "You're on the small side. I can fit you inside or on top."

Anna looked at her silk gown and moire slippers. Surely the man could see she was not a passenger meant for an "on top" seat.

"Inside, of course!"

He nodded then quoted her a ridiculous sum. She eyed him with suspicion, but when he glanced at his watch again, she reached into her reticule. Thank heavens she hadn't spent all her pin money yet. She handed over the required sum, and he provided her with a ticket.

"The porter there will see to your trunks," he said, motioning to a man standing behind her.

"I don't have any trunks," she said, and then the enormity of what she was doing hit her. She would be traveling with strangers, on a *common stage*. With no maid to accompany her, no clothing beyond her wedding finery, and worst of all, no curling tongs. Had she taken leave of her senses?

A horn blast sounded from the stable yard. "Hurry, miss. The stage is leaving."

CHAPTER THREE

NEWFORD, CORNWALL

Six of Jory Tremayne's sturdiest cousins held ropes to steady a massive bronze bell over Weirmouth's town square. Forty feet above, Jory leaned over the bell's smooth metal to secure the last bolt in the oak headstock.

"Are you nearly finished, Jory?" James shouted.

"What's wrong?" Jory turned and looked out the tower's open window to the cobbled ground below. All appeared in order. Uncle Alfred stood with his arms crossed, supervising the operation silently while Jory's cousins stood around the tower, shoulders and arms straining to hold the pulley ropes steady. Trout, Jory's black collie, waited patiently for his return, tongue lolling to one side.

"Aye! Hurry!" Gavin shouted. "We've all of us pints to lift at the Feather."

The price of cheap labor, it would seem, was suffering his cousins' company. Not that he would complain, for he was looking forward to a pint as well once they returned to Newford, and his cousins were better company than most.

With one more twist of his wrist he set the bolt in the thick wood, then he wiped his hands on a rag and took his time collecting his tools. He let his cousins strain a bit longer on the ropes before he told them to let up.

It had been a good day's work, mounting the tower bell in the neighboring village, and tomorrow the clockmaker would connect the striking mechanism. Jory had spent the last weeks tuning the pitch of the bell, and while he was proud of the result, he was sorry to see the project end.

His uncle preferred foundry work—the shimmering molten metal, the smell of the forge, the hiss of steam.

All of that was well and good, but Jory's satisfaction came from shaving and shaping the inside of a bell to achieve the perfect note. The craft required mathematical precision and a good ear, and the feeling of transforming something ugly and dissonant into a rich, full-bodied tone was enough to make a man weep. Not that Jory would ever admit as much to his cousins.

He wiped his brow with the back of one arm,

slung his knapsack over his shoulder, then descended the tower's wooden ladder.

"Many thanks, gentlemen," he said when he reached the square below. Trout ran alongside him, giving his hand a lick with her long, pink tongue. Jory gave her a quick scratch behind the ears, getting another lick for the effort.

"You're a fortunate man," James said.

Jory's brows dipped as Alfie fell in step with them. "How d'you figure such?"

"He's right, you know," Gavin said. "Not many cousins would assist you the way we do."

"There's no need to remind me how fortunate I am," Jory said as they approached Uncle Alfred's wagon. "I told you the first round was to be your payment for today's work, and so 'twill be."

Gavin clapped an arm about Jory's shoulder. "You're the best of cousins, old man." Just a month younger than Jory, Gavin never failed to remind him of his advanced years.

Jory shrugged off Gavin's arm. "You should be buying *my* ale," he told them. "'Tis my birthday, after all."

Cadan studied him with a thoughtful expression. "I've a better idea, lads," he said, which caused no small amount of alarm for Jory. Cadan was always looking for a way to save a farthing. "Let's find our Jory a lass to mark this momentous day."

Jory snorted. His cousin's offer was little more than wishful thinking, as unattached lasses were few and far between in Newford, but still he felt the need to make his position known. "No lasses," he said with a shake of his head.

He thought of his birthday five years before when he'd confessed his love to a particular lass with silky golden hair... who'd later left him holding his hat. He'd been a fool then, and he had no wish to repeat the experience, so he had a strict no-lass rule for his birthday.

Not that his cousins needed to know the reasons behind his thinking. He'd never hear the end of it if they knew how witless he'd once been.

"He's still sore about Betsy Carew," Cadan said. "He never could let a grudge go," he grumbled.

"What has Betsy Carew to do with—" Jory stopped. If his cousins believed the Betsy Carew incident was behind his reticence, who was he to argue? "Never mind," he said.

He'd always suspected Cadan had been behind the dead-snake-in-the-picnic-basket jest that had resulted in his humiliation in front of the squire's eldest daughter.

Granted, Jory had been thirteen at the time, and Betsy a mere twelve, but warmth still spread along the back of his neck whenever he recalled his own high-pitched squeal on finding the snake coiled about a bowl of strawberries. And he'd been so set on impressing the lass....

His cousin's grumbling now was as much of a confession as he was likely to get, and he narrowed his eyes on the back of Cadan's head.

"Jory, you can't be content with our company forever," Merryn said. "Much as we'd like to, we'll not keep you warm like the arms of a willing lady. Nor will this light-skirt."

Merryn raised his eyebrows at Trout and looked to the others for confirmation. All heads nodded at Jory, save Gryffyn, who brought up the rear as usual.

The tallest of the group, Gryffyn was also the quietest. Judging by the intent look on his face, Jory suspected his stone-carver cousin was contemplating a new piece of marble while they walked.

Trout jumped into the front of the wagon, and Jory took the seat next to Uncle Alfred while his cousins climbed into the back.

"As distasteful as I find you lot," he said, "I'll suffer your company. No lasses."

"THAT BEAST AIN'T SETTING foot in my inn, Jory Tremayne," Wynne said, her nose wrinkling beneath a faint smattering of freckles. "She reeks of the river."

Jory looked at his cousin with mock affront, then at Trout, who gazed at him expectantly, tongue drooping to the side.

Wynne merely crossed her arms and remained silent.

Jory sighed and spoke to the collie. "Sorry, old girl. Wynne is being unreasonable today." He lowered his voice to an overloud whisper. "But I have it on the best of authority that you'll find a new pair of shoes in her room."

He stroked the dog's black head with one hand and gave Wynne an innocent look. She rolled her eyes and threw her hands up then spun away from him.

"Only because 'tis your birthday," she threw over her shoulder.

"She doesn't reek of the river," he called after her. "Much," he muttered, although he thought the smell of the river would have been an improvement.

"Trout, you need to stop rolling on dead fish if you wish to impress," he told the dog. "I fear no amount of bathing will rid you of the stench."

She grinned and trotted ahead of him into The Fin and Feather, cutting a direct path to the coffee room where his cousins were already seated. She turned a few times then, satisfied, curled up next to

Jory's usual chair with a sigh. Wynne might make a fuss, but Trout was as much a fixture at the Feather as the polished oak bar and the uneven slate floor.

The familiar din from multiple conversations was already growing loud but not unpleasant when he reached his cousins. Jory always enjoyed the chaos of family gatherings—the shouts and laughter and teasing that made one feel connected to a greater whole, no matter how much or how little one participated in the conversation.

Alfie, who served as the inn's cellarman, collected an empty cask from behind the bar. He passed them on his way to the cellars as Gavin clapped Jory on the back and pressed him into his seat.

"Was that the sound of creaking bones I hear?" he asked.

"No," Jory said. "You must have mistaken the sound of your own rusty gears."

"Jory." Roddie Teague approached from the bar, wiping his hands on a linen. "This sorry lot says you're to buy the first round."

"Aye, 'twas the agreement. Brew for brawn."

Roddie shook his head. "'Tis good that brawn is all you bargained for, Jory, as 'tis all this lot's good for."

An uproar rose at Roddie's comment, and a piece of bread sailed through the air. Jory ducked, and the bread bounced off Roddie's chest. Jory toed it toward Trout, whose tongue snagged it before she sighed and rested her head on his foot.

Roddie stalked off, grumbling, but Jory saw him motion to Wynne. She winked at her husband and went to draw their ale.

Not for the first time, Jory found himself amazed at the silent communication that passed between his cousin and her husband. He'd witnessed Wynne and Roddie exchange entire conversations before with only a glance and a tilt of one eyebrow.

How remarkable, he thought, that two such perfectly matched people had found one another, and in such a tiny corner of the world, no less.

"Jory!"

He realized his cousins had been calling him, and he turned back to their table. Someone made a poor joke about him having his head inside too many bells to be able to hear them properly.

"Speaking of bells," Cadan said, "Uncle Alfred says you're finally to replace the parish bells."

"You had to ask about it, didn't you?" Alfie said as he joined them. "Now he'll go on all night about bells, as if I don't hear enough about them from my father," he grumbled.

"Aye," Jory replied, ignoring Alfie's complaint. "We inspected the belfry last week. We're to replace the timbers and all eight bells. Uncle and I have already begun the molds, and Merryn's firm will build the new mounting frame."

"Are you lodging here at the Feather then?" James asked.

"'Tis much more convenient for the hours I'll spend at the foundry. I'll return to Oak Hill once Uncle and I complete the casting."

"'Twill be nice to hear the bells ring over Newford," Cadan said. "Grandfather's the only one of us who's ever heard the full peal—"

"—the year he and Grandmother wed," they all said at the same time.

"Fifty years is a long silence," Jory agreed.

Cracks had been discovered in Newford's bells five decades before, brought on by age and poor casting. Since then, the ropes had been removed from all but one, and Sunday worshippers were summoned with a single, mournful tone.

Every time funds had been raised to replace the bells, they'd been reallocated to sustain Newford through a difficult winter or assist survivors of a shipwreck or supplement a poor fishing season.

But the vicar had just received approval to move forward with the long-awaited repairs, and after much convincing, Uncle Alfred had agreed to let Jory take on the project.

Once the new bells were in place, each perfectly cast and tuned to a different pitch, cascading sound would ring over Newford and the surrounding valley again.

Trout sighed at his feet and turned onto her side, clearly unimpressed with the significance of the coming endeavor.

Wynne brought their ale, balancing a tray on the edge of the table and appearing more harried than usual.

"Where's Peggy?" James asked.

Wynne sighed. "The foolish girl has gone and broken her foot," she said. "A flirtation misadventure, it would seem."

"How—" Jory said then stopped with a frown.

"How does one break a foot while flirting?" Wynne asked then answered. "You didn't hear it from me," she said, "but 'twas at last week's bonfire. Apparently, she was trying to impress the butcher's son by dancing atop a fallen log. You can imagine the rest. As 'tis, I'll have to bring this one up from the cellars"—she motioned toward Alfie—"to don a barmaid's apron soon."

Alfie's eyes widened in horror as his cousins mocked him. Eventually, conversation around the table shifted from Peggy's disastrous flirtation to his cousins' usual cycle of topics: fishing, lasses, then fishing again.

He'd told his cousins no lasses tonight, but he couldn't deny that he envied what Wynne and

Roddie had. If the truth be told, he wanted gentle arms to return home to each night and silent conversations spoken across entire rooms.

He'd thought to have it once, but he'd misread the situation. He'd misread *her*.

Miss Anna Pepper.

He scrubbed a hand over his face. He was six and twenty today. He'd mourned Miss Pepper long enough, and he didn't think he was being overly dramatic. *Mourned* was the correct word, for he'd grieved her loss—privately—as surely as if she'd died.

But she'd made her feelings known by her silence. It was time he moved on.

He thought of Miss Keren Moon, one of the mayor's daughters who'd flirted with him at last week's assembly. He shifted in his chair, not sure that the lovely Miss Moon, with her forward manners, was the type for silent conversations across crowded rooms.

And, regardless of Miss Moon's amiability, Jory had heard the mayor had a powerful right hook. That was a stream he wasn't certain he wanted to fish.

But Miss Moon was only one lady. Their numbers weren't great, but there *were* other lasses in Newford.

Then he thought of his hordes of unwed male

relations and frowned. He could broaden his search to the surrounding county, if need be. Or to Wales. He'd just need to apply himself and keep an open mind. Set Miss Pepper from his mind once and for all.

CHAPTER FOUR

~~~~

NEWFORD, 1814 - FIVE YEARS BEFORE

ANNA MARCHED ALONG THE BANK of a winding stream, irritation staining her cheeks. She'd only had a tiny piece of pound cake—hardly enough to warrant her mother's criticism—and yet here she was, taking exercise to prevent herself from growing too soft.

She and her mother had arrived at Penhale, Mrs. Steward's Cornwall residence, the previous week after traveling from their home in Berkshire.

As nice as the lady's manor was, Cornwall was a poor substitute for the glitter and sparkle of a London Season.

Granted, her first season the previous year had been less than successful, but she'd rallied with dreams of a better, second season.

Then her father's death a few months later had

put a halt to her plans. And now, rather than flirting and dancing at balls and routs, Anna found herself plodding along in the grass and mud.

She lifted her hem and eyed her velvet slippers. Ruined, as she'd suspected. At least she'd managed to keep the hem of her dress—her current favorite—from the worst of the mud.

She loved the rich, golden hue of the muslin. Like spring sunshine, it never failed to lift her spirits, and with a deep breath, she allowed its vibrancy to improve her mood.

She pushed a crooked branch aside and plodded on, grimacing as a patch of mud sucked at her foot. A copse of trees nestled in a curve of the stream ahead. She'd walk as far as that, then return to Penhale. Perhaps by then her mother would have forgotten about the pound cake.

As she neared the trees, a brace of birds squawked and took flight. Anna stumbled and held a hand to her throat at the sudden noise, watching as the pair soared toward the brilliant sapphire sky.

Then a louder rustling sounded from the trees, and a masculine voice commanded, "Trout!"

Confused, Anna looked down in time to see a dark shape lunging toward her from the shadows. Her first thought—that she was about to be set upon by a fish—quickly yielded to horror as two paws landed on her chest, knocking her to the ground.

Hands shielding her face, she peered between her fingers to see sharp, white teeth. She squeezed her eyes shut and braced for certain death, only to receive . . . a wet swipe across her hand.

Slowly opening one eye, she spied the beast's pink tongue and recoiled while its hot, moist breath fanned her curls. Was it *smiling* at her?

"I'm proper sorry, miss. Are you all right?"

A large hand reached down to assist her. She lifted to her elbows and looked up—then up some more—into the face of its owner, and her breath caught. He was hatless, and sunlight glinted off tousled hair the color of wet sand.

But what captured her attention were his eyes. Clear and blue, the same shade as the sea, they shone from a face lightly weathered by the sun.

At last, something of interest in Cornwall.

Then her eyes moved down. He wore simple clothing—coarse trousers and a rough linen shirt. No waistcoat. Boots and a plain kerchief about his neck. A laborer of some sort, then. Perhaps a servant from Oak Hill, the neighboring estate.

Disappointed, she pushed her interest down while mud seeped through her favorite dress, through her petticoat and shift to dampen the backs of her legs.

"Miss? Are you well?" he asked again, backlit by the sun, hand still extended.

Ignoring his assistance, she stood on her own and shook out her skirts.

He pulled his hand back. "I apologize. Trout's young, and she's still learning her manners. But right now, she's a proper heller." He scowled at the dog, who sat next to Anna, tongue hanging from grinning dog lips.

Anna took a breath to assure him she was all right, then she gasped. "What—what is that awful smell?" she asked.

He winced and flicked a finger to call the dog to his side. "'Tis merely Trout. She rolls on dead fish."

"She rolls on—why on earth would she do that?" Anna asked, holding a hand to her nose.

She smelled damp earth then—an improvement over dead fish, to be sure—and pulled her hand away to see it covered in mud. Mud that now covered her face. She tried to brush it off, but there was no part of her that was clean.

"'Tis a question I'd dearly love to know the answer to myself," he replied as he stretched a linen handkerchief toward her.

She hesitated before taking it with her thumb and forefinger, but it appeared clean. When she lifted it to wipe the end of her nose, she was surprised by the linen's bright scent. It reminded her of fall, of sunshine and apples, and she was sorry to see she'd stained it with mud.

Wait... She wouldn't have stained his handkerchief if his dog hadn't mauled her in the first place. She frowned. Now she'd have to see it laundered and returned to him.

"Keep it," he said as if he'd read her thoughts. "And please, allow me to reimburse you for your ruined dress." His voice was rich and smooth, Rs rolling as he motioned toward her bodice with reddened cheeks.

Anna glanced down and gasped on seeing two very distinct paw prints at the top of her dress. That, combined with the wetness at the back, confirmed it. The dress was ruined.

She doubted the man had the funds to reimburse her for it, though, and she didn't wish to embarrass him. She only wished to leave, to return to Penhale and forget this dreadful afternoon had ever occurred.

"There's no need," she responded crisply.

He swallowed and nodded, a furrow creasing his brow.

Anna spun on her heel in the mud then began the march back to Penhale. She held her skirts away from her, the scent of dead fish competing with apples and sunshine as she walked.

―――

THE NEXT DAY, ANNA SET out for her exercise promptly after luncheon. Despite the maids' attempts, there had been no saving the yellow gown from its muddy demise.

Today she wore a pale blue muslin with a darker ribbon beneath the bodice—not her favorite, but it was still a lovely shade. If it reminded her of the blue-eyed man she'd encountered yesterday, she ignored the fact.

She'd given yesterday's slippers to one of the maids, who'd cooed appreciatively over the stained velvet. Anna thought of the mud along the path and considered donning a sturdier pair of half boots. They would be the more sensible choice, but they would hardly do justice to the blue dress.

She shook her head and donned blue satin slippers instead. She'd just have to be more cautious of the mud.

She thought of the fish-scented beast and her master with the rough clothing. What were the odds she'd encounter them again today?

Slim, if she was one to wager. The stream was long and meandered through vast fields and thickets along the edge of Newford until it reached the Penryn River. It was unlikely that she'd happen upon the pair again.

She looped the ribbons of her bonnet beneath her chin and set out from Penhale with a bounce in her step. As she neared the curve in the stream and the stand of trees, she smiled to herself.

She'd skirted much of the mud and her slippers had survived thus far. And without the ravening beast to knock her to the ground, she might just make it back to Penhale with her clothing—and her pride—intact.

She turned at the trees to begin the return trip, then a rustling sounded behind her moments before a dark shape crashed from the shadows.

"Trout! Heel!"

Anna's heart raced and she began to turn—to brace herself for attack—but her foot caught on a root, and she landed in the mud. Face down.

The stench of dead fish was overwhelming as a cold, pink tongue licked the back of her neck. She squealed and brushed it away, earning another lick to her hand.

"Trout, heel," the man repeated.

Anna pushed up from the mud, noticing he didn't offer a hand to help her this time.

She looked down at her dress. Mud coated her from tip to toe. Perfect. Another ruined gown. At this rate, she'd be walking in her chemise before the week was out.

She looked up and caught the tiniest hint of a smile on the man's face. It wasn't as broad as his dog's grin, but it was a smile, nonetheless. She scowled, and he pressed his lips together.

"My apologies, miss," he said. "Are you all right?"

She shook her head and held her skirts away from her to gauge the extent of the damage. "Your dog is a menace," she said.

The animal must have sensed she was the topic of discussion because her grin grew wider, her tail swiping the ground where she sat at Anna's feet.

Anna frowned at her. "A lady would behave with more decorum," she told her. Wait. Was she speaking to a *dog*?

He stretched another handkerchief toward her, and she took it after a small hesitation. Wiping the square across the tip of her nose, she inhaled and resisted the urge to close her eyes on the warm scent of apples and sunshine.

Why hadn't any of the gentlemen she'd met in London smelled as nice?

Then she stared in consternation at the muddy streak she'd created and debated the propriety of accepting two handkerchiefs from the same man. She could hardly walk about with mud on her face, but neither could she return the linen to him in its current soiled state.

"Keep it," he said.

The appearance of confidence, she reminded herself. She nodded briefly then closed the linen in her fist and turned to leave.

"Good day to you, miss," he said behind her.

She lifted one hand in farewell and kept walking.

THE NEXT AFTERNOON, JORY CAST his line and wedged the angling rod between two rocks. He leaned against a boulder to tie a new fly while bugs skipped along the water, dimpling the smooth surface while his line floated undisturbed.

He wondered if the prim and fancy miss would invade his favorite spot again. Trout had assumed her usual position to nap at his feet, at least until a clean dress paraded itself before her muddy paws.

Jory chuckled as he recalled the squeak of astonishment the lady had emitted when she'd landed in the mud a second time. Even though Trout had stopped short of planting her paws on the lady's person, he still felt accountable. She'd landed in the mud trying to escape Trout's attentions, after all. He was fair certain his dog's exuberance had ruined her pretty dresses.

He scowled down at the collie, wondering if she would ever learn her manners. He'd been working with her since his uncle had found her shivering outside his foundry last winter. She'd shown improvement, so he knew she could learn, but sometimes she simply . . . forgot herself.

She was downright pathetic in her wish to love and be loved, and Jory's scowl instantly softened. It seemed cruel to begrudge the animal her need for affection, her wish to share her joy with the world.

She must have sensed his thoughts, for she rolled over and stood then butted her head against his hand for a scratch behind the ears.

Footsteps sounded beyond the edge of the trees and Trout stiffened, nose in the air. "Stay," he said with a motion of his hand.

Trout's ears perked forward, but she heeded his command.

When he felt confident of her manners, he stood and left the shade of the trees, Trout following at a ladylike pace for once.

The lady of the mud stood before him, dressed this time in a brown linen dress and half boots. His lips twitched. No satin slippers today? No fancy skirts?

She eyed him and Trout warily, no doubt braced for attack. He wondered whether she was local to the area or merely visiting. He guessed visiting, as he knew most everyone in Newford and the surrounding countryside. Plus, she had the look of an incomer about her.

"*Dohajydh da*," he said. At her confused look, he had his answer. "Good day," he translated.

Her face cleared. "Good afternoon."

The broad brim of her bonnet shaded her eyes, but he recalled they were a pretty green. Everything about her was small, from her pert nose all the way to her dainty feet.

"D'you stay at Penhale?" he asked.

She hesitated, understandably uncertain about the propriety of speaking with a man to whom she'd not been introduced. He didn't think their previous discussions counted as she'd been covered in mud.

Finally, she reached a decision and replied. "Yes, my mother and I are visiting Mrs. Steward."

"Where d'you go every day?" he asked, motioning to the path behind her.

"I just walk. For the exercise. Why are you here?"

"I just fish. For the enjoyment."

She pressed her lips together, whether in amusement or annoyance at his mimicry he wasn't certain.

"Would you like to join me?" he asked.

Her brows lifted. "Join you? To fish?" She wrinkled her nose, nibbling her bottom lip.

He rubbed the back of his neck. "Or you could simply enjoy the stream. 'Tis clear and peaceful, at least when Trout's asleep."

She eyed the dog at his feet, then gave him a short nod. "Perhaps just for a moment."

CHAPTER FIVE

※

1819 - THE PRESENT

ANNA SAT WEDGED BETWEEN A middle-aged matron who smelled of camphor and a portly man who smelled of tobacco and sweat. An elderly couple took up the opposite seat along with a sixth passenger, a lone gentleman with the look of a barrister. She estimated his age at about thirty, so he wasn't quite ancient. He seemed to have all his teeth and most of his hair, although it was heavily pomaded.

The coach lurched and lumbered through London's noisy streets to the wider stretches of road beyond. Anna shifted uncomfortably and held a handkerchief to her nose.

It had long since lost the scent of apples and sunshine, but the linen was soft and calming. She idly rubbed a finger over the small, entwined "JT" embroidered in one corner.

As more of the city passed beyond the windows, she asked the portly gentleman for the time. His elbow poked her ribs as he shifted and reached for his watch. "Half past nine."

Half an hour, then, until her wedding. She nibbled her bottom lip and eyed the carriage door. She thought of Greenvale. Meg, waiting with her slipper. The guests they'd invited to the wedding. She probably should have sent a note around to her mother.

Her aborted wedding to Signor Rossi had been small, with only her mother and his cousin there to serve as witnesses, but this one with Greenvale . . . .

There were plenty who would know of her cowardice. The scandal would be uncomfortable, to say the least. She had no doubt that Mary Riverton would gloat about her own successful wedding. Anna closed her eyes and forced the thought aside.

Was she making a mistake? She could demand the driver to stop, but then what? It would take entirely too long to travel to St. George's. She'd not make it on time, and she truly didn't wish to. It was best to treat this excursion as a lark and worry about tomorrow . . . tomorrow.

She inhaled deeply, the breath stuttering in her chest, then she crossed her hands in her lap.

The barrister gentleman on the opposite seat

caught her eye and curved his lips in a shy smile.

She mentally calculated her remaining coins and decided an ally on this journey couldn't hurt. Calling up her flirtation skills, she returned his smile, ignoring the matron at her side who sniffed and turned to face the open window.

"Do you travel all the way to Falmouth?" the barrister asked.

———

When the coach stopped at yet another posting inn—the fifth by Anna's count—the driver again instructed everyone to disembark while the horses were changed.

The passengers had been bounced on the rutted road for an inordinate amount of time, and her energy for this endeavor was flagging. Surely it couldn't be much longer.

She stepped down from the coach and approached the driver while the other passengers crossed to the inn. "Sir, are we nearly to Newford? When will we arrive?" she asked.

He gazed at her with a twitchy left eye then sucked his teeth and spat into the dust. Anna stepped back and gripped her hands while she awaited his response. It didn't escape her notice that if she'd had the foresight to bring Meg with her on this jaunt, the maid could have handled these distasteful interactions.

"Four o'clock, just like the schedule says."

Four o'clock. Anna sighed with relief. That couldn't be too much longer. "Thank you, sir," she said and started to turn away.

"Wednesday."

She stopped and turned, cocking her head. Surely, she'd misheard him. "Pardon?"

"Four o'clock *Wednesday*."

Anna stared at him for a beat during which the blood slowed in her veins. Her eyes widened.

"Wed—Wednesday?! But that's two days from now!"

The man shook his head and spat again then stepped aside as an ostler unhitched the horses.

ANNA SUPPOSED SHE OUGHT TO have paid better attention to her geography lessons. When she and her mother had traveled to Newford five years before, it hadn't seemed so very far from their home in Berkshire.

Clearly, London was another matter altogether.

She rubbed a finger along the top of her hand and cringed at the feel of grit on her skin.

Heavy leather curtains at the glassless coach

windows kept out some of the road dust when they were closed, but they kept *in* the sour stench of the passengers. Accordingly, they were open most of the time, and a never-ending cloud of dust billowed about them.

The gentleman across from her—Mr. Tompkins—shifted on his seat and tried to read a book despite the rough jostling of the carriage.

His pomade had attracted an impressive amount of English dirt, and Anna lifted a tentative hand to her own limp curls beneath the brim of her bonnet. Fortunately, her pelisse protected her lovely gown from the worst of the dust, and she was careful to keep her slippers tucked beneath her hem to maintain the pristine cream moire.

She licked her bottom lip, tasted dirt, and added "excessive dust" to the scathing letter she was mentally composing to the stagecoach company. She'd post it straightaway once she reached Mrs. Steward's.

Her stomach rumbled, and she pressed a hand to silence it. She was surprised and a little dismayed to realize the extent to which her pin money had dwindled since she'd left London, so when Mr. Tompkins invited her to share his meal at the next coaching inn, she readily accepted.

The matron next to her gave another disapproving sniff, which Anna ignored.

She'd hesitated to provide her own name to any of her fellow passengers. She may have been an impulsive gudgeon, but she wasn't an idiot.

An unwed lady of quality traveling alone on the public stage was bound to raise an eyebrow or two, but a *married* lady might pass without too much notice.

But that reasoning, sound as it was, couldn't explain the brainless moment when she'd introduced herself to her traveling companions as Mrs. Tremayne.

She closed her eyes at the recollection. She'd been rubbing the initials on her handkerchief, and Tremayne had been the first name to come to mind. It escaped her tongue before she could call it back.

But it was no matter, she told herself. She'd leave the coach in Newford, and no one need know of her foolishness.

She grimaced to think that Mary Riverton had certainly never done anything so harebrained.

ANNA AWOKE FROM A SHORT doze to the warm, briny scent of the sea. She straightened, turning her head left then right to work out the stiffness in her neck. Her breath caught at the view framed beyond the coach's open windows, and she stilled, her sore neck quickly forgotten.

The coach traveled along a high ridge, and the sea sparkled in the distance under a brilliant sun. It was a rich shade of blue she'd only seen in Cornwall, the color of peacock feathers.

Or a boy's eyes as he leaned in for a kiss.

White cottages clustered below near a small harbor, and boats bobbed and dipped on the water.

She inhaled deeply, and the familiar, salty tang of the air flooded her with memories that she struggled to put back in their place.

The other passengers stirred and shifted, and Mr. Tompkins smiled at her from the opposite seat. They must be nearing Newford. Indeed, if she squinted, she could see Penhale atop a rise in the distance.

She lifted a hand to her bonnet and tried to right herself but sighed when she realized nothing but a bath and hot curling tongs would help her appearance.

Presently, the coach pulled beneath an arched gate into the stable yard of The Fin and Feather. The driver ordered everyone off as a man rushed from the stables to change the horses.

Mr. Tompkins descended first then turned to assist Anna from the coach.

"Mrs. Tremayne," he said. "It's been a pleasure to make your acquaintance. Are you quite certain you'll be all right on your own in Newford?"

Anna winced at the name then smiled up at him. "Yes, Mr. Tompkins," she assured him. "I'll join my mother's friend shortly and shall be quite all right, but I thank you for your concern."

His dusty, pomaded hair notwithstanding, the man had been kind to her. Anna was glad to have had his company, if only to distract her from her own frantic thoughts.

She watched him return to the coach, then she shook out her pelisse, dismayed at the amount of dust that billowed from the folds.

The outer garment had done an admirable job protecting her gown. Indeed, a little attention to her gown's exposed hem, and it should be like new again.

She lifted her skirts slightly, pleased to see her diligence had also kept her slippers in pristine condition. All would be well.

CHAPTER SIX

≫∞≪

THE SOUND OF A HORN heralded the arrival of another stage from London. Jory looked up from his ale and watched as Mr. Malvern and his stable boys rushed to change the horses.

The man had long been in friendly competition with the ostler at The White Dove to see who could turn a coach the fastest. His cousins placed quick wagers while Merryn monitored his watch.

The first of the passengers stepped down from the coach, a thin man who looked as though he'd, well... traveled for days on a coach. His hair was stiff and caked with dust, his attire wrinkled.

He reached a hand to assist a lady down the steps, and Jory's heart stuttered in disbelief before skipping painfully. Her profile was hidden by a wide-brimmed bonnet, but he'd recognize her petite frame anywhere.

Or had his earlier thoughts merely conjured her

in the next petite lady he encountered?

He focused more intently, and Trout raised her head at the shift in his attention. He stilled her with one hand and waited for the lady to turn.

After what seemed an eternity, she raised her head to cast a flirtatious smile at the dusty-haired man. Jory's heart stopped skipping and began racing.

It *was* her. Miss Anna Pepper had returned, but why? Was the man her husband? His insides turned hot and queasy as he watched her dimple at the dusty-haired passenger.

When the pair parted ways with a brief bow from the man, he exhaled. His relief evaporated, though, when he realized she approached the inn.

He was torn between equally strong impulses to hide and confront. He opted for somewhere in the middle and remained motionless where he was, striving to contain his expression amidst his cousins' laughing banter as they watched Mr. Malvern's ostlers.

Why had she returned? Had he not just determined to forget about Miss Anna Pepper?

"Two minutes, fifty-seven seconds!" Merryn said.

Shouts went up at the table as his cousins reached into their pockets to settle their bets. Gavin pushed a pile of coins toward Jory, and he gazed at them in confusion.

"You have the devil's own luck, old man!"

———

ANNA ENTERED THE FIN AND Feather through a narrow, flagged hall and went to seek the innkeeper, intent on continuing her journey to Penhale as soon as possible. A bath and a good night's rest were what she needed.

As she passed the inn's coffee room, a tall man with rich, auburn hair approached.

"Good afternoon, ma'am. I'm Mr. Teague," he said. "How may I be of service?"

She smiled prettily at the innkeeper as he led her to a low desk. "I need to secure a chaise to Penhale, Mr. Teague. Can you assist me?"

The man's eyes widened, and he rubbed his jaw. "Ah, Penhale. Are you the new owner then?"

"The—the new owner? Doesn't Mrs. Steward reside there?"

"No, ma'am. She sold the property some weeks agone and has removed to Bath." The man waited patiently while Anna's insides turned to ice.

She rubbed the corner of her handkerchief nervously. Mrs. Steward had left? She'd just spent three days—days!—on a public coach, sustained only by thoughts of finally reaching Penhale.

She held a pleasant smile on her face as questions raced through her mind. Had her mother mentioned something about Mrs. Steward relocating to be closer to her son? A daughter, perhaps?

She inhaled deeply. Yes, she rather thought her mother might have shared such an event. Why couldn't she have recalled that bit of information sooner?

WYNNE APPROACHED HER HUSBAND WITH wide eyes. "Mr. Teague, might I have a word with you?"

Roddie looked at her with raised brows, clearly wondering what couldn't wait while he assisted the London lady. At Wynne's continued silence, he turned back to the lady and excused himself.

"Pardon me, ma'am," he said. "I won't be but a moment."

Wynne pulled Roddie aside, and he leaned down to hear her whispered words.

"When Mr. Malvern went to change the horses, he overheard one of the passengers refer to this lady as 'Mrs. Tremayne.'"

She stressed the name and gave Roddie a meaningful look before darting a glance at the crowded coffee room beyond his shoulder.

"And?"

"And," she continued, "my cousin is right this moment trying to melt the back of the lady's head with his eyes."

She pressed her lips together while he chewed on that. When he was silent, she added the final, telling bit. "And the lady carries one of his handkerchiefs."

Roddie scoffed. "What are you saying?" he asked.

"Jory has never formed an attachment to any lady, but if he were *already married*, he wouldn't, now, would he?"

Roddie choked back a laugh. "Wynnie, that's a stretch, even for you. The Tremayne name, 'tis a common one in Newford. Indeed, there must be hundreds of them in this part of the duchy."

She stared over his shoulder again. "You can't argue tain't a little strange, Roddie. Not when you see the eyes he's casting this way. No—don't turn!" she hissed as she gripped his arm.

Roddie winced and crossed his arms. "What would you have me do then? Shall I ask him? Or her? If he's married to the lady, don't you think he'd speak to her? Don't you think she'd be traveling to Oak Hill instead of Penhale?"

Wynne chewed her lip as she considered Roddie's questions. He made good points, but if their new arrival was Jory's Mrs. Tremayne, then clearly something had occurred to set them apart. It was obvious the lady wasn't aware that Jory sat not more than twenty feet behind her.

Wynne's eyes narrowed as she studied the incomer's delicate frame and London finery. Her fussy bonnet and flawless skin.

If she had to guess, she'd lay the blame for any romantic misadventure at the lady's feet. Jory was too guileless to be at fault. Too sweet for his own good, Wynne had always thought. Then her husband's words registered.

"She's staying at Penhale?" Wynne asked with surprise. "Is she the new owner then?"

"No," Roddie frowned. "She seemed unaware that Mrs. Steward has gone to Bath."

Wynne frowned, tapping her lip. "That's perfect, then. Give her a room, Roddie. Number eight, I should think."

"Wynne . . ." Roddie said with a suspicious squint.

"I'll handle the rest," she said, "so you can set your mind at ease." Wynne nodded decisively then forcibly turned her husband and gave him a nudge back to the desk.

―

Noisy revelers crowded the room behind Anna, and she wished nothing more than to escape to a hot bath and a comfortable bed. Although, given her change in circumstances, she should probably begin crafting a plan for her next steps.

She'd never been much of a planner—*planning* was a poor substitute for *doing* as far as she was concerned—but she conceded that perhaps now was a good time to try her hand at it.

The innkeeper returned to the desk along with the lady. His wife, Anna presumed. Mr. Teague and his wife cast such intent stares upon her person that she wondered if she had a smudge on her nose. She reached a tentative hand to her cheek but dropped it with a grimace when she felt the dust there.

"It seems there's been some confusion with my . . . my correspondence with Mrs. Steward," she said to Mr. Teague. "If you've a room available, I would be most grateful."

A beat passed while the Teagues continued their staring, then Mr. Teague looked beyond her shoulder to the coffee room. A tiny frown appeared between his brows, and Anna took a step back before stiffening her spine.

"Of course, of course," Mr. Teague said. "Let's get you settled straightaway, Mrs. . . . ?"

It was Anna's turn to stare as she frantically sought a name to give him. Something *not* Tremayne. Her eyes shifted to the wall behind him where several keys hung. To the desk where a ledger sat with the words "The Fin and Feather" boldly inked across the top.

"F—Feather," she blurted.

"Mrs. . . . Feather?" he asked with a steep lift of his brow.

"Featherton," she amended, nodding decisively. *The appearance of confidence* . . . she reminded herself. "Now, about that room . . ."

Mr. Teague collected a ridiculous sum from her for the night then removed a key from the wall behind him.

"You'll be pleased to know we're one of the few establishments with locking doors, Mrs. Featherton."

Anna's eyes widened. She'd never traveled alone before, so she'd not considered the possibility of a room without a lock. Gads.

"'Tis a luxury, to be sure," the innkeeper continued as he handed her the key. "Number eight. My wife can show you the way."

"Thank you. And please have a bath sent up, Mr. Teague," Anna said before turning to follow his wife.

Mrs. Teague led the way upstairs then to a narrow door at the end of a wide hallway. She handed the key to Anna and stepped back to allow her to enter.

Anna pushed on the door, but it hit something and stopped halfway. She peered around the wood to see a tiny bed taking up most of the room.

"Why, it's not much bigger than a larder!" she said with dismay.

"I'm sorry, Mrs. Featherstone," the lady said as she handed her a candle. "The hurling brings many guests, and this is the last room we have available. You can try to secure accommodations at The White Dove, but I'm afraid they'll be full up as well." The lady gave her a closed-mouth smile, hands folded before her.

Anna recalled several keys hanging on the wall behind the innkeeper, so it stretched the bounds of credulity to think this was the only room available. She narrowed her eyes on Mrs. Teague, but as she was too tired to argue, she simply nodded and turned sideways to enter the room.

Only after Mrs. Teague left did she realize there was no amount of engineering that would see a full-sized tub into the tiny space.

———

ANNA TURNED IN A SLOW CIRCLE to survey her accommodations. It didn't take long.

Candlelight from her lone candle bounced off all four walls, illuminating the tiny cot with its thin covering, a small bedside table and an armless wooden chair with part of one leg missing. One corner held a wooden bucket and mop, along with a crate of broken . . . crockery?

Why, it was nothing more than a closet!

There wasn't even a proper vanity, much less a mirror. How was she to know if her hair was presentable? Was this how common people traveled? Truly?

With a sigh, she sat on the edge of the bed and tested the mattress. It was thin, but the light of the candle showed it to be clean. There were no obvious moth holes or active vermin crawling about that she could see. She shuddered as a knock sounded.

Anna opened the door as far as possible to see a maid in the hall with a linen towel, pitcher and bowl.

"Yer bath, ma'am," the maid said, lifting the blue and white porcelain.

Anna's brows rose in disbelief then collapsed. It was water, after all, and hopefully clean. She'd take it.

The maid tried to hand her the wash set, but the basin was too wide to fit through the narrow opening. Pressing her lips to stifle a scream, Anna took the pitcher and set it on the table then returned for the basin. Turning it sideways, she brought it into the room as well.

As she started to close the door, she recalled her plan to, well, create a plan. "Please have paper and ink sent up as well." she said.

The maid bobbed a curtsy and offered the linen, which Anna snatched in irritation.

JORY WATCHED HIS COUSIN LEAD Anna upstairs, and the unfamiliar weight of indecision settled on him. He'd no wish to speak with Anna, but neither could he ignore the fact of her presence in Newford. They were bound to see one another eventually, much as he might wish otherwise.

Why had she come *now*, with flagrant disregard for his no-lass rule, when he'd just decided to set her from his mind once and for all? The question wouldn't stop circling his thoughts.

His neck prickled with awareness, and he turned to see Wynne had returned. She and Roddie watched him from their positions behind the desk. They couldn't know of his foolishness five years before, could they?

His cheeks grew warm, and he brushed his embarrassment aside.

No. He'd not told anyone of Anna or his ill-fated elopement. Gryffyn was the only person who might have suspected anything, as Jory had requested the loan of a carriage that night—a carriage for which he'd never had a need.

But Gryffyn was not one to tell tales. If he

suspected anything, he'd keep his own counsel. Jory looked to his cousin, but Gryffyn's eyes were distant, fixed on the opposite wall. He was probably fantasizing about some rock or another.

Jory pocketed his winnings and stood as his cousins continued their boisterous banter. Trout lifted her head to watch him cross the room then settled onto her side once again, secure in the knowledge that he wasn't going far.

Wynne's lips twisted as Jory approached her desk. "Your key, Jory?"

He nodded and stopped short of inquiring if they'd received any guests from the London stage. The question would only rouse Wynne's curiosity, and Anna's purpose here was no concern of his.

Instead, he called for Trout and made his way to his room.

———

ONCE JORY LEFT, WYNNE HURRIED to her cousins' table. They looked up at her approach, a collective question in their eyes.

"Here, wait 'til I tell you . . ." she said.

CHAPTER SEVEN

ANNA TURNED OVER AND PRESSED the thin pillow to her head to muffle the sound of yet another stagecoach arrival. Last night, she'd consoled herself with the fact that her room boasted a window. But as it turned out, the window afforded an unobstructed view of the inn's stable yard, and the glass rattled with the sound of horns as drivers entered through the arched gate. All night long, it would seem.

She flopped onto her back once the horn ceased, twisting the rough linen sheet about her legs.

Was she puffy? She patted the skin around her eyes with light fingers. Yes, she was most definitely puffy, but as the sun's rays were starting to crawl across the planked floor, it was unlikely she'd find any more sleep. Anna stretched a hand to the bedside table and retrieved the plan she'd drafted the previous night. She was rather proud of herself.

She'd originally titled the list "Problems," but that had a bit of a desperate ring to it. She'd crossed through the word and rewritten "Solutions" above it. Below that, she'd listed each of her dilemmas and next to them, the solutions she'd decided upon.

She held the page toward the floor to catch the sunlight and re-read her list.

No. 1: Funds. She'd counted her remaining pin money last night. By her calculation, she had barely enough for another night at The Fin and Feather. She'd post a letter to her mother straightaway and ask her to send the family's solicitor with funds and a carriage, thus eliminating the need for another torturous journey on the public stage.

She thought requesting Mr. Gramercy to bring a carriage when he brought the funds was an inspired touch, as it would solve multiple problems. She'd placed a little star beside No. 1.

No. 2: Clothing and Hair. She'd hung her dress and pelisse over the broken chair last night and slept in her chemise. She couldn't continue wearing the same gown, so she'd simply have to find a modiste. Which, she acknowledged, would have a further downward effect on her funds.

As to who would curl her hair . . . There was no fireplace in the tiny room, so there was no way to heat curling tongs, even if she had them. Although it pained her to do so, she drew a line through *and Hair*.

There would not be a solution for this particular problem any time soon. She closed her eyes and inhaled a calming breath then released it slowly.

No. 3: Jory Tremayne. She'd given this one quite a bit of consideration the night before, as she had no notion how to go about learning his fate.

She knew very little about him, for all that she'd nearly eloped with him. Five years before, they'd spent their days idling beside his favorite fishing spot.

She thought back to that summer and was surprised to realize that, despite their time together, she knew only his name, not his direction or any of his family or acquaintances. And even if she had known his family, she could hardly inquire of strangers whether he'd married or not.

Inspiration had finally struck as she'd thought of her failed wedding—the most recent one. If the wedding had gone off, she and Greenvale and their witnesses would have signed the church register, so... A visit to the parish church to review the register should tell her whether Jory had married.

If he had—and she was fairly certain he would have by now—then her work here was done. She could dust her hands of this uncomfortable guilt. But nothing could erase the fact that she'd left behind another jilted fiancé, which led to her fourth and final problem...

No. 4: Rest of life. What was she to do with the rest of her life? Where would she go, what would she do once she left Cornwall?

She wouldn't be marrying Greenvale, that much was certain. And truth be told, she probably wouldn't be marrying anyone after her flight from London, so where did that leave her?

London was out of the question.

Her French had never been particularly good, so Paris wasn't a logical choice.

She and her mother had visited an uncle in Berlin after the incident with Signor Rossi. Perhaps she could rejoin him there. Or . . . could she escape to America and pass for a widow?

All of these solutions seemed a bit extreme. She acknowledged that, in the end, she'd probably retire to the Pepper home in Berkshire. Disgraced and alone. There was no ready solution for this dilemma. She'd drawn a friendly little heart around No. 4 in an attempt to make it less daunting. Puffing out a breath, she told herself she could fix this. No challenge was insurmountable, and these were no different. They were simply . . . four tiny problems.

She pressed the pillow over her face and let out a frustrated, muffled groan. Immediately, she regretted the unladylike sound, but her mother wasn't there to hear. In fact, there was no one at all to censure her actions.

She blinked in surprise then groaned again, simply because she could. Despite her lengthy list of problems (*solutions*, she reminded herself), she smiled.

JORY LEFT TROUT TO WARM the stone floor at the front of the parish church while he led Merryn along a complex path to the belfry: up a set of winding steps, down a stone-lined passage, then up more straight steps to the ringing chamber. From there, they ascended another set of winding steps to the belfry above.

"Where did you disappear to last night?" his cousin asked as he unfolded a wooden measuring ruler. "Did you run off to hoard your winnings?"

Jory snorted. "Our stakes on Mr. Malvern's speed are hardly worth hoarding."

Merryn pulled a pencil from his pocket and flipped to a clean page in his notebook. "Tell that to Cadan," he said with a chuckle. "He'd have invested the sum before the coins stopped spinning. If you weren't hoarding your winnings, then it must've been a lass."

"There's no lass," Jory said. He'd long since learned not to rise to his cousins' bait, although Merryn's words hit a little too close to home. He moved to the tower's open window to avoid his cousin's probing gaze. Rubbing his eyes, he stifled a yawn. He'd lain awake much of the night, wondering in which room Anna slept. How long would she stay? Could he avoid her for the duration of her visit?

"Grandfather is dying again," Merryn said to his back.

Jory chuckled and turned back to face him. "The old man will outlive us all."

"And yet, every month 'tis a new ailment."

"Despite being surrounded by family, I fear Grandfather suffers from loneliness," Jory said. He crossed his arms and turned back toward the street while he waited for Merryn to complete his measurements.

"A wife," Merryn said.

Jory grunted. "What?"

"Grandfather needs a wife."

Jory dropped his arms and looked at his cousin in disbelief. "Grandfather will never marry again. He's always said—"

"I know, I know," Merryn said.

"'Don't marry one you can live with. Marry the one you can't live without'," they said in unison.

Anna's image rose in Jory's mind again, and he tried to press it down. As if to mock his efforts, the lady herself emerged from The Fin and Feather at the end of the street.

Jory stepped back from the tower opening to observe without being seen. She looked left and right, then marched past the town green toward the post office, her reticule swinging from one wrist and a bonnet shielding her face from his view.

She wore a fancy dress with flowers adorning the hem, and he recalled the fussy, society lady he'd met in their first encounters by the stream. The one who wore fancy dresses and insensible slippers to traipse in the mud.

He shouldn't have been surprised by her attire now. As he'd learned later that summer, the sensible, companionable Anna he'd fallen in love with had been an illusion.

He thought of his earlier resolve to keep an open mind when it came to lasses. Firming his jaw, he turned to his cousin.

"Your sister's friend—Miss Parker," he said to the back of Merryn's head.

"What of her?"

"Is she attached?"

Merryn turned to look up at him. Jory rubbed the back of his neck and resisted the urge to drop his eyes from his cousin's assessing gaze.

"She's not attached to my knowledge," Merryn said slowly.

Jory nodded but stopped short of requesting an

introduction. He'd need to think on it before he made his interest known. Not that Merryn wouldn't blather to all of their relations now anyway . . .

"Here. Make yourself useful," Merryn said, handing him the end of the ruler.

Jory left the tower window and forced himself to stop thinking about ladies. Merryn jotted more figures in his notebook, then they adjusted their positions to take additional measurements.

"How many pulley blocks d'you think will be needed?" Jory asked.

Merryn tugged on his lower lip, thinking. "Three, I think. Two for lifting bells inside the tower, and one to move materials outside."

"And you still think the work can be completed in a year's time?"

"A year or less," Merryn said, "if the bells are ready on time."

"They'll be ready," Jory said.

After Merryn had the information he required, they retraced their steps back to the front of the church, where Trout rose to give them enthusiastic hand licks.

"Ugh," his cousin said, backing away. No words were needed to convey his displeasure as he wiped a hand on his trousers.

"She missed us," Jory said in defense of his dog, chuckling at the look on Merryn's face.

"We weren't gone above ten minutes," Merryn said. "You," he pointed at Trout, "need to learn the subtle art of flirtation. Don't lay out all your charms so readily. 'Tis unseemly."

Trout cocked her head as she listened earnestly to Merryn's guidance, then she ruined the effect with one final, wet lick of her pink tongue.

Jory grinned and shrugged, tossing his cousin an apologetic look. Trout stiffened at his side, and he looked to where a shadow had appeared in the entrance. A petite, distinctly Anna-shaped shadow. He stilled, wondering if it was too late to hide behind the pulpit.

For the briefest of moments, the cruel irony of their positions struck him. Him, standing at the front of the church looking down the aisle. And Anna, poised in the entry, haloed by the sun behind her. Almost like an eager bride. Then Trout ruined the moment and bounded down the aisle.

"Trout, no!" he hissed.

ANNA WAS DISTRACTED AS SHE approached the parish church. The postmaster had stared at her in a most disconcerting manner when she'd inquired about sending a letter to London. After some hesitation, he'd held a hand for her correspondence, but Anna couldn't shed the feeling that she'd been measured. And found wanting.

She'd glanced down at her folded and sealed missive and examined her penmanship. It was impeccable, as always, so certainly he could find no fault there. And her mother's address was entirely respectable, so that couldn't have been the reason for his regard, but nevertheless, he'd shaken his head as he tossed her letter into a mail bag.

The dressmaker's shop was still dark, so Anna brushed aside thoughts of the postmaster's scrutiny and crossed to the stone church. She needed to find the vicar so she could inspect the parish register. Once she confirmed that Jory had indeed married, she could mark No. 3 off her list.

The interior of the aged structure was dark after the bright morning sunlight, and she paused to allow her eyes to adjust.

Then, as shapes materialized, she spied two men at the front of the church. One looked remarkably like . . . She squinted. No.

Her breath caught as she recognized the all too familiar form of Jory Tremayne.

His head came up then, and she froze. She thought of turning and fleeing the church, but he'd already seen her. No, no, no.

He wasn't supposed to know she'd come to Newford. She'd no wish to see him—to suffer the awkwardness that was sure to paint any reunion—but it seemed what she wished didn't account for much in the eyes of providence.

The blood rushed in her ears as she stared at him, and her feet refused to move. At least, until his beast of a dog began racing toward her, jolting her from her frozen state. Instinctively, she raised her hands and braced her feet.

"Trout, no!" Jory said, but the dog was deaf to his command.

Anna squealed and stumbled backwards as two large black paws landed on her chest. Then she gasped at the sound of rending lace as the dog's paws raked her dress.

Stunned, she gaped at her tattered overskirt while the dog sat before her, grinning, tail sweeping the stone floor. A dirty paw print decorated the top of one slipper.

"Wha—?" Words failed her at the swift destruction of the lovely gown. At the effort wasted effort to maintain her pristine slippers on the journey to Newford. Torn lace hung loosely before her, fluttering in the breeze from the open door.

Jory reached her, the other man not far behind, and she looked up, up, into his beautiful sea-blue eyes. Her memory hadn't dimmed in the slightest, and he was just as she recalled. Better even.

Tall and broad, with hair the color of wet sand.

Soft hair with a tendency to curl at the ends when dampened by a summer shower. Faint lines fanned from his eyes, even as he frowned. Which he was doing now. Frowning and staring.

Despite her perfect recollection of his features, she'd forgotten how much he made her heart pound and her stomach twist. Gads.

Seconds passed before she found her tongue.

"I see Trout still hasn't learned her manners," she said with a small smile. She instantly regretted the words. She'd not meant to sound so disparaging, but absent any witty or sophisticated greeting, it was the best she'd been able to fashion. Why could she never think of the right thing to say?

Jory's jaw firmed as he continued to stare at her. Finally, he said, "No, but you can't fault her loyalty. She's nothing if not constant in her affections."

Anna swallowed at his not-so-subtle criticism. It was well deserved, as was the chill in his voice, and her smile slipped.

"I—I should go," she said. She could hardly review the church register with him here, and it seemed sort of silly now anyway. Could she not just ask him how he fared? Perhaps another time when he wasn't looking at her with such intensity.

The man behind him cleared his throat, and Jory closed his eyes briefly.

"Anna," he said. "Please accept my apology for

Trout's unladylike behavior. Allow me to reimburse you for the gown. And your slippers." His voice still flowed like his beloved stream over smooth boulders, his Rs rolling across her skin.

"There's no need, truly." The choking feeling was back in her chest—the feeling she could no longer deny was guilt. She couldn't allow him to suffer remorse over something so trivial as *a dress* after her poor treatment of him.

The man behind Jory watched them. His stare was remarkably like that of the postmaster—probing and slightly accusatory—and Anna frowned. Her limp curls must be worse than she thought.

Reluctantly, Jory motioned to the man. "May I present Mr. Merryn Kimbrell?" he said. "Merryn, this is Miss Anna—"

"Feather—Featherton," Anna interjected. Or was it Featherington? Featherstone? Blast.

Jory's brow furrowed, and he swallowed. "*Mrs.* Featherton."

JORY STARED AFTER ANNA AS she left the church. "Let me know what more you need to begin work on the tower," he said, rubbing a hand on the back of his neck.

"I will." Merryn cleared his throat again, clearly

awaiting information.

Jory ignored him and called to Trout, who'd begun sniffing around the pews. At his continued silence, Merryn took matters into his own hands, as expected. Indeed, Jory would have been surprised if he'd remained silent.

"So . . . Mrs. Featherton is a friend of yours?" his cousin asked.

Friend? No, Jory didn't think the appellation fit.

Friends didn't leave one waiting beside a stream at midnight, without a word or explanation.

Friends didn't make one's stomach queasy, as if one was being pitched about on stormy Cornish seas.

Friends didn't take one's heart with them then marry men named Featherton.

No, Anna was not his friend.

"I made her acquaintance years agone when she visited Penhale," he said. It was all the explanation he was willing to give.

"Oh, is that all? Because it seemed—"

Jory spun and cut him off. "I'd like an introduction to Miss Parker. If you can arrange it, that is."

His cousin's brows dipped, but he gave a short nod and remained blessedly silent.

Jory strode from the church, his boots ringing on the stone floor as Trout followed him.

"Wynne," Merryn said, once he'd tracked his cousin down in her office at The Fin and Feather. "You were right. Jory is acquainted with the lady." Then he thought of Jory's request for an introduction to Miss Parker. "But I don't think they're married as you suggested."

Wynne's lips twisted as she gave the matter further thought. "Married or not, I recognize a broken heart when I see one. And that woman, she broke our Jory's heart."

Roddie approached, standing behind his wife's shoulder. "How d'you know *she* broke *his* heart? Maybe 'twas the other way around," he said as he thumbed through a stack of correspondence.

"You've a tender heart, Roddie Teague," Wynne said, leaning up to kiss his cheek. "Always giving the benefit of the doubt, even when 'tis clear as the nose on your face that the lady is up to no good. But she'll know soon enough you can't trifle with one of ours and not answer for it."

"Wynne," Merryn said. "Perhaps you ought to let things lie. Allow Jory and the lady to address whatever's between them on their own."

Wynne stared at the two of them then gave a snort of disbelief before disappearing behind the bar.

CHAPTER EIGHT

∽

1814 - FIVE YEARS BEFORE

JORY HAD BEEN SURPRISED WHEN Anna agreed to join him at the stream the first time—and amazed at his own desire for her company as the weeks passed. She was fussy in temperament and clearly accustomed to fine things, but next to the stream, beneath the shade of the birch and alder trees, she was just a companion to share the sublime peace and sparkle of the trickling water.

She met him every day without fail, even when the weather turned mizzly. He started bringing a wool blanket to spread on the bank, and she'd sit quietly while he fished, or they'd talk about anything and nothing at all. He took extra food, and they shared picnics of cheese and fruit and cold chicken.

His grandfather had commented more than once on Jory's sharpened dedication to angling, but he'd kept his own counsel, preferring to hold his afternoons with Anna to himself.

For the first time, he wished for an income of his own. As much as he enjoyed spending time with Anna beside the stream, he wished for her to see him as more than an aimless idler. His grandfather owned much of Newford, and Jory and his uncles and cousins would inherit his holdings one day. But the desire to create an independent living grew stronger as he thought of providing for his own family.

He decided to approach his uncle Alfred about learning the bell founding business. His uncle often spoke of the mathematics involved in casting and tuning a new bell, and Jory had always had an aptitude for numbers. Perhaps Alfred would agree to teach him the craft.

But that was the future. Today, he thought to steal a kiss.

When Anna arrived, his dog trotted to her side with her own welcoming kiss. Anna accepted the lick with a grimace as Trout pressed against her leg.

"Good afternoon, lass," Jory said. He stretched his arm and watched with satisfaction as the horsehair line sailed ahead then settled gently atop the water's surface.

"Good afternoon," she said, smiling shyly. She wore another simple gown and leather half boots that peeked from beneath her hem. A fanciful bonnet with a wide brim was at odds with her more sensible attire. He smiled to see that while she may have abandoned her fine muslins and slippers, some of her fussiness remained.

"You profess an aversion to Trout, but your frequent ear rubs say otherwise."

Confusion clouded her features for a moment, until she followed his gaze to where she scratched the dog behind one ear. She laughed, a light, bubbling sound that trickled over him.

"She's hard not to like, isn't she?"

"Aye, she's shameless, that one." Jory watched as Anna lowered herself gracefully onto his blanket, folding her legs beneath her. Trout settled contentedly at her side.

He wedged his fishing pole between heavy boulders at the edge of the stream and joined them. The bank was shady enough that Anna had no need for her bonnet, so he reached over and slowly untied the ribbons. She watched him with wide eyes until he set the bonnet aside.

Her golden curls shone, even in shadow, and he wished to thread his fingers through them. He imagined they'd flow over his hands like warm honey. He leaned back on his hands and stretched his legs before him instead.

"I've brought you something," she said, reaching

behind her. "For your birthday."

She'd remembered? He straightened as she handed him a paper-wrapped bit and a folded linen. "What's this, lass?"

"It's not much," she said with a shrug. "Just some pound cake from Mrs. Steward's kitchens, and a handkerchief to replace the one you gave me. The two you gave me, actually."

He unfolded the cloth and studied the embroidery decorating one corner of the linen square. It appeared to be a tiny, silver-threaded . . . eel?

"It's a trout," she said, rising on her knees to lean toward him.

"Ah, I see. 'Tis probably the only one I'll catch today. I shall treasure it always," he assured her with a smile, and her pleasure warmed him.

Next, he unwrapped the paper to find the pound cake. Breaking off a corner, he offered it to her. She settled back on her heels and chewed slowly, eyes closed. Her tongue licked a crumb from the corner of her lip, and he swallowed before breaking off a piece for himself.

She opened her eyes and smiled, one dimple appearing in her cheek. He leaned closer, his gaze trapped in hers, but Trout roused herself and pushed between them as she headed to the stream.

Anna dropped his gaze, and Jory turned to

watch his dog sniff around the boulders where his fishing pole rested. The stones were smooth and warm from the sun, and Jory, suddenly alert, called Trout back to the blanket.

She came reluctantly, and he rose to see what had captured her interest.

"What is it?" Anna asked as he returned and settled back on the blanket.

"Naught but a bird after a grub," he said. "I thought she might have found an adder—they can be plentiful about the stream in the summer months—but 'tis nothing to worry about."

Her eyes widened, and the pitch of her voice climbed. "An adder? As in, a *snake*?" She watched the bank over his shoulder, anxious, until his voice pulled her gaze back to him.

"Aye, but 'tis nothing to fret over," he repeated. "I shall protect you. And besides, adders are more afeared of you than t'other way around."

"I'm not so certain," she said as she sidled closer.

He smiled, enjoying the warmth of her so near to his side.

"Perhaps you should have a bench here," she said, and he laughed.

"A bench, to fish?"

"Yes, then you wouldn't need to sit on the ground." She eyed the bank beyond the edge of their blanket with worry. "Surely a bench would be better in winter, too, when the ground is cold."

"I'll give it some thought," he said. "Perhaps a bench is just what this bank needs."

"Why do you like to fish in the stream?" she asked. "Instead of the ocean, that is. It's not as if you ever catch anything here."

He grimaced. "D'you not like the stream, lass?"

"Oh, don't think that," she assured him hastily. "It's lovely and peaceful. I was simply curious, when so many of Cornwall's fishermen favor the ocean."

He hesitated then admitted, "I become seasick. I can't set foot on a boat. Just ask my cousins; they'll be happy to tell you all about my foolishness." For a man in an entire *county* of fishermen, Jory's ailment had long been one of endless amusement.

"I'm sorry you become ill," she said, touching a fingertip to the top of his hand, the subject of snakes forgotten. "I become queasy before a ball," she admitted.

He scoffed. "I hardly think 'tis the same," he said, turning his hand up to receive hers.

"It is," she insisted. She swirled a fingertip over his palm, leaving a trail of fire to scald his skin, before settling her hand in his.

"No," he said. "You become queasy out of worry. My ailment—'tis nothing to do with the thoughts in my head, only with the motion of the boat. You can quiet the thoughts in your head, but you can't change the swells of the ocean."

She frowned at him for a moment. "I suppose so," she said, and he instantly felt contrite. She'd attempted to comfort him, and he'd belittled her worries.

"No," he said. "Forgive me, lass. Regardless of the cause, I think we both suffer for it. But I've no wish for either of us to fret over boats or balls. I'd rather enjoy this fine day."

Her frown fell away at his words and his heart lifted. Her leaf-green eyes shimmered in the dappled shade beneath the trees, and he tugged on her hand, pulling her closer.

She placed a hand on his chest, more to steady herself than to push him away. He reached up and covered her hand with his own before inching closer. Her eyes widened but she didn't pull away, so he gently pressed his lips to hers.

He closed his eyes at the contact. She was soft and smelled of lemons, and his heart swelled with emotion as he tasted her lips.

―――

ANNA INHALED, REVELING IN THE feel of Jory's mouth against hers, in the fresh scent of apples and sunshine that swirled about him. A tiny part of her had been imagining his kiss since the first time she'd joined him beside the stream, but a larger, more sensible part had tempered the foolish desire.

But the reality of his kiss was much better than her imagination could have painted it. The reality of *Jory* was much better than she could have imagined.

She wore old dresses and sensible shoes, and still he smiled at her. She didn't primp or preen or flirt, and yet he seemed content in her company. She confessed to her pre-ball anxiety, and he *kissed* her.

Surely the man was addled. What man in his right mind would feel affection toward such a pitiable creature? She knew it was foolish to allow hope to grow unchecked, but when Jory's hand cradled the side of her cheek, she leaned into him like a flower bending toward the sun.

"Anna," he whispered, although there was no one to hear them but Trout.

She opened her eyes to see his own studying her. They were as clear and blue as the Cornish sea, and she smiled.

"In case you haven't noticed," he said, "I'm quite besotted, and fair on my way to loving you."

The words startled her like a splash of icy water from the stream, and her eyes widened. Love? He *was* addled. But, foolishly, the hope in her chest burned brighter.

"I love your persistence—how you returned to

the stream despite Trout's attacking you, and despite the damage to your dresses." He lowered his lips to hers once more, nibbling one corner while she breathed him in and tried to make sense of his words.

"I love your pretty bonnets and sensible shoes." He moved his mouth to nibble the other corner. Surely, he was quite mad.

"I love this dear freckle," he whispered. He stroked a thumb over her cheek then leaned in and kissed the spot.

Freckle? She lifted a hand to her cheek, but his next words distracted her from her worry.

"And I especially love how you hear me without us speaking a word." He angled his lips over hers again, and she gripped his forearms.

She slid one hand to the back of his neck, and his hair curled over her fingers as his smooth lips caressed her own. Her breath was shallow when he finally pulled away, as if he'd stolen it.

Then she recalled his words and stopped breathing altogether.

Love. The poor man didn't know what he was talking about. He couldn't love her. And yet, the affection shining from his blue eyes caused her heart to stutter and skip.

CHAPTER NINE

❦

1819 - THE PRESENT

ANNA SHIFTED THE PARCELS IN her arms as she returned to The Fin and Feather. She'd just been to the dressmaker's where she'd acquired a new, ready-made dress to replace her ruined rose silk. And of course, a new dress required new slippers, so her funds were much less now than they'd been before.

The thought brought her back to her present circumstances. Her eyes burned, and she blinked. She wished for nothing more than to forget about Jory Tremayne and her ridiculous quest and return to London. Or to her home in Berkshire. She'd even go to York if it meant she could leave Newford. But as she didn't have sufficient funds for a ticket to anywhere—at least until her mother dispatched Mr. Gramercy—she was stuck in Cornwall.

With effort, Anna smoothed the frown from her face. Wrinkles never solved anyone's problems. She entered the inn and approached the desk to find Mrs. Teague making notations in her ledger.

"Good morning, Mrs. Teague," she said, fighting to put a smile in her voice. She was determined not to let her circumstances erode her good manners.

"Mrs. Featherly," the lady said in greeting.

Anna opened her mouth to correct the lady, but she couldn't recall the name she'd given her last night. Perhaps it *had* been Featherly? Shaking her head, she focused on the matter at hand.

"I'll need to secure a room for another night. And if you have one that's a bit larger, that would be preferable."

Mrs. Teague consulted her ledger. "I'm afraid that's the only room we have at the moment. As I told you, the hurling, you see . . . But I can let you know if another room becomes available."

Anna suppressed a sigh and resigned herself to another night in the tiny room. "That will be fine, thank you." She reached into her reticule for one of her precious few remaining coins.

"Let me just check your balance," Mrs. Teague said, consulting the ledger again before quoting an amount significantly more than Anna had expected.

"I beg your pardon?" Anna lowered her voice as her brows dipped. "Why is it so much?" she asked.

"I paid for last night's lodging already."

"Aye, but this balance includes your bath."

A snort of disbelief escaped Anna before she realized the lady was in earnest.

"And the ledger shows you also requested two sheets of paper. And ink. That's an additional charge."

"You can't be serious," Anna said.

"I'm afraid I am," Mrs. Teague said without apology.

Anna stared at the woman, momentarily speechless. Aunt Catherine would have cringed to hear her disputing the cost of anything, much less something as common as lodgings at a coaching inn. She would advise her to hold her head high and give imperious instruction to place the expenses on credit, thereby ending the discussion.

A lady—merchant's daughter or not—did not distress herself with financial matters, after all.

"Very well," Anna said. She held her head high and looked Mrs. Teague in the eye with her most imperious stare. "Please place my charges on credit. For the bath, the paper and tonight's room."

"I'm sorry," Mrs. Teague said. "We don't offer rooms on credit."

"You don't offer—well, what's to be done then?" Anna asked, her shoulders rounding. "I'll have more funds presently, I assure you." She wondered how long it would take for Mr. Gramercy to arrive.

Mrs. Teague narrowed her eyes. "You can hardly return your bath or the paper and ink you've used. Are you saying you don't currently have the funds to settle your balance?"

Anna thought that was exactly what she'd just explained. "Yes, but I will soon," she assured her.

Mrs. Teague pressed her lips together, then motioned to someone behind Anna. "Constable," she beckoned.

Constable! Anna spun and watched a man approach the desk. He was tall and imposing— everything a constable should be, in short. He gazed at Anna with a disconcerting curiosity, and she resisted the urge to step back. She would not allow them to intimidate her.

"This *lady* is unable to pay her bill," Mrs. Teague said.

The constable turned to Anna. "Is this true, ma'am?"

"Well, yes, in a manner of speaking" she admitted as an uncomfortable warmth spread over her face and neck. The feeling of complete and utter mortification, she assumed. "But I'll have sufficient funds soon," she promised.

"How much is the balance?" the constable asked, and Mrs. Teague quoted the ridiculous sum again.

The constable rubbed his jaw and turned to

Anna. "I'm sorry, ma'am," he said. "There's nothing for it."

"Wha—what do you mean?"

"I'll need to remand you to the Newford gaol."

"Gaol?!" she shout-whispered to the man.

"What's the problem?" a new voice said from behind Anna.

Jory. *Now* her mortification was complete.

AGAINST HIS BETTER JUDGMENT, JORY approached the discussion taking place at the desk. Anna had clearly caused some sort of to-do for which he felt partially responsible.

Why he felt such accountability when he'd neither seen nor heard from the lady in five years, he couldn't say, but there it was.

After Wynne explained the situation, he pressed a hand to his jaw to hide a grin. Anna, detained in gaol? Gavin was well respected as constable, and she wouldn't be mistreated in his custody, but Jory didn't think she'd appreciate his thoughts on the matter. Or his amusement.

But the notion was too entertaining not to relish. If he'd been a vindictive man, he would have enjoyed the poetic justice of the moment—was he daft? The poetic justice was *magnificent*.

He coughed to cover a laugh.

But no matter how much he might wish to see Anna carted off to gaol, he couldn't allow it. The uncertainty in her eyes was his undoing. His foolish heart still held an affection for her, it would seem.

"Certainly, there must be another solution," he said, and the uncertainty in Anna's eyes lightened to something more closely resembling hesitant hope.

Wynne watched them, and Jory smoothed his features to remove any sign of interest in Anna or her fate. He was merely an objective bystander, nothing more.

"Well . . ." Wynne said, tapping her lip with one finger.

"Yes?" Anna asked, leaping on Wynne's hesitation.

"Peggy is out with a broken foot, and with the hurling coming up, I'll need more help. D'you have any experience?"

"Experience? With what?"

"Working at an inn."

"Working?!" Anna shook her head. "No, I couldn't . . ."

Wynne looked at Jory as if to say, *There. I tried.*

Gavin sighed and reached for an inner pocket of his waistcoat. He wasn't truly going to put her in shackles, was he?

"Wait," Jory said, holding up a hand and turning

to Anna. "Surely you can try. Wouldn't it be better than gaol?"

She gazed at him, a tiny furrow between her green eyes. Her hesitancy—her anxiety over the situation—nearly broke him. He was about to offer to pay her bill, but then she straightened and looked Wynne in the eye.

"Yes, I can do it. I can"—she swallowed and waved a hand over the room but stopped short of saying *work*. "I can help," she said.

"YOU'LL NEED A MORE SENSIBLE dress," Mrs. Teague said, eyeing the torn lace of Anna's rose silk gown.

Anna lifted the paper-wrapped parcels she carried, pleased that she'd had the foresight to acquire a new gown. "I'm prepared," she said.

"Very well. Go change and return in fifteen minutes, then I'll show you what to do." Mrs. Teague handed her the key to room eight.

Stunned, Anna contemplated her change in circumstances as she climbed the stairs. She was three shillings from gaol and about to begin a life of drudgery working at an inn.

Helping, she reminded herself. Thinking of *work* as *help* was the only way she'd been able to swallow the notion of herself as a common inn person.

Gads, if Mary Riverton—if her father—could see her now... And yet, the pleased half-smile on Jory's face when she'd accepted the challenge had warmed her insides.

She wondered what tasks Mrs. Teague would have for her. Perhaps she could mend the linens, she thought. She enjoyed needlework, although her stitches had never been very straight. Then the notion of touching another person's bed linens sent a small shudder through her, so hopefully the lady had another task in mind.

She wasn't very good with sums, but perhaps she could help with the ledger. Mrs. Teague spent an inordinate amount of time perusing the large book at her desk. She supposed she could assist there, although ... she thought of the ink that would stain her fingers and forced the frown from her face.

She had experience entertaining and planning menus with her mother's cook. Surely an inn had a need for such skills, if the stringy mutton and overcooked potatoes she'd experienced on the journey to Newford were any indication. That wouldn't be so bad. Perhaps she *could* do this.

Anna pushed the door of her room open as far as she could, but she couldn't fit through the small opening with her parcels in hand. She tossed them in one by one then sidled into the room.

Fifteen minutes wasn't much time to change, so

she hurried to unwrap her packages. The dress was a soft, sprigged muslin in pale pink, and the slippers were precious with a little heel and dusky pink rosettes on the toes. She might not know how to work at an inn, but at least she'd have the most darling shoes while doing so.

Not for the first time, she wondered what her mother would make of her experience. She'd probably expire on the spot to see her daughter living in a common inn, wearing a common, ready-made dress, preparing to work for her lodging.

She inhaled and forced her brown thoughts aside. Time was short, after all, and Mrs. Teague was waiting.

She'd never purchased a ready-made dress before, but the shop owner had assured her it would fit. She pulled it over her chemise and petticoat then tied the ribbon beneath the bodice. Straightening, she looked down at herself in dismay.

The gown was much too long for her petite frame and puddled on the floor. It would need to be taken up at least two inches. Why on earth had the dressmaker believed it would fit her? And where was Meg when she needed her?

Anna carried needle and thread in her reticule, so she hurriedly undressed and set to taking up the hem. When she finished, she shook out the garment and admired her work. It wasn't perfect—her mother would have made her pull all the stitches and start over—but it would do.

When she finally descended the stairs, Mrs. Teague looked up from her desk with a frown. "You're late, Mrs. Featherson," she said.

Anna narrowed her eyes. She may have been a gudgeon, but she was certain she'd not given the lady such a ridiculous name as *Featherson*.

―

"Gaol was an inspired touch," Wynne said to Gavin with a little smile.

"I thought so," he replied.

"Were you truly going to place her in shackles?"

"Of course not!" he assured her. "I was merely reaching for my watch."

Wynne tapped her lip, thinking. "Did you see how quickly Jory defended her?"

Gavin chuckled. "Indeed."

CHAPTER TEN

Mrs. Teague, as it turned out, didn't need anyone to mend the linens or manage the ledger or coordinate the menu. Anna, it seemed, was to be a barmaid.

A barmaid. Gads.

Her eyes burned at the thought, and she blinked rapidly to prevent tears from falling. The pink slippers were a mite snug on her feet, so she concentrated on the pinching of her toes to take her mind off her other troubles.

Mrs. Teague reached behind the bar and retrieved an apron, which she handed to Anna. Then she explained her responsibilities in exquisite detail, from how to take a customer's order to how to draw a pint of ale without filling the glass with too much foam to how to count out a customer's change.

Anna was exhausted before her duties began, but she thought that with diligence, perhaps she could see the day through and settle her bill. She'd worry about tomorrow . . . tomorrow.

Gazing at the near-empty coffee room, she didn't quite understand Mrs. Teague's emphasis on efficiencies. What difference did it make if the snoring gentleman in the corner received his ale in three minutes or five?

As Mrs. Teague droned on, Anna took the tray from her and interrupted. "I think I'm ready, Mrs. Teague."

The lady stared at her for a beat, then nodded. "Very well. The next coach is due in"—she consulted a clock behind the bar—"four minutes."

And in five minutes, Anna began to comprehend the lady's obsession with efficiency.

The coach clattered into the inn's stable yard, horn blaring, and discharged its passengers. They entered the inn *en masse*, demanding ale and bread and cheese.

None of them had the correct change.

All of them were irritable, travel-worn and dripping water onto the stone entry as it had begun to rain.

Two ladies requested rosewater to refresh their handkerchiefs and were vocally disappointed to learn The Fin and Feather had only lavender water.

The coach's horn blared again, and four passengers had yet to receive their ale. They glared at Anna before storming out to the stable yard to resume their journey. She sighed to see the back of the last passenger, only to turn and find Mrs. Teague handing her a mop.

"For the puddles in the entry," she said.

Anna's shoes pinched more tightly than before, and she felt a bead of perspiration form along her hairline. Perspiration! But she took the mop from Mrs. Teague and sopped up the puddles.

When she returned to the coffee room, she was surprised to see the table in the window collecting a crowd of boisterous gentlemen. As she watched, two more arrived from the street-side entry.

She approached the table and recognized the postmaster who'd stared at her so rudely that morning. The constable was also present, and she frowned.

"Good afternoon, Mrs. Featherton," a voice said from behind her.

Anna turned and recognized Jory's acquaintance, Mr. Merryn Kimbrell. Relieved to see a familiar face—one which wasn't set on critiquing her penmanship or casting her into the Newford gaol—she smiled.

"Good afternoon, Mr. Kimbrell." She greeted him with a shallow nod, then she noticed the faces of the remaining men gathered around the table. They studied her with an intensity that gave her pause, their scrutiny not unlike the postmaster's. The town's citizenry truly wasn't accustomed to visitors it would seem.

Resisting the urge to step back from their inspection, she straightened instead and began collecting their orders.

"Whisky."

"Ale and one of Wynne's raspberry tarts."

"Ale and a copy of the *Times*, please."

"Whisky."

"Change mine to ale," the first gentleman said.

Anna blew a fluff of hair from her forehead and mentally tried to keep track of which seat ordered which beverage.

A thump against her leg caused her to turn, where she found Trout grinning at her, black tail swishing against Anna's skirts. And where there was Trout . . . She looked up into Jory's blue eyes.

"Ale, please," he said as he took the remaining chair.

Perfect. She bit her lip and nodded, an uncomfortable warmth flooding her insides. How much longer would it take to settle her debt?

―

JORY TRIED TO ATTEND TO his cousins' banter, but his eyes kept straying to Anna. She was as lovely as he recalled—his memory hadn't exaggerated there—although her apron nearly swallowed her whole.

Once or twice he caught her limping, as if her shoes were too small. He wasn't surprised to see delicate pink slippers beneath the sagging hem of her (also pink) gown. Had she not learned anything, then, about sensible footwear?

He turned back to the table to find his cousins watching him in rare silence, their faces shining with varying degrees of amusement. Even Gryffyn wore a half-smirk.

Jory cleared his throat. "Alfie," he said. "I hear you've gotten yourself into a spot with the Stanton sisters."

His cousins responded as expected, with jeers and taunts at Alfie's expense. Jory crossed his arms and tipped his chair back as Alfie smirked and doffed an imaginary hat in his direction.

Once the initial uproar began to settle, James leaned back and spoke casually. "Forget about your troubles with the Stanton sisters, Alfie. Wynne's newest barmaid is quite comely, don't you think?"

The legs of Jory's chair came to the floor with a heavy thud, and Trout perked her ears at him. His neck heated, and he felt a scowl forming despite his efforts to maintain a bland expression.

"Indeed, she is," Cadan agreed. "Although she seemed a little stiff when she came to the post office this morning. She's not quite as friendly as Peggy, but I imagine a wink and one of your grins would loosen her up a bit, Alfie."

"Stubble it, lads," Merryn said. "Our Jory is acquainted with the lady."

Jory's scowl broke free as he glared at Merryn.

"Do tell, cousin," James said, brows lifted as he leaned forward on his elbows.

At that moment, Anna arrived with their orders, and Jory relaxed at the reprieve. She balanced her tray on the edge of the table and began passing whiskies and ales around. The *Times* for James and a raspberry tart for Merryn.

"Thank you, lass," Alfie said with a wink and a grin.

Anna blinked at his blatant flirtation, and Jory couldn't help wishing he'd let Gavin lock her in gaol. She might not have preferred it, but his sanity would have thanked him for it.

The whisky and ale silenced his cousins temporarily, but it did nothing to dim their memories. It wasn't long before Cadan brought them back around to the topic on everyone's minds.

"What's the tale with the lovely barmaid, Jory?" he asked. "How are you acquainted with the lady?"

"There's no tale to tell," Jory said, crossing his arms again. "'Twas naught but a passing acquaintance years agone when she visited Penhale.

And I believe she's married now, so you may as well look elsewhere."

He directed the last bit toward Alfie, but he feared he protested too much. His cousins weren't idiots—generally speaking. He was certain they'd see through his nonchalance if he didn't tread carefully.

"Married, you say?" Alfie asked. "Where's her husband?"

Jory's cousins watched him for a beat longer than was comfortable. "How should I know?" he asked.

Finally, Alfie turned his attention to James, and conversation shifted to the headlines in James's paper. Jory relaxed when Alfie said, "Pass the society page, cousin."

James snorted but divided his paper. "I don't know why you read that dribble."

"'Tis entertaining," Alfie said. "Far more exciting than the financial bits. Take this, for example: 'This author was shocked to discover that Lady Q launched a physical assault on Lady M in retaliation for aspersions against her prized Persian's character.'" Alfie lifted a brow then frowned at his cousins' unimpressed reactions.

"No? Here's another: 'The author has it on good authority that the colorful Lord G is blue after one salty Miss P left him at the altar.' Heartless!" Alfie said, clutching his chest. "The poor man is well rid of her, I say. He should be thanking providence rather than bemoaning his lost love."

A cold heaviness settled on Jory's chest. The "poor man" probably was well rid of his lady, but that didn't mean he wasn't miserable, as Jory well knew. He stared into his ale and sought another topic. Anything other than tales of foolish men and fickle ladies.

"Merryn," he said. "Tell us about the new lending library you're to build."

Merryn grinned and launched into his favorite topic—building—as he outlined the library's design on the table with one finger.

Jory sat back and listened, one ear tuned to Merryn's overly detailed monologue and the other to the whisper of pink slippers on the planked floor. His attentiveness was the reason he was the first out of his chair when Anna tripped over the sagging hem of her gown and upended a tray of empty glasses.

He reached her side as she stood amid the shattered glass, eyes round, one hand pressed to her mouth.

"Anna," he said. "Step away from the glass before you're injured."

She looked up from the destruction at her feet, and he thought he saw the shimmer of tears before she inhaled and lifted her head. After a moment's hesitation, she took his hand and gingerly stepped over the glass to stand at his side.

A jolt fired from his fingers to his stomach at the contact, much like the clear vibration of a perfectly tuned tenor bell. Her hand was soft and small in his larger one, just as he remembered, and if he held it overlong . . . Well, he had no excuse.

He dropped her hand as Wynne approached with a broom and brass dustpan. He took them and bent to sweep up the glass.

"I can do it," Anna said from his side as she held her hand for the broom.

He looked over his shoulder and spied raw determination in the set of her jaw. A force of will completely out of scale with the task at hand.

Every male instinct shouted at him to do the task for her, to be gallant and comfort her. But his human instinct recognized that, for whatever reason, this was a task she needed to do herself. He nodded and stood, handing her the broom.

"You don't have to do this," he whispered.

"Yes. Yes, I do." She nodded and began sweeping.

ANNA'S HAND STILL BURNED WHERE Jory had held it. She pressed it against her waist and savored the tingling sensation. Her feet were blistered in her pink slippers, and she was more exhausted than she'd ever been in her life—even more than after the Effingham's masquerade last season when she'd danced every set. But despite her fatigue, her hand felt oddly alive.

It was well past midnight. Her shift had ended, and the coffee room was nearly empty. Only Jory and one of his companions remained at the large table in the window.

She stood before Mrs. Teague's desk as the lady tallied figures in her ledger. Certainly, given Anna's labors of the past hours, she'd earned enough to settle her bill. With luck, she'd gained enough to sustain her until Mr. Gramercy arrived with the carriage and more funds.

"One farthing," the lady said as she straightened.

"One—one farthing? That's all I've earned?" Anna chewed her lip nervously. One farthing would not pay her bill, much less secure lodgings until Mr. Gramercy arrived.

"No," Mrs. Teague said with a wry twist of her lips. "One farthing is how much I've added to your bill."

What?! Anna narrowed her eyes on the lady. "What do you mean?"

Mrs. Teague calculated, ticking figures off on her fingers: Anna's wages and tips, less her room and board for the day, less the cost of six broken glasses and five mugs of ale that had to be discarded for "excessive foam."

"Fortunately, the gentlemen left generous tips." She motioned with her head to the tip box affixed to the wall. "But still, your balance for the day comes to one farthing."

"I—It *cost* me money to work here?" Anna asked with disbelief. She'd failed miserably then.

A complete gudgeon with more hair than wit. Her father had been right in his assessment. She didn't think he'd had barmaiding in mind when he'd uttered the criticism, but if she couldn't manage even the most elementary of tasks, what use was she to anyone? Mrs. Teague would probably send for the constable, and she could hardly say she blamed her. Would Mr. Gramercy be able to find her in gaol?

"That it did," Mrs. Teague said with censure, pulling Anna back to the conversation. Then, to Anna's surprise, the innkeeper's expression softened. "But you did well for your first day. You'll do better tomorrow."

She'd done *well*? Was the woman daft? Then she heard the rest of her statement.

Tomorrow. She had to do this *again*?

Mrs. Teague seemed to expect a reply, so Anna nodded slowly. She supposed she ought to be thankful she had a place to sleep for the night. She turned her heavy, blistered feet toward the stairs.

The darkened hallway, lit only by a brace of flickering candles, fit her mood perfectly. Long shadows danced on the walls and chased her as she passed. She slid sideways into her room then frowned in surprise. There, on the small bedside table, was a fresh linen towel next to a pitcher of steaming water.

IT WAS WELL PAST MIDNIGHT, past the time when Jory would normally have retired to his room. He had an early day at the foundry tomorrow, but he'd waited to be sure Anna made it through the rest of the night without further mishap.

The look of dismay on her face as Wynne tallied her wages had been amusing, but he sobered to see her limping up the stairs. The urge to follow, to comfort her, was strong, so he turned back to Gryffyn instead.

Of all his cousins, Gryffyn was the one for whom he felt the greatest affinity.

A stone carver by trade, Gryffyn had aspirations—and talent to match—to become a sculptor. An appreciation for craftsmanship was something they had in common, aside from their shared hordes of relations. Gryffyn's love of the smooth beauty carved from stone well matched Jory's for the sweet sounds carved from the inside of a bell.

Of all his cousins, Gryffyn was also the most perceptive, so Jory resisted the urge to shift in his chair as his cousin watched him.

"Is that her?" Gryffyn asked.

Jory lifted his brows in question then drained his ale.

"The lady you planned to elope with?"

Jory set his mug down. Denial sprang to his lips, but then he saw the smug certainty on his cousin's face.

"You knew?" he asked.

Gryffyn snorted into his own mug. "You asked to borrow a carriage, then you didn't need it, then Grandfather said you were teasy as an adder for weeks afterward. I'm not a scholar, Jory, but it didn't take one to put the pieces together."

Jory sighed. "Aye. That's her."

Gryffyn nodded.

"Do the others know?" Jory asked.

"I've not said anything, but that doesn't mean they won't reach their own conclusions." His cousin paused before adding, "And I should tell you, Wynne suspects something."

Jory nodded. He wasn't surprised by her suspicions—Wynne was a suspicious sort by nature—but he *was* surprised she'd not confronted him yet about Anna.

"D'you mind if I ask what happened?" his cousin said.

Jory stared into the dregs at the bottom of his mug, wishing he'd ordered whisky instead. He scrubbed a hand over his face, remembered pain and wounded pride burning the back of his neck.

"I wish I knew, Gryff. I was a fool and fell in love with an illusion, I suppose."

CHAPTER ELEVEN

~~~~

1814 - FIVE YEARS BEFORE

"Is—is that a freckle?" Her mother's mouth curled down in disgust, and she leaned in to peer at Anna more closely. Anna lifted a hand to her cheek self-consciously and rubbed, as if she could wipe the offending spot away.

"*Ach*, have you not been wearing your bonnet? Perhaps you should spend less time out of doors. No gentleman of quality will wish to take a freckle-faced miss to wife. We must call for a lemon straightaway." Her mother marched to the bell pull and gave it a sharp tug.

"Perhaps . . ." Anna began haltingly. Her mother waited, one brow lifted expectantly. "Perhaps a freckle isn't so bad?" Anna finished. She'd meant the words as a statement, but they squeaked out with a question mark at the end.

Jory liked her freckle, so it couldn't be such a horrid thing. No, he *loved* her freckle.

Her mother gazed at her, lips puckered as if she'd sucked on the lemon she'd just requested.

"Don't be a gudgeon, my dear. You know how much your father always despised silliness."

Gudgeon. Her father's words were rarely far from her mind. *A complete gudgeon with more hair than wit. What man in his right mind would willingly tie himself to such a creature?*

What man, indeed?

IT HAD BEEN THREE WEEKS since Jory's declaration, and while Anna had permitted—and enjoyed—more of his kisses, she hadn't allowed him to speak of love.

She knew it was horrid of her, but whenever he gave her *that* look—the one that said he was about to speak words she longed to hear—she found an excuse to examine a rock at the side of the stream, or to scratch Trout behind the ears, or to inspect a loose thread on her skirt.

Because whenever she thought of his confession of love, her breath stopped. He couldn't love her, not truly. His inevitable disappointment when the illusion faded wasn't something she thought she could bear. Just the thought of it was enough to cause her own heart to crack painfully in her chest.

Once or twice, he'd cast looks of confusion her way, but she'd merely distracted him with another kiss or a well-aimed smile.

She didn't know how much longer she could continue to distract him, or herself. How much longer could she resist the enticing promise of his words?

She needed to end this, before the waiting became any more unbearable, but she'd been unable to say the words.

Trout's short bark brought her attention back to their surroundings. Jory's fishing line danced on the water, the cane rod bending slightly from where it anchored in the rocks, and Jory jumped to tend to it.

He turned to face her, his broad grin lighting the shadows around them. "Bring the net, lass," he said, and his excitement caused her heart to turn over.

She scrambled from her place on the blanket and hurried to him with the net. He dipped it into the water beneath his line and brought up a thin fish no more than two or three inches long. Its wet scales shimmered as it bounced in the net, and Anna smiled, pleased that he'd finally caught something.

Then she saw his crestfallen face and frowned.

"Ah, lass, 'tis naught more than a gudgeon."

A gudgeon? "What"—she cleared her throat—"what do you mean?"

"And a small one at that. Tain't fit for the table."

He unhooked the fish and tossed it back into the stream then moved to stand. On seeing her downcast expression, he relaxed his own frown to smile reassuringly.

"Worry not, lass. We anglers are optimists by necessity. Something better will come along."

Her throat tightened. "Jory."

She pressed her lips together, determined to resist his pull. To say what she'd been trying to tell him for the last three days.

"My mother and I—we're returning to Berkshire."

His smile collapsed. "You're leaving, lass? When?"

"Tomorrow," she lied. They planned to leave the following week, but she couldn't bear to see Jory another day. The weight of his looming disappointment was crushing her.

His eyebrows shot toward his hairline. "So soon?"

She nodded and turned her attention to Trout so she wouldn't have to see Jory's confusion.

"Anna," he said, reaching for her hand and pulling until she faced him. "Don't go."

"I can't remain here indefinitely, Jory. I have

acquaintances back home." She swallowed. "Another London Season to anticipate."

He studied her, and her eyes burned. She blinked, but the sting didn't ease.

"Marry me," he said.

"Marry you?" Her heart skipped, and she commanded it to settle. At Jory's earnest expression, she said, "I'm not certain my mother would approve." That much, at least, was the truth. Her mother would not wish to see her wed to a Cornish fisherman, no matter how blue his eyes.

"Then we'll elope." He lifted her hand and kissed the backs of her fingers.

"Elope?!" she squeaked.

"We'll do it tonight. I can secure a carriage, and we'll ride north. Say yes, Anna."

He gripped her hands and waited, gazing at her through thick lashes. Trout's tail swished and thumped Anna's skirts, the dog as eager for her answer as her master.

Elope with Jory? Surely it was madness to consider such a thing, but her heart picked up its pace again. Could she do it? *Should* she do it? She nodded her reply before she could stop herself.

Jory's grin widened, and he moved his hands to her face. His blue eyes caressed her face in the second before he pressed a hard kiss to her lips. Against her better judgment, she responded. He angled his head to deepen the kiss, and Anna's eyes burned with the sense of heartbreak yet to come.

What man in his right mind would tie himself to such a creature?

THAT NIGHT, ANNA PLED A headache and requested supper in her room. A maid left a tray with a curtsy and asked if she required anything further. Anna declined and dismissed her, anxious to be alone again.

She couldn't quite believe she was actually doing it. Eloping with Jory. Turning to the armoire, she studied her clothing, unsure what was considered proper attire for an elopement. She placed dresses, shifts and stockings into a small bag and stared at it.

Her heart pounded, and her palms grew damp. She pictured a life where Jory would come to despise her. Or worse, ignore her and turn to another. Much as her father had ignored her mother. Much as he'd turned from them in favor of his other family.

And how miserable would she be then, when her hopes came crashing down and that which she longed for above all else remained firmly out of reach?

She drew a heavy, shuddering breath and sat on the end of the bed. The clock on the mantle ticked, overloud in the silence. It was nearly midnight, the time she and Jory were to meet by the stream. The moon had risen to cast its silver beam on the floor of her room. It would light her way along the path to Jory, if only she would let it.

She couldn't do it.

She remained on the end of the bed, watching the moon crawl across the night sky. Tears traced twin paths down her cheeks, and she wondered what Jory must be thinking as he waited by their stream.

JORY WAITED UNTIL WELL PAST midnight, Trout's soft snores rumbling beneath the high-pitched sounds of night. Finally, he acknowledged the truth. Anna wasn't coming.

His stomach was hot and rolling, much like it felt when he set foot on one of his cousins' boats. For the first hour, he'd told himself she was merely late. Perhaps she'd had difficulty escaping her mother and Mrs. Steward. Or trouble selecting which slippers to pack.

But the second hour came and went, then the third, and he could no longer delude himself. She wasn't coming.

He lifted his bag and trudged back to his grandfather's house, silently letting himself in the servants' entrance.

He lay awake on his bed, moonlight streaming through his window as he relived every touch, every conversation he and Anna had shared. As he tried to determine what had gone wrong.

Had he imagined her regard and the sweetness of her kiss? Had he done something to upset her?

When the moon had set and the sun began lighting the horizon, he decided to return to the stream. Just in case she'd had a change of heart. He went earlier than his usual time, and he stayed much later than he normally would have, but still she didn't come.

The following week, he learned that Mrs. Pepper and her daughter had not, in fact, left Cornwall as he'd been led to believe. Hurt and angry, he stomped through the woods to Penhale.

As he reached the edge of the estate's broad lawn, he slowed his steps, unsure what he would do, what he would say if he saw her. Could he still convince her to come away with him? Did he even wish to? Why would she lie to him about returning to her home?

As he stood in the shadows of the trees with his unanswered questions, the doors of the manor opened, and a striking older lady emerged. She strode down the steps to a waiting carriage and paused while a footman let down the steps.

Anna emerged next, dressed once again in fussy

silks and lace, and his heart cracked a little more. The urge to go to her, to convince her to stay, was strong, but he forced himself to remain still.

She moved to the carriage slowly, eyes shadowed by her fanciful bonnet. He pled with her to look up, to see him. Surely, she couldn't miss him if only she'd look up, but her head remained down, focused on the tips of her slippers.

She entered the carriage behind her mother, skirts disappearing in a swirl of blue silk, and he watched the coach drive away.

CHAPTER TWELVE

1819 - THE PRESENT

ANNA WOKE AGAIN TO THE trumpeting horn of an arriving stagecoach and groaned. She tilted her head back and looked out the window above her. It was still dark. She rolled her eyes then rolled from the bed.

Pain shot through her feet as they made contact with the floor. She lit her candle with a flint and sat on the bed staring at her feet in the meager light.

They were swollen and blistered. Where had her ankles gone? She turned one foot to the side and examined it. Could she have done permanent damage? Would she never walk again?

A panicked fluttering started in her chest. She closed her eyes as anxiety rolled over her, then she pushed herself up from the bed. Her feet throbbed and burned, but it was a positive sign that she could feel them, wasn't it?

She turned to the porcelain basin at the little table. She was surprised to find that the longer she stood, the more accustomed she became to the pain in her feet. It wasn't a pleasant feeling by any stretch, but the discomfort brought an unexpected sense of satisfaction.

Surely so much pain was a sign that she'd accomplished *something*.

As she washed, she thought of Jory. She'd come to see if he was settled, if he was happy. She still didn't have an answer, but she suspected by his lingering at the inn well into the night that he wasn't eager to return home to a wife.

The thought caused an odd blend of sadness and relief to swirl about her. Sadness, she could understand. She wished for his happiness, after all. But relief? Why would she feel relief when she'd come to Cornwall for the express purpose of assuring herself he was settled? Relief was an emotion clearly at odds with her intention.

Regardless of Jory's state of happiness, her recent trials felt like an odd sort of penance. Not that he would forgive her—she'd never expect that—but her work the day before had had an unexpected cleansing effect. If she didn't look forward to today's duties with eagerness—she wasn't mad, after all—she might welcome them with acceptance.

She thought again of that dreadful night five years ago. The night she'd left Jory alone, waiting for her by the stream. Her stomach turned at the memory, as it always did. It would take more than a few shifts in the coffee room to atone for her treatment of him. She dressed then pinned her hair, forcing the memory from her mind.

A knock sounded at her door, and she moved slowly to answer it. A maid thrust two packages through the narrow opening then hurried away. Anna turned them over, but there was nothing to identify the sender.

She chewed her lip, thinking, then hesitantly opened the first parcel. And was surprised to find a soft blue muslin dress. Simple but respectable. She held it up to her small frame, noting the length was perfect. No hemming required.

After a short hesitation, she exchanged her pink dress with the deadly hem for the blue and glanced down at herself. Sadly, she thought her blue satin slippers would have been perfect with the dress, were they not days away in London.

Then she recalled the second package. She opened it with more eagerness, surprised and mildly disappointed to find . . . sensible shoes. Half boots, to be precise.

Her forehead creased in confusion, and she forced it to smooth as she studied the boots. They weren't blue satin—far from it—but this was Newford after all. She doubted anyone would give her a second look if she wore sensible footwear. Indeed, she'd come to appreciate such necessities five years ago. Delicate slippers and fine dresses were not the thing for lounging beside a muddy stream.

She removed the pink slippers and tried on the boots, sighing in relief. They were a much better fit than the slippers, although not nearly as dear. But she thought about the hours ahead, and she decided in this situation, *sensible* was infinitely preferable to *dear*.

She descended to the public rooms and approached Mrs. Teague. The lady's red hair was perfectly curled and styled, and Anna felt a moment of envy as she touched a hand to her own limp curls. She waited before the desk for several moments while Mrs. Teague consulted her ledger. Finally, Anna cleared her throat.

"Aye, Mrs. Featherbill?" Mrs. Teague asked without looking up.

"How much for the dress and boots?"

Mrs. Teague's head did come up then. "Aye?"

Anna motioned to the dress and shoes she wore. "How much will this add to my bill?"

Mrs. Teague eyed her attire in confusion, then her expression cleared, and she smiled. "I take it you received the parcels that arrived this morning."

At Anna's nod, Mrs. Teague returned her attention to the ledger. "They came from Mrs. Williamson's shop, but I can assure you they're not from me."

Anna frowned. "Then who sent them?"

"Perhaps your husband?" Mrs. Teague asked with a wave of one hand.

Anna knew when she was trapped. "Oh, yes," she said. "Perhaps."

THE GENTLEMEN FROM THE TABLE at the front window had returned. Honestly, had they nothing better to do than spend their evenings at The Fin and Feather? Nevertheless, Anna took their requests and went to pour whiskies and ales.

When she returned to distribute their orders, she stopped short. Mr. Kimbrell, who normally sat in the fourth chair, was now in the second chair. The postmaster had moved from the fifth chair to the first, and the constable was not where he was supposed to be either.

They gazed at her with innocent looks, and she pressed her lips together. She'd memorized their orders by their positions at the table as Mrs. Teague had taught her, but that was before they'd rearranged themselves.

From the corner of her eye, she caught sight of Mr. Kimbrell's twitching lips as they awaited her reaction. They thought to fluster her with their childish prank?

Very well. She could do this. She balanced her tray on the edge of the table and concentrated on recalling their original places.

"Coffee for the constable," she said, passing him a steaming cup of dark coffee.

"Ale and a raspberry tart for Mr. Kimbrell." She handed him a full mug then considered the remaining orders.

"Ale for Mr. Postmaster."

He nodded as she placed his order in front of him. "Mr. Cadan Kimbrell," he said with a smile.

She nodded then moved to the next order, tapping her lip. "Whisky for Mr. Flirt."

The group laughed at the gentleman who'd flirted with her the previous day, and he gave her another broad grin and a wink.

"Mr. Alfred Kimbrell," he said. "But my father is also Alfred, so my friends call me Alfie."

"Heavens, another Kimbrell?"

"Aye," he said. "We're some prolific, but I'm from the desirable side of the family."

The constable jabbed him with his elbow, and Mr. Alfie Kimbrell lifted his whisky defensively.

"Am I to suppose then," she said, narrowing

her eyes on the constable, "that you're Constable Kimbrell?"

He grinned. "Aye. Constable Gavin Kimbrell."

She acknowledged him with a short nod before turning back to her tray. She had one whisky and one ale remaining.

Twirling a curl at her nape, she twisted her lips to the side, considering. The quiet gentleman who'd stayed late with Jory had left an overly generous tip in the box.

"Whisky for the generous gentleman with the large tip."

Someone coughed and the generous gentleman murmured, "Gryffyn Kimbrell."

"And that leaves ale and the *Times* for you, sir," she said as she handed the remaining mug and a newspaper to the final gentleman.

"Mr. James Kimbrell," he said with a smile.

Heavens, six sturdy Kimbrell men. The family was very prolific indeed. She chewed her lip, thinking.

"Are you related to the Kimbrells of Oak Hill, near Penhale?" she asked the table.

"Aye, Mrs. Featherton," the postmaster replied. "Alan Kimbrell is our grandfather. Are you acquainted with him?"

"I've not had the pleasure," she replied. "My mother and I visited Penhale some years ago, but we never met your grandfather. I believe he was in mourning at the time. My condolences on the loss of your grandmother," she said.

They nodded as one, warm smiles on their faces in remembrance, then Mr. James Kimbrell said, "She was a lovely woman. You remind me of her."

Anna's eyes widened as the other gentlemen nodded their agreement. "Thank you. I can tell you held her in great affection." She returned their smiles, then ducked her head before collecting her tray.

She was ridiculously pleased with the compliment and with herself for beating the gentlemen at their own game. Oh, she knew the achievement was a small one—she'd not cured smallpox or ended a war or fed a village after all—but the gentlemen's approving grins made her feel as if she'd passed some sort of test.

She glanced at Jory's empty seat, and her elation flagged. She may have enjoyed his companions' banter and compliments, but she would much rather have had a single approving glance from him instead. She turned from the table and encountered the object of her thoughts, arms crossed as he took in the gentlemen's merriment with a frown.

She hesitated, then asked, "Ale?"

He nodded and followed Trout to his chair.

Jory's hands were clenched in tight fists, and he forced himself to relax as he greeted his cousins. They'd been *flirting* with her.

When he'd arrived to witness their harmless prank, the impulse to scowl at all of them had been strong. The urge to take Anna's hand—to kiss her senseless and show them that her affections were spoken for—was as irrational as it was unwelcome. As pathetic as it was untruthful.

She was married after all. To someone else. She was very clearly *not* his.

She'd made her thoughts known five years ago, so why couldn't he let it go? Why must his heart feel like the cracked parish bells—hollow and damaged?

When she returned and placed a mug of ale before him, he nodded his silent thanks, and she moved to another table.

He should have stayed at the foundry. He could be working on the new bell molds instead of... instead of torturing himself with thoughts of a life that would never be.

His cousins grew quiet until he couldn't ignore their stares any longer.

He sat straighter, stretched his mouth into a grin and asked, "How will we defeat Jago Simmons and the rest of the southern lads in the hurling this year?"

ANNA SHOOK OFF THOUGHTS OF Jory's frowning irritation and joined Mrs. Teague at the bar. "You appear to be woolgathering, Mrs. Featheringill."

Anna's brows lifted, but she let the ridiculous name pass as she set down her empty tray.

"What is the hurling that everyone speaks of?"

"What is—why, hurling is the sport of Cornwall! 'Tis the most anticipated event of the year by any Cornishman's calendar."

At Anna's look of confusion, Mrs. Teague leaned on the bar and continued. "Here, 'tis like this. The men of Newford will form two teams according to which side of the river they reside upon. The aim for each team is to get a little silver ball across their goal." She shrugged as if the explanation made perfect sense.

"Last year's winner, Mr. Flirt"—she motioned with her head to the window-table—"will toss the ball in the town square, then the teams will compete to carry it to their respective goals."

"That—that's it?" Anna asked. "They just have to move a little ball?" She thought it sounded quite unremarkable, and at odds with the frequency with which the event was discussed.

The lady sighed. "You'll have to see it for yourself, Mrs. Featherwood. 'Tis quite something to behold."

Anna nodded, unconvinced. "Where are the

goals?" she asked.

"That's part of the excitement," Mrs. Teague said, eyes shining. "The goals are about a mile beyond Newford. The teams will have to cross field and stream, hedges and ditches and briars to reach them. The gentlemen will need to display quite a bit of strength and stamina to win, and they always look deliciously rumpled after the event."

"Oh," Anna said, holding back a sigh. She nibbled her lip, thinking a "deliciously rumpled" Jory would indeed be a sight worth seeing. "Will the inn have a part in the festivities?" she asked.

Mrs. Teague nodded. "We'll close the coffee room 'til the teams move beyond the town proper. Then we'll need to prepare for a crowded night after the game is completed. Many of the gentlemen—and townswomen as well—will return here to celebrate." The lady's eyes lit with anticipation while Anna's feet throbbed at the thought of more crowds to serve.

―

LATER THAT EVENING, ANNA TAPPED a finger on her lip and pondered again the mystery of her new dress and boots. If Mrs. Teague hadn't sent them, then who had? Had her mother received her letter? If so, why did she not just send funds? Why send a dress and boots?

She looked down at her ensemble. It was simple. Unremarkable. Definitely not in the first stare of fashion. No, she could say with certainty her mother had not sent the items.

Jory. That was the only explanation. It was wholly inappropriate for him to send her a dress, but who else could it have been? And inappropriate though it may have been, she couldn't help the warm fizzing in her veins at the thought.

She watched him at the window table, grinning with his companions. Trout sighed and rolled onto her side, content to nap at his feet. Jory laughed at something one of the gentlemen said, his blue eyes bright. He looked up then and caught her watching him, and his grin slipped.

Anna swallowed and turned to tend another patron. Why shouldn't his grin falter on seeing her? She'd done nothing but treat him ill, so his displeasure on catching her gaze shouldn't come as a surprise.

But if he was so displeased to see her, then why had he sent the dress? Though she'd no reason to expect it, was it possible he was beginning to soften toward her?

Warmth bloomed in her chest. Hope. She hurried to push it down. Nothing would be accomplished by allowing herself to hope for Jory's good opinion. Only certain disappointment lay in that direction.

Nevertheless, when he pushed back from the window table, she hurried after him. She needed to know.

"Jory," she said.

He looked up and stopped, one foot on the stairs as Trout waited at his side. "Anna."

She chewed her lip and tried to think how to bring up the question of the dress. Finally, she offered, "I can get you more ale, if you'd like."

"No, thank you. I have an early morning at the foundry, so I'm retiring."

Anna looked at the stairs behind him, confused. "You live here?" she asked, dismayed that she knew so little about him.

"On occasion. When I've a large commission at the foundry, 'tis more convenient to stay here."

She nodded.

"Good night, then," he said and started to turn.

"Jory," she said again, reaching for him.

He turned back to her, and she dropped her hand. "Did you send me the dress?" she said on a whisper, aware of the crowded coffee room behind her.

"What dress?"

She rolled her eyes and held her skirts to the side. "This one. It arrived this morning. Did you send it? And the boots?"

His eyebrows came together, and he shook his head. "I didn't send it."

Disappointment swiftly drowned her tentative hope. Of course he hadn't sent it. Anna nodded and dropped her head.

"Perhaps it's from your Mr. Featherton," he said.

She looked up. His blue eyes were intent on her. She couldn't lie to him. Again, that was. She couldn't lie to him *again*.

"Jory, I'm not married," she said, her heart skipping. He remained silent for so long she thought he must not have heard her. "I'm sorry, I should have been honest, but I'm traveling alone, and it didn't seem prudent..." Her voice trailed off as he continued to stare at her.

"I didn't send the dress," he repeated.

"Oh. Well, all right," she said. Then, mustering her courage, she asked, "Are you? Married, that is. Did you ever—"

"No." He stared at her for a beat longer then turned and climbed the stairs.

―――

JORY ENTERED HIS ROOM AND closed the door before he remembered Trout behind him. He opened the door again to find her sitting in the hall, head cocked, gazing at him in confusion. He waved her in, and she trotted to curl up before the fireplace. Settling her head on her paws, she watched him curiously for a moment before her eyes drifted shut.

And just like that, he was forgiven.

He scrubbed a hand over his face. If only people—if only *he*—could forgive as easily. He thought if he could just forget his time with Anna, he might find some peace. He might be able to move forward. But unfortunately, his memories were clear and sharp, not likely to be forgotten anytime soon, much less forgiven.

He pulled his shirt over his head and splashed cold water on his face and neck.

She wasn't married.

She wasn't married.

The refrain played over and over in his mind. But as much as he might wish otherwise, the fact that there wasn't a Mr. Featherton didn't change anything.

She'd still left him waiting five years ago.

She'd still left *him*.

But if her fictional Mr. Featherton hadn't given her the dress . . . and Jory hadn't sent it . . . which of his idiot cousins had?

CHAPTER THIRTEEN

TWO DAYS LATER, ANNA CHEWED her lip as Mrs. Teague completed her calculations in the ledger. The lady muttered softly as she made tidy notations in the margins, head bent toward the page.

Anna tried to be patient, but she couldn't help shifting her weight from one foot to the other. Her feet were considerably improved in the new half boots, but that wasn't to say they were pleased with the day's work, and she thought longingly of her hip bath in London.

Fortunately, the hem of the blue dress had performed admirably, and she'd neither tripped nor dropped any more glasses. Just the three soup crocks today . . .

Mr. Teague entered from the coffee room and reached for a key on the wall.

"Good evening, Mrs. Featherton," he said.

Anna greeted him with a short nod. "Mr. Teague."

He rounded the desk and glanced at her feet. "I see you've opted for more sensible shoes. Excellent choice," he said with a wink.

Anna stared after him as he left to greet a new arrival.

"Do you enjoy working in your husband's inn?" she asked Mrs. Teague.

The lady spoke while she continued tallying figures in her ledger. "You have it backwards, Mrs. Featherstine. *He* works in *my* inn. And," she added, "I'd hazard to say he enjoys it very much."

Anna wasn't sure what to say to that. She'd never met anyone quite like Mrs. Teague. She wanted to hate her—certainly, she had cause—but she found herself liking the lady just a little.

Finally, Mrs. Teague looked up from the ledger, and Anna straightened. The lady was smiling. That was good, wasn't it? Anna smiled back and rocked on her heels.

"Much improved," Mrs. Teague said. "Your credits offset your debits."

Anna blinked. "What does that mean?"

"It means you don't owe anything."

"But—but I didn't earn anything, either?"

"No," Mrs. Teague said, closing the ledger. "But the gentlemen's tips were even better than the previous nights, so that's something."

Anna sputtered. "How am I ever to repay my debt?"

"The hurling."

"Pardon?"

Mrs. Teague shrugged. "The hurling. I told you we'll have quite a crowd that night, and half of them will be euphoric with their win. Flirt a little, and you'll be surprised how large the tips will be."

Who knew her mother's lessons in strategic flirting would prove so prescient?

LATER THAT EVENING, WYNNE CORNERED her husband in the inn's small office as he addressed some correspondence. She crossed her arms and waited, admiring his hand as it moved across the page. He glanced up and hesitated at the look on her face before turning his attention back to the letter before him.

"What's on your mind, love?" he asked.

"My cousins all deny sending Mrs. F the dress and boots," Wynne said casually.

"Do they now?"

"They do. I doubt there's a Mr. F who could have sent them, and I know *I* didn't send them. Which leaves Jory. Unless . . ."

"Unless?"

"Unless my husband has taken an interest in the lady's welfare."

"Why would he do that?" Roddie asked, setting his pen aside and sanding the page.

"I can't imagine why he would do such a thing," Wynne mused. "Other than the simple fact that he has a soft heart." She turned to leave then stopped.

"Was there something else, Wynnie?" he asked.

She loved when he wore (what he considered) his innocent expression. She started to mention that his left eye was twitching, then she thought better of it. If he didn't know how she could tell he was fibbing, who was she to enlighten him?

She smiled and surprised him with a kiss instead. "No. Just that I love you," she said.

———

A FEW DAYS LATER, JORY contemplated returning to Oak Hill. Sleeping at the Feather may have been convenient for his work at the foundry, but it was wreaking havoc on his senses knowing Anna lay somewhere nearby. The very unmarried Anna.

As he finally began to drop off to sleep, Trout whined at the door. He groaned then turned over. "Trout," he mumbled.

She whined in response. Sighing, he rolled from the bed and pulled on trousers and a shirt.

"This had better not have anything to do with the cur down the street," he told her as he stabbed his feet into his boots. He opened the door to his room, and Trout shot toward the stairs, her nails clattering on the wooden treads as she descended to the main floor.

He started to follow but stopped on seeing Anna at the end of the hall. *Unmarried* Anna. She looked up, green eyes shimmering beneath thick lashes, and her candle cast its warm glow on her soft cheek. The cheek that he longed to touch again. He clenched his fist and nodded at her instead.

She smiled hesitantly as she opened her door. "Good night," she whispered, then she slid into her room. Sideways.

Frowning, Jory stared at the closed door. Once he'd retrieved his dog, he went in search of his cousin.

"Wynne," he called from the desk. There was no answer. "Wynne!" he called again.

Finally, she emerged from the office at the back. She looked at him with a bored expression, brows lifted. "Aye?"

"What game are you playing?" he asked.

"What d'you mean?" Her innocent stance was at odds with the shrewd gleam in her eye.

He enunciated in case she was hard of hearing. "Why is Miss—Mrs.—Featherton sleeping in your broom closet?"

She gave him a closed-lip smile. "Cousin, I don't know what you're going on about. You know as well as I that the hurling brings a lot of guests this time of year. I must improvise to accommodate them all."

"Wynne . . ."

"If she were a relative, or a close friend of a relative, perhaps I could have found a better room for her. But she's just a fancy Londoner passing through. A Londoner with a debt to pay, mind you."

"Wynne, this is beneath you."

"Oh stuff, Jory." Wynne crossed her arms. "What concern is it of yours?"

Jory inhaled through his nose. He wasn't sure what his cousin was up to, but he didn't like it. "Put her in a proper room, Wynne. And send her a proper bath to make up for what you've done."

The slightly smug twist of his cousin's lips contradicted her glare. The slightly smug, *calculating*, twist.

"And don't charge her for it," he clarified.

———

THE NEXT EVENING, ANNA WAS stunned and not a little pleased to find she'd earned a farthing. An entire farthing. But that was nothing to her astonishment on Mrs. Teague's next words.

"Mrs. Featherington, the occupant of room twelve has gone, and I've had your things moved there. You'll find the accommodations are a bit more spacious than room eight." She reached for a key on the wall behind her and handed it to Anna, then resumed marking items in her ledger.

Anna stared at the key, then at Mrs. Teague. Suspicious, she asked, "How much does it cost?"

"Same as room eight," the lady said without looking up.

Still suspicious, Anna chewed her lip. If the room cost the same as room eight, she thought it couldn't be much more spacious. It was probably worse, in fact, if such a thing were possible. What if there were mice? Or bugs? As tiny as room eight was, at least it was clean.

"Is there something else, Mrs. F?"

"Can I not remain in room eight?" she asked.

Mrs. Teague puffed a put-upon sigh. "Room eight is no longer available."

Anna trudged up the stairs, dreading what she would find. As she inserted the key to room twelve, Jory reached the landing. He looked up and stopped when he saw her, then he gave her a short nod before disappearing down the opposite hall to his own room.

Anna twisted the key then pushed on the door, expecting to encounter resistance—a bed, a table, a mop and bucket. But the door flew back on smooth, silent hinges to hit the wall behind, and Anna gasped.

The room was easily three times the size of room eight. Four, perhaps. A low fire burned in a small fireplace, and a bed—a real bed, not a cot—beckoned along one wall. Velvet curtains framed the window and two candles—two!—added their light to the fire's glow. But the best part: a small tub sat in front of the fireplace, steam rising above it in beautiful, flowing tendrils.

Anna squealed and ran into the room. She flopped onto the bed with a short bounce and looked left, then right, taking in everything. She rose and went to inspect the tub, swirling one hand in the warm water. A short stool stood next to the tub with a clean linen towel and a fresh cake of soap. She lifted it and inhaled, closing her eyes. Orange blossoms.

Pulling the curtains against the night, she made short work of her boots and dress. As she placed one foot into the water, she hesitated. Certainly, there'd been a mistake. One for which she'd receive a bill on the morrow. But she'd worry about tomorrow... tomorrow. Tonight, she was having a bath.

———

JORY CHUCKLED TO HEAR ANNA'S delighted squeal followed by the heavy thud of her door closing. He entered his own room with a smile, then quickly wiped it from his face.

He was pleased that Wynne had done as he'd asked. It was the proper thing to do. Why she'd placed Anna in the broom closet in the first place was a mystery, but he had his suspicions. His cousins were nothing if not loyal, and if Gryffyn was correct, then Wynne suspected something of the events from five years before.

So yes, he was pleased that Anna had been given a proper room, but that didn't mean he needed to turn warm and brainless as a Christmas pudding on hearing her joy.

Trout watched him from her spot near the fireplace. "Her joy doesn't concern us in the least, does it?"

The dog perked her ears toward him but didn't offer an answer.

CHAPTER FOURTEEN

~~~

THE ANTICIPATED HURLING HAD FINALLY arrived, and Jory felt an odd fizzing in his veins—not unlike sparking metal—that he feared was due to more than just the competition. Anna and Wynne watched the festivities from the top balcony of the inn, and his neck burned with awareness. Would this ridiculous infatuation never end?

Anna would leave soon, wouldn't she? She'd return to London, and perhaps then he could resume his life. Days filled with molten metal, out-of-tune tenor bells, and fishing with Trout. Peaceful days free of this unwelcome, burning ache. This frustrating conflict in his heart, forged of equal parts hurt and longing.

He wished to hit something. But as that wasn't his way, he turned his energies instead to the hurling.

He anticipated the coming dash over hill and

dale, through hedges, ditches and streams. The scrambling and scratching and wrestling as both teams fought to get the ball to their goal. Whoever was fortunate enough to carry it would need to be swift of foot and strong to withstand the inevitable flattening from the opposing team. And from Jago Simmons, whose play was often less than fair.

His cousins surrounded him, and taunts were exchanged with the southern team as everyone gathered in the street to await the start of the game.

It wasn't unusual for the winner to receive a victory kiss. Alfie had received a number of them the previous year, if he recalled. The proprieties were somewhat more relaxed on hurling day. If the more rigid matrons sniffed their disapproval, they were far outnumbered by the revelers.

For a moment, Jory enjoyed a fleeting fancy in which he returned with the silver ball to Anna's smiling face. He imagined she would clap and squeal her delight, and then he would swoop down and capture her lips beneath his. Cradle her head in his hands and breathe her in. And not let go this time. His heart pounded, and the game hadn't even begun yet.

"LOOK, THERE'S RODDIE," MRS. TEAGUE said, pointing

to the growing crowd of males gathered below their balcony vantage point. Her expression softened as she watched her husband and, without a word of summons, the man looked up. His gaze unerringly found his wife, and he gave her a soft smile before his teammates secured his attention once more.

Anna turned away with an uncomfortable lump in her throat, both intrigued and embarrassed to witness such obvious affection between the pair.

Unable to dampen her curiosity, she glanced back at Mrs. Teague to see the lady's cheeks were pink and her eyes bright as she watched her husband, and Anna was surprised by a flash of piercing envy. She tried to smile but it felt more like a grimace, so she focused her attention on the proceedings below as more gentlemen joined Mr. Teague.

They were down to linen shirtsleeves, vests and coats discarded for the hurling. She recognized the cobbler, Mr. Kitchens, and the baker's son. Then several of the Kimbrell gentlemen arrived. Finally, Jory appeared with Trout at his side.

Mr. Kimbrell—Merryn Kimbrell, that was—pointed to where Anna sat with Mrs. Teague. Jory looked up and gave Mrs. Teague a broad smile, then he nodded politely at Anna.

She swallowed. Would he always be so reserved toward her? She knew she'd done him a horrible turn, but she longed for the easy friendship they'd shared so many years before.

Mrs. Teague explained again that Alfie, as last year's winner for the northern team, would start the play. After an inordinate amount of banter and shoving between the two teams, he strode to the center of the street and dealt the silvered ball with a deft toss into the air.

With shouts, North and South clambered for possession of the little ball, tossing it from player to player up and down the length of the high street. The play was rough, as Mrs. Teague had promised, with players slamming into buildings and each other and the assembled crowd down below.

Earlier that day, Anna had assisted Mrs. Teague in securing boards over the inn's lower windows. She now saw the reasoning behind such a precaution as well as Mrs. Teague's high vantage point.

Then Anna gasped. "Did you see that man hit Jory?"

"Aye, 'twas Jago Simmons," Mrs. Teague said with a frown. "But fear not. His poor behavior won't go unrewarded."

Indeed, as they watched, Mr. Teague's elbow found its way into Mr. Simmons's ribs. Mrs. Teague cheered and clapped for him, and Anna caught herself squealing when Jory made a particularly impressive catch from the postmaster.

Jory looked up at the balcony, and she pressed a

hand to her mouth and tried to regain some decorum. What would her father have said to see her carrying on so?

She pushed down thoughts of his displeasure—he could hardly criticize her now—and squealed again when the North broke free with the ball and headed for the goals beyond the town.

"Oh," she said, fanning herself. "This is exciting!"

Mrs. Teague quirked her lips in amusement. "Come, Mrs. F," she said. "They'll return this way soon, and we'll learn who's won. In the meantime, let's make sure all is in readiness."

Together they pulled down the boards securing the street level windows, then they set out extra chairs and glasses while they waited for the teams to return.

Some time later, the sound of distant shouting reached the inn, and they went to wait at the entrance.

"'Ere, they're coming!" a spectator shouted. And indeed, they were. Unrestrained shouts came from the end of the high street and grew louder as the crowd of men approached.

Anna lifted onto her toes to see, but the crowd was too thick. Several other spectators had perched on wagons and railings, so she hurried into the inn and dragged a chair to the porch. Climbing on top, she gained an unobstructed view of the gentlemen.

The constable led the way, a wide grin on his face, and Trout danced at his side, barking happily. And in the middle of them all, atop Kimbrell shoulders (those of Mr. James and Mr. Alfie Kimbrell), sat Jory.

"Oh, look!" Mrs. Teague said. "Jory reached the goal!"

He laughed and grinned with his compatriots, then cuffed Alfie on the ear when they threatened to drop him. His joy was contagious. Indeed, Anna's insides squirmed with it.

His companions set him in the middle of the street, and well-wishers swarmed to congratulate the men. Anna clapped her hands and bounced on her toes in the chair, sharing a grin with Mrs. Teague.

But when she looked back up to find Jory, it was to see a lady with her arms locked around one of his as she offered smiling felicitations.

As Anna watched, the lady pressed Jory's arm tighter beneath her hands and Anna flinched. Her stomach plummeted to her sensible shoes, and every inch of her skin burned.

"Come, Mrs. F," Mrs. Teague said softly. "Let's go inside."

But Anna couldn't move. She couldn't breathe.

What had she expected? She'd come to Newford to assure herself Jory was well settled and happy.

She could hardly fault him for receiving the attentions of another, could she? But as rational as the argument was, it didn't ease the pitching roll of her stomach. Or the crushing sense of all that her cowardice five years before had cost her.

"Mrs. F, let us go." Mrs. Teague repeated as she pulled gently on Anna's hand.

Anna forced a smile to her face. "Yes. Let's prepare for the crowd," she said.

WHEN JORY RECOVERED FROM THE surprise of finding Miss Moon's arms attached to his own, he disentangled himself and looked up, but Anna was gone. He gave a short but polite nod to Miss Moon then stepped away before she could offer a congratulatory kiss.

"Proper job, old man," Gavin said, handing him the silver ball. "'Tis yours 'til next year!" He clapped Jory on the back and ushered him toward the inn. Jory stretched his aching jaw and glared at the back of Jago Simmons.

His hurling elation had evaporated, and he tried in vain to recapture it. While his team had been racing toward the goal, then on the exuberant return to town, he'd managed to forget Anna. The energy and excitement of the challenge had supplanted all thoughts of her, at least until his cousins set him down. Then his first impulse had been to find her, to share his celebration.

His fanciful musings from before the hurling had returned, and the image of greeting her with a thorough kiss wouldn't leave his thoughts, despite Miss Moon's ill-timed welcome. What was wrong with him that he couldn't forget Anna?

He entered the inn, ignoring his cuts and bruises, but before he could join his cousins at their table, Wynne stormed toward him. "What is wrong with you?" she hissed, poking a finger in his chest.

As he'd just been wondering the same thing, he didn't have a ready answer for her. He lifted his hands in surrender as she leaned closer.

"Keren Moon? Truly?" Wynne threw her hands up and left him.

CHAPTER FIFTEEN

A NNA WATCHED AS YET ANOTHER group of gentlemen entered the crowded inn. The Teagues had joined her in taking and delivering orders, and she relinquished the window table to them as she had no wish to see Jory. Yes, she'd come to Cornwall to satisfy herself that he was well-settled and happy. He seemed happy enough, she thought, setting down an ale with more force than necessary.

"My apologies," she said to the gentleman as she offered him a cloth to wipe foam from his coat.

As she unloaded a tray of empty mugs at the bar, Mrs. Teague thrust another full tray into her hands. "Take this to the Kimbrell gentlemen, please," she said.

Anna stared at the mugs in dismay, but the lady had already spun in the other direction. It seemed she wouldn't be able to avoid Jory after all. She sighed and carried their orders to the window table, where she was surprised to find an older gentleman seated with the Kimbrells.

"Mrs. Featherton, there you are," Mr. Merryn Kimbrell said with a smile. "We thought you'd abandoned us."

"Never, sir," she said with a tight smile.

"Allow me to introduce my grandfather, Mr. Alan Kimbrell of Oak Hill. He's come to celebrate with us tonight."

Anna offered the gentleman a shallow curtsy, balancing her tray and silently praying the drinks didn't slide off as she rose. "I'm pleased to make your acquaintance, Mr. Kimbrell."

He studied her, much as the rest of the gentlemen had done when she'd first made their acquaintance.

"Have we met before, Mrs. Featherton?"

"No, Mr. Kimbrell. I visited Mrs. Steward some years ago, but I believe you were in mourning then, and my mother and I didn't wish to impose upon your hospitality. My condolences on your loss, sir." She cringed to think how she must appear to him — once a guest of Mrs. Steward at the luxurious Penhale estate and now a lowly barmaid.

"Thank you, my dear. You remind me of her. My wife, that is. She was a little thing and quite lovely, just as you are. You have a brightness about you that's more than just your pretty hair."

Anna's mouth rounded for a moment before she found her voice. She was accustomed to empty flattery, but the sincerity of the elder Mr. Kimbrell's words, the kindness of his smile, made her cheeks heat. She felt Jory's eyes upon her, and she carefully avoided his gaze.

"Thank you, sir."

She swallowed then began distributing orders from her tray. As she greeted each man in turn, she was surprised to see the effects of the hurling upon their persons.

Mr. Merryn Kimbrell's knuckles were bruised, and Mr. Alfie Kimbrell's eye had begun to swell. Mr. James Kimbrell's sleeve showed long green streaks from the grass as well as darker stains that she hoped were mud. Goodness, if it weren't for the broad grins they wore, she'd think they'd been in a common brawl. On the losing side.

When she reached Jory and passed him his ale, she couldn't resist looking up as he took the mug from her. Then she gasped.

"You're injured!" she said, resting the tray on the table before she dropped it. He sported a thin cut above his left eye and a darkening bruise on his jaw, probably from the despicable Mr. Simmons.

He ducked his head and lifted a hand to his brow. "'Tis nothing," he said. "Merely the price of victory."

"Yes, well I hope the little silver ball was worth it," she said with some tartness.

"The rewards of victory are always worth the sacrifice," Mr. Alfie Kimbrell said before drawing a long swallow of ale.

Anna recalled the lady she'd seen congratulating Jory, and she pressed her lips together. Rewards, indeed. Then she inhaled, reminding herself she'd come to Newford to see that he was happy.

Mrs. Teague approached with a bowl of water and a linen cloth, which she handed to Anna. "For the cut on his brow," she said, motioning to Jory.

Anna stared at the linen. Was she meant to tend his injury? While everyone watched? She looked up and found his blue eyes trained on her, his mouth turned down.

"Anna," he said.

"Yes?" she whispered.

"The linen, please."

She looked down to where he held his hand for the linen and bowl. "Oh! Of course." A flush heated her cheeks, and she passed him the cloth. His fingers grazed hers, warm and rough and so familiar, even after five years. She pulled her hand away quickly.

"Mrs. Featherton," the elder Mr. Kimbrell began. "My family is gathering at Oak Hill for luncheon on Sunday. If the weather holds fair, we'll make it a picnic. Please say you'll join us."

"Oh, I couldn't, sir." He was inviting a barmaid to his home?

"Nonsense," Mrs. Teague said from her side. "Sunday is your half day. You must go."

What? She had a half day? She looked around the table, and all the gentlemen were nodding their encouragement, save one. Jory was busy blotting the cut on his brow.

"You'll ride with me," Mrs. Teague continued.

"Oh ho! You risk your life to ride with this one at the reins," Mr. James Kimbrell said, to which he received a heated glare from Mrs. Teague. He ignored her and said, "You may ride with me."

"Or me," Mr. Gavin Kimbrell said.

"You're to go as well?" Anna asked Mrs. Teague.

"Of course. I rarely miss luncheon with Grandfather. Alfie will assist Roddie here. We shall attend church together, then you'll ride with me to Oak Hill." She gave a short nod to set their plan.

Anna opened and closed her mouth on a denial, but the Kimbrell gentlemen gazed at her expectantly. Their grandfather watched her with a smile, waiting. Finally, she recalled her manners. "Thank you, Mr. Kimbrell, for the invitation," she said. "I'd be delighted to attend."

Then Mrs. Teague's words registered further. Grandfather? "You're related to the Kimbrells then?" Anna asked her.

"Aye" Mrs. Teague said. "Before I became a Teague, I was a Kimbrell. I'm sorry to claim this lot, but they're my cousins."

Frowning, Anna turned to Jory. "Are you related as well?" she asked.

He looked at her in surprise before nodding. "Aye, my mother was a Kimbrell," he said.

"I . . . see." And suddenly, she did. The constable who'd threatened to toss her in gaol. The innkeeper who'd given her lodgings in a broom closet. The postmaster and all the others who'd scrutinized her so closely.

They were his cousins. They *knew*. She didn't know how, but they knew what she'd done to him five years ago, how she'd left him. Had he told them? The innkeeper had given her lodgings as soon as she'd arrived, so she didn't think so. And even if he had told them, it was no less than she deserved. Her cheeks burned, and she swallowed.

"Jory, will you ride with us?" Mrs. Teague asked.

His eyes darted to Anna, then he shook his head. "No, cousin. I've no wish to die just yet. The last time I rode with you, you nearly landed us in the river."

———

JORY WATCHED ANNA LEAVE THEIR table and wondered how he was to suffer through Sunday luncheon with her present. What had become of his very sensible plan to put the past behind him and focus on his future? Keren Moon caught his eye from across the room and smiled—undeterred by his less than enthusiastic reception. He should be keeping his mind open to possibilities, but he couldn't muster more than a polite nod of acknowledgment in her direction.

The cut on his brow pulled when he frowned, so he smoothed his features and brought his attention back to his cousins. As conversation ebbed and flowed around him, he drank his ale and interjected when necessary, but always he was aware of *her*.

Anna hurried back and forth across the room, delivering orders and greeting patrons. Smiling pleasantly, twirling a curl here and tossing a dimple there. Never too bold or outside the bounds of propriety, but still he ground his teeth as appreciative gazes followed her. As bad as it had been to hear her flirting with his cousins, he didn't think he could bear to see her making eyes at strangers much longer. He'd leave and return to his room if he thought his cousins wouldn't remark on his low mood.

Anna approached a noisy table of gentlemen from the southern team, and a jittery unease rolled through him as Jago Simmons eyed her. She tossed the group a bright smile and balanced her tray on the edge of the table while she dispersed their orders. As he watched, Jago's hand reached up and rested on her backside. Anna stiffened and sidled away, and Jory came out of his seat.

He reached the table in three steps and took the tray from her. "Go," he said in a low tone, and after a brief hesitation, she did.

"You've had your last round, lads. You'll be leaving now."

He reclaimed their orders with angry movements, sloshing ale onto the tray as he replaced the mugs. The men seated around the table watched him with a mixture of surprise, amusement and affront, but he ignored their blustering protests.

Simmons stiffened and made to stand. Jory longed to hit something, and he flexed his fist. Then Simmons looked past him and slowly sank onto his seat. Disappointed, Jory glanced over his shoulder to see his cousins standing at their table, arms folded and tense. Simmons had more sense than he'd credited the man with.

Anna hovered in a corner beyond his cousins, watching Jory with wide eyes, and something shifted in his chest. He relaxed his fist and turned back to the table where the men eyed him warily.

"Come, lads." Simmons said. "The maids at The White Dove are more accommodating."

After they'd gone, Jory took the tray and crossed

to the bar. Wynne met him, lips pressed in a thin line, and he pulled her aside.

"What are you on about, Jory? You're driving away my paying customers," she said.

"How much does she owe?" he asked, ignoring her complaint. Anna wasn't a barmaid. She didn't belong at the Feather, and he didn't think his heart could take more nights like tonight.

"Cousin?"

"How much does Miss—Mrs. Featherton—owe you?"

She frowned for a moment then told him, one brow raised in question.

"I'll pay it," he said. "Consider it a tip. Tell her she's earned enough to settle the debt, and release her from your employ."

Wynne studied him for a beat then nodded. "If that's what you wish."

"I do," he said, not at all sure he did.

ANNA'S LEGS WERE SHAKING FROM her encounter with the rude gentlemen at the far table, and her knuckles whitened where she gripped the sides of her apron. She resisted the urge to rub her hip, if only to dispel the sensation of Mr. Simmons's hand.

She stood in a shadowy corner and watched

Jory, her heart twisting in her chest to see anger in the rigid line of his posture. Her throat tightened at his cousins' ready defense of him. Jory may not have married, but he wasn't without love. He had an entire town behind him, while she had . . . what?

An abandoned fiancé. A mother more concerned with her daughter's wedding than her marriage. A half-sister she didn't—couldn't—acknowledge, no matter that they'd once been friends.

Her eyes burned, and she squeezed them tight. When she looked up, Mr. Cadan Kimbrell was approaching her corner.

"Are you well, Mrs. Featherton?" he asked.

"Yes," she said. Then, because her whisper had lacked certainty, she nodded.

"Pay them no heed," he said, motioning to the table at the far side of the room. "The southern team has always lacked sense, but 'tis no excuse for their poor behavior tonight."

She smoothed a hand across her stomach, pulling in a breath. Her face burned to know they'd all witnessed her mortification, but she dipped her head in reply. "Thank you."

He nodded and watched her for a moment before taking his leave to rejoin his cousins.

"Mr. Kimbrell," she said, halting his departure. "Have you by any chance received a letter for me?" She'd instructed her mother to write to her under the name "Mrs. Featherton." While it was probably too soon to expect a reply, she had a sudden, desperate wish to know she wasn't quite as alone in the world as she felt.

Mr. Kimbrell rubbed his jaw. "No, Mrs. Featherton. I'm sorry to say I've not received any post for you."

She tried to smile, but the corners of her mouth wouldn't quite turn up. "Thank you."

Much later, well into the early hours of the morning, all the patrons had left except Jory and the constable. The silence rang without the inn's boisterous crowd.

"Good evening, Mrs. Featherton," the constable said, tipping his hat as he left.

"Good evening, sir."

Anna retrieved a broom and began sweeping the floor, the rhythmic swish of straw on slate the only sound in the near-empty room. Presently, Jory stood, and Trout roused herself to follow him up the stairs. He'd not spoken to Anna since the incident with Mr. Simmons, and his silence as he left was a heavy weight on her heart.

Mrs. Teague stood at the desk, tallying figures in her ever-present ledger. Mr. Teague leaned down and spoke softly to his wife, one hand at her waist, before disappearing into the office.

Swallowing, Anna approached the desk and

leaned the broom against the wood.

"How long have you and Mr. Teague been married?" she asked.

The lady glanced up then returned her attention to her notations. "Oh, Roddie and I have been married nearly two years now, but I've loved the man quite hopelessly my entire life. He's both my greatest strength and my greatest weakness."

"How—how nice," Anna said.

"Love is no fairy tale," Mrs. Teague continued, and Anna's eyes widened at the vehemence in her voice. "'Twill make even the most certain of us doubt ourselves. 'Tis difficult and messy, a game without rules, and just when you think you've figured it out . . . Well, I don't suppose I need to tell you any of this."

Anna frowned and sought to turn the subject.

"Have you finished tallying the day's receipts?" she asked, although she dreaded to hear the poor sum. After the incident with the southern team, she'd ceased flirting with the patrons. She'd made a concerted effort to deliver their orders in as cool a manner as she could, in fact. Although she'd not been rude, she'd been efficient and impersonal, and her jaw ached from the effort of not smiling.

"I have," Mrs. Teague said, her forehead wrinkling.

Anna cleared her frown and waited, forcing her hands to relax their grip on one another.

"Congratulations are in order," Mrs. Teague said in a flat voice. She hesitated, then added, "You've earned enough tonight to settle your debt, and more besides for your room. Your services at the Feather are no longer needed."

Anna stared at her, eyes wide. "I don't understand," she said. "I'm sure the tips couldn't have been that generous."

"They were generous," Mrs. Teague said as she counted out Anna's wages on her desk.

Anna eyed the coins as they glinted in the candlelight. Her debt was settled then. The thought should have pleased her, but instead she felt hollow.

With nowhere to go, she'd nothing to do but . . . what? While away the days waiting for her mother to send the carriage? She stared at the toes of her sensible shoes, dismayed at the thought that she was no longer needed.

"But—I did drop that glass," she said. "Did you account for that?"

"I didn't forget about the glass," Mrs. Teague said with a twist of her lips.

"What about the crock I broke yesterday? Did you remember to include that?"

"Aye, Mrs. F. I assure you, I've not missed any of your expenses."

Anna continued staring at the coins as she chewed her lip.

Mrs. Teague tapped her chin with one finger. "Peggy's not fully recovered, though..."

Anna straightened hopefully and blinked.

"I could still use some help in the coffee room," Mrs. Teague said, "if you'd like to remain, that is."

Relieved, Anna smiled. "Well, if you still need help..."

CHAPTER SIXTEEN

JORY WOKE WITH THE HEAVY stiffness that came from being flattened by hordes of healthy Cornishmen. His ribs ached, the skin above his eye pulled, and his teeth hurt when he breathed. Trout offered comfort in the form of her long, pink tongue sweeping the side of his face.

"Trout," he mumbled. "You need tooth powder, lass."

She grinned, panting hot, foul breath in his face, then nuzzled his shoulder with her wet nose.

Jory rolled onto his back, threw an arm across his face and winced at the pain. He pried one eye open to see Trout resting her chin on the edge of the bed, watching him.

Foul breath notwithstanding, he couldn't deny her loyalty. Or her stamina, for she'd run as much as he had yesterday. He threw an arm about her neck.

Judging by the darkness in his room, it was still

early. He'd poured the bronze for the remaining church bells two days ago, and it would still be several more days before he could remove the molds. Today would be a perfect day to fish. If he could move.

Trout must have divined his thoughts as she gave a soft whine and looked to the corner where he kept his cane fishing pole.

"Very well," he said, rolling from the bed with a groan.

He packed fruit and cheese from Wynne's kitchen then went in search of his cousin. He found her counting linens in a back cupboard.

"Good morning, Wynne."

"Oh, you look some pitiful, cousin." Her broad smile was at odds with her words, and Jory wondered how Roddie suffered her cruel nature. Before his mind could worry too long over questions without answer, he turned it toward other, more pressing, topics.

"'Tis done then? Did you release Anna from your employ?" His cousin lifted her brows at his use of Anna's given name, but she held her tongue for once. His heart thumped as he awaited her reply. The sooner Anna settled her debt at the Feather, the sooner she would leave Newford. He still didn't know why she'd come, but his heart would rest easier when she'd gone.

"I did as you requested," Wynne said.

He breathed a heavy sigh and forced his jaw to relax while he waited for the thumping in his chest to ease. That was it then. Free of her debt to Wynne, Anna would surely make plans to leave for . . . well, wherever she would take herself off to. His throat felt tight, and he cleared it then nodded. "Thank you."

"I did as you requested," Wynne repeated as he started to turn, "but the lady wishes to remain in my employ. She wishes to continue her work at the Feather. 'Tis curious, don't you think?"

Jory's heart resumed its painful thrumming in his chest, and he rubbed it with a fist.

"What has passed between you and Mrs. Feath—whatever her name is?"

Jory looked at Wynne through his lashes. "Nothing of interest, I assure you."

"I doubt that to be the case, cousin. I'm sure I'd be some interested, and I'm a good listener," she said softly. "And a woman."

"A fact that has not gone unnoticed," Jory said, "however irrelevant it may be."

"My point," she said, "is that I may have insight into how other women think. If you were interested in such insight, that is."

Jory stared at her, tempted and yet afraid to open that door. In the end, he settled his hat on his head and took his leave of his cousin.

"*Dha weles*, Wynne. I'm going fishing."

"Watch for adders," she called behind him. "I hear they're some bothersome this summer."

ANNA FINISHED DRESSING AND FOUND she still had two hours before her shift. The morning promised to be a pleasant one, so she tucked a piece of pound cake from the Feather's kitchens into her handkerchief and walked.

It wasn't long before she found herself on the hillside path near Jory's stream.

She'd not returned to the place since coming to Newford, and she wasn't certain she wished to now. What if it had changed? What if it hadn't? But her feet moved of their own accord, making the decision for her.

Pushing aside the familiar crooked branch, she crossed the stand of trees to the burbling water beyond. The sun had risen just high enough to catch the stream. Its white light twinkled and shimmered as water tumbled over smooth stones and bent the long grasses along the bank.

She quickly found her favorite flat boulder, removed her bonnet and settled her skirts around her, enjoying the peaceful sounds of water and birds. She'd never been one for nature, preferring ballrooms and drawing rooms to hill and dale, but she couldn't deny there was something soothing about this stream.

She felt cocooned, wrapped in the security of the trees and stream and the soft sounds of the hillside. Gone were the scents of Newford—of horses and fish and sawn timbers. Instead, a warm, mossy fragrance folded around her, bringing with it sharp memories.

She could picture Jory standing on the bank as clearly as if it had been yesterday. Casting his line to rest atop the water, joyfully content with his persistently empty hook. Grinning at her as she fed a piece of cheese to Trout. Kissing her with the strength and gentleness she'd come to adore about him.

Soon she became aware of footsteps approaching on the path beyond the trees. She stood and turned, anticipation twisting her stomach as she waited to see who would arrive.

Trout emerged first then bounced toward her with an excited bark. Anna reluctantly accepted a sloppy kiss on her hand then looked up as Jory appeared. He stopped short at the edge of the trees. Indeed, his consternation on seeing her would have been humorous if it didn't break her heart so.

A bruise shadowed his jaw, and the cut above his eye must have pained him. She itched to soothe it with her finger. He wore simple trousers and a grey kerchief above his linen shirt. His favorite cane pole rested on one shoulder, the pose so familiar it was as if the past five years had never occurred.

Then she returned her gaze to the intent look on his face and discarded that notion. Jory didn't look pleased to see her, and she couldn't blame him. She'd invaded his favorite fishing spot. Swallowing, she brushed crumbs from her hands.

"I was just leaving," she said.

He rubbed a hand along the back of his neck. "You needn't go."

She hesitated, struck by how much she longed to stay, but his words had been strained, spoken out of courtesy rather than a desire for her company. The silence lengthened until she finally said, "I should return. Mrs. Teague will be ready for me to begin my shift soon."

He nodded, and she began to leave until he lifted a hand. "Stop," he said.

Surprised and a little heartened by his request, she stopped.

"Don't move."

Confused by his abrupt tone, she stilled until she realized his gaze was trained on the ground behind her. Her stomach sank. With dread, she turned to see what had captured his attention, then she squealed.

A grey snake uncoiled and stretched toward her, a dark jagged pattern on its back, red eyes watching her. She squealed again then lifted her skirts (lest it was a skirt-climbing sort of snake) and scrambled atop the boulder, her bonnet tumbling to the ground in her haste.

"Kill it!" she yelled, heart pounding.

"I told you not to move," Jory said in exasperation.

"*Not move?* There's a *snake*, Jory. Of course I'm going to move." She danced atop the boulder, pulling her skirts in to assure herself her ankles were snake-free.

Jory motioned Trout to his side—essentially saving his *dog* before he saved her—then he reached for a long stick in the grass.

"Kill it," Anna begged again with a shudder. This—*this*—was why she didn't like nature. What had she been thinking? All thoughts of the soothing stream behind her evaporated like raindrops on hot cobbles.

Jory approached slowly, keeping one eye on Trout as he neared the snake. Anna turned away in time to hear a loud rustling sound. She squeezed her eyes shut and wrinkled her nose as she listened to Jory's movements in the grass.

"You can come down, now," he said.

She drew in a shuddering breath. "Is it gone?" She opened one eye to see him standing before her.

"'Tis gone." He lifted his hands to her waist to help her from the boulder, and the touch of his broad palms seared through her layers of muslin.

She placed her hands on his shoulders, and when her feet were on the ground again, she looked up into his blue eyes. Her heart beat in her throat, and she thought for certain he must hear it. His scent, familiar and uniquely his, folded around her, and she could hardly hear the burbling of the stream anymore for the pounding in her ears.

He leaned closer, eyes dropping to her lips, and their breaths mingled. She waited, lips parted expectantly, then he stopped.

Straightening, he dropped his hands and turned away. She shivered from the loss of warmth where his hands had been. Wrapping her arms about her middle, she waited for her heart to slow.

"Th—Thank you," she whispered. "For dispatching the snake."

He nodded but didn't speak. She stared at his back, wondering what she should do next. Finally, he broke the silence.

"Why, Anna?"

She opened her mouth, but no sound came out.

"Why didn't you come that night?" He removed his hat and ran a hand through his hair. He kept his back to her, his face in profile as he spoke.

She unfolded her arms and considered her words. She'd been expecting his question ever since she'd boarded the stage in London, but still she had no ready answer. He deserved a proper response, though, not some half-truth.

But how could she explain the doubts that had plagued her the whole of her life? How her hopeful longing for him had been crushed beneath the brutal certainty that he couldn't truly love *her*? Her heart had done battle with her mind and lost.

"I'm sorry I said I would go with you that night. It was unfeeling of me to leave you waiting," she said simply. Her words dropped to a whisper as she repeated, "I'm so sorry."

"I loved you," he said. "Did that mean nothing?"

His use of the past tense was nothing less than she expected, but still her heart twisted. Surely this rough handling couldn't be good for the organ.

But all she said was, "How, Jory? How could you have loved me? And how disappointed would you have been to find your love was nothing but an illusion?"

How disappointed would *she* have been, to have been tempted with such a gift only to lose it? But, she realized with a start, was she not precisely where she'd feared to be?

———

JORY'S HEART WAS CRACKING ALL over again. She'd apologized, not for leaving him, but for agreeing to go with him in the first place. He didn't think he could have felt worse than he had that night, but he did.

Five years ago, at least he'd had hope, some shred of optimism that she might yet change her mind. Now, he had none, and he was surprised to find that there'd still been a glowing ember deep within that had waited for her return.

But her words had effectively extinguished it, and he felt something shift and slide inside.

He turned to face her, but her head was down, her features hidden from him. She'd asked how he could have loved her, but he couldn't explain it. He'd just felt it, deep in his core, with gut-solid certainty, and he feared the feeling would never go away.

Perhaps with time and distance, it would fade, but he knew in that moment that he would always love her, even if she couldn't return the sentiment.

Regardless, her uncertainty in herself, in her ability to inspire love, tore at him. He lifted her chin so he could see her eyes.

"Anna, your question . . . 'tisn't how could I have loved you. 'Tis how could I *not* have. You brought me joy. You were a beautiful, heavenly bell that rang true across my soul, and you made me wish for more from this life. From myself."

Her eyes shimmered as she gazed up at him. "Oh . . . That's lovely," she whispered with a delicate sniff. "Thank you."

A tear spilled over her lashes, and he reached up to brush it away. But even that intimacy was too much to bear, so he handed her his handkerchief instead and retreated a step. She dabbed at her cheek then twisted the poor linen between her hands.

The anger and disappointment he'd carried with him for so long was a heavy weight, and he wished nothing more than to be free of it. Like an anchor caught on the reef beyond Falmouth, it pulled and threatened to capsize him if he didn't cut it loose.

He took a large breath and held it before asking, "D'you think we can forget the past, Anna? Forget what's gone before and simply be . . . friends?"

She hesitated then gave him a shaky smile. "I'd like that," she said as she held the linen square to him, now impossibly crumpled.

"You may keep it, lass."

He retrieved her bonnet from where it had fallen. Lifting it, he placed it on her head then slowly looped the ribbons beneath her chin.

―――

JORY DIDN'T JOIN THE KIMBRELL gentlemen at their table that night. His chair was conspicuously empty, and Anna avoided looking at it as she bustled around the coffee room. If she stayed busy, perhaps she wouldn't dissolve in a puddle of tears.

Their table was noticeably quiet and lacking their good-natured banter. She wasn't sure if they were feeling the effects of their hurling injuries, or if they missed Jory as much as she did. She suspected it was as much the latter as the former, as they kept casting oblique glances at her when they thought she wasn't looking.

For her part, her emotions were still raw from their encounter by the stream. She wasn't sure her heart could take much more buffeting without a reprieve, so she accepted the respite Jory's absence afforded. That didn't mean she didn't recall their meeting over and over in her mind, though.

Friends. He wished them to forget about the past and be friends. The thought caused a lump to form in her throat.

She'd come to Cornwall to put Jory Tremayne behind her. To assuage her guilt. His forgiveness, his willingness to set the past behind them, was a heavy weight lifted from her shoulders. She should have been satisfied, but she only wished to curl up in her bed.

She set her empty tray on the bar and carefully unfolded his linen handkerchief. It carried his scent, and she drew in a shaky breath as she ran her thumb over the tiny embroidered trout.

CHAPTER SEVENTEEN

ANNA AWOKE EARLY THE NEXT day and groaned at the sunlight spilling into the room. Her throat ached from unshed tears, and she was tempted to plead a headache to avoid seeing anyone. It wouldn't have been a stretch, as her eyes were itchy and tired, her neck tense from holding her head at a confident, not-about-to-cry angle the day before.

But it was Sunday, the day she'd agreed to attend Mr. Kimbrell's luncheon at Oak Hill. She thought of the man's kindness in extending his invitation, and she couldn't repay him with such an ill turn. And if Jory wished for them to be friends . . . well, surely friends could attend the same luncheon without the world collapsing.

Straightening, she resolved to focus on the day's promise as the early morning fog evaporated beneath the sun's warmth. She donned the pink dress, which she'd repaired the day before, and gazed longingly at the too-small pink slippers resting near the hearth. She thought of the picnic to come at Oak Hill, and the walking that would certainly entail. Sighing, she realized nothing could improve on the shoes' tight fit, so she pulled on the sensible half boots once more.

A short knock sounded on her door, and she found Mrs. Teague standing in the hallway with a grin. The lady lifted one hand, and Anna saw that she held a pair of curling tongs. Anna looked from the tongs to Mrs. Teague, a question in her eyes.

"I thought you might like to curl your hair," the lady said.

Anna waited for the rush of euphoria that such a statement would normally have prompted and was surprised to feel nothing. But Mrs. Teague had such an expectant look on her face, so she pulled the door wider and smiled.

"That would be nice," she said. Anna sat at the room's mahogany vanity while Mrs. Teague placed the tongs on the fire. While they heated, she took Anna's hair down and began brushing it.

"Are you well this morning?" she asked, watching Anna in the vanity's mirror.

"Yes, quite well," Anna said. "And you?"

Mrs. Teague's lips twisted before she responded. "I'm also well."

Moments passed while Anna sought a topic of conversation, but all thought seemed to have fled her mind. Mrs. Teague didn't seem to have such a problem, though.

"I saw Jory this morning," she said. "He left early for the foundry to check on his bells before church. That boy has such a passion for his craft."

Anna suppressed a snort on hearing Mrs. Teague, who seemed of an age with Jory, refer to him as a "boy."

"I've never seen anyone with such enthusiasm, other than perhaps Gryffyn for his stone. Although Gryffyn's is a more restrained temperament, don't you think?"

"I suppose so," Anna said uncertainly. Mrs. Teague's brow furrowed as she pondered her next words, and Anna waited, curious to know what additional insights she would share.

"Not, Jory, though. There's nothing restrained about him. He can be a little fierce in his emotions. It can be overwhelming, if you want the truth. When he feels something, he feels it strongly, and his conviction is formidable. He's much like Grandfather in that way. It must be nice to be so . . . so certain of one's sentiment, don't you think?"

She released a perfect spiral and wrapped another lock of Anna's hair around the tongs.

"Yes," Anna said as a spark of envy zipped

through her. To know oneself with such certainty would be quite remarkable indeed. "But I'm certain even Jory has been mistaken in his sentiment before."

Mrs. Teague studied her in the mirror, and Anna watched her nervously, wondering if the lady had forgotten about her hair. Presently, though, she released the curl and let it bounce before setting the tongs back on the fire.

"I suppose there's always that risk," Mrs. Teague said as she began pinning up Anna's new curls. "But I'm thinking Jory's affections would be worth the venture, for anyone willing to chance it."

An unwelcome blush began at the base of Anna's throat. Who had said anything about affections? She caught sight of her frowning image in the mirror and smoothed her features.

Outside, the church bell rang from the end of the high street, one solitary note calling Newford's parishioners to worship.

"We must hurry," Mrs. Teague said, pinning the last of Anna's hair.

———

THE CHURCH WAS FULL WHEN they arrived, and Mrs. Teague pulled Anna along to sit with her and Mr. Teague in a pew near the front. Anna greeted a number of parishioners along the way, surprised to realize how many of the townspeople she'd come to know through her work at The Fin and Feather.

She looked for Jory but didn't see him amid the sea of dark hats and Sunday coats.

"Jory should hurry," Mrs. Teague said, and Anna wondered if her thoughts were that transparent. "He'll be late, and our vicar doesn't suffer latecomers."

However, once the sermon began, Anna felt a tingling in her neck that told her he'd arrived. She glanced to her left and caught his eye as he watched her. His lips tilted up on one side, then he returned his attention to the vicar.

After the service, Mrs. Teague retrieved a cart from the stables. Anna eyed the pony with hesitation—she'd expected something a little more refined than a pony cart for traveling to Oak Hill. A curricle, perhaps, or a barouche. But at Mrs. Teague's urging, she climbed aboard, and they set off for Mr. Kimbrell's luncheon.

Before they reached the end of the high street, they encountered Jory and Trout. Mrs. Teague pulled the cart to the side, and Jory stopped to await them, jumping back with a deft step when the cart threatened to run over his foot.

"Are you certain you don't wish to ride with us?" Mrs. Teague asked him.

He gazed at Anna and the narrow spot on the

bench next to her then shook his head. "I'll walk, thank you just the same."

"Suit yourself," Mrs. Teague said, flicking the reins.

"Have a care, Wynne." Jory jumped again to avoid the cart's wheel. "'Tis not a race!" he called as the pony broke into a trot and the cart lurched forward.

Anna squealed and gripped the wooden side with one hand and her bonnet with the other. Mrs. Teague navigated around another cart and took them up the hillside toward Oak Hill.

If their pace wasn't quite breakneck—it was a pony cart, after all—it was exhilarating, and Anna could understand Jory's hesitation. But she soon found herself laughing alongside Mrs. Teague.

OAK HILL WAS A MUCH grander estate than its simple name suggested. Anna caught her breath as the rambling Tudor manor appeared at the end of an oak-lined drive. Built of heavy granite and slate, it perched atop a grass-covered hill. Beyond the sprawling house and gardens, through a cut in the terrain, Anna could just make out the shimmering blue of the sea.

Mrs. Teague pulled the pony cart around the

manor's circular entrance and handed the reins to a groom while a servant assisted Anna to the ground. She adjusted her bonnet, which had gone askew in their dash up the hill, and shook out her skirts before joining Mrs. Teague on the wide entry steps.

A butler admitted them with a greeting. "Good afternoon, Mrs. Teague," he said.

"Hello, Parsons. Are we the first to arrive?"

"I'm afraid not, ma'am. Several are here before you. They're gathered on the back lawn with Mr. Kimbrell."

Mrs. Teague pulled Anna through the spacious entry then along a wide, whitewashed hall buttressed with dark oak timbers. Finally, they reached a set of doors leading to a rear terrace.

"Things will make much more sense if you remember that 'Mr. Kimbrell' is my grandfather," she explained. "All the other Kimbrells are referred to by their given names to avoid confusion. You'll find the Kimbrells far outweigh everyone else in this family—in number if not in consequence."

"Good afternoon, Mrs. Featherton," Merryn Kimbrell said when he spied them. Anna cringed at his greeting. She'd come to count the Kimbrell gentlemen—and the Teagues—as friends, and to hear them continue to call her by the false name, especially in such a convivial setting, didn't sit well. But she didn't know how to resolve the problem she'd laid for herself, so she simply smiled and dipped her head.

Then she looked beyond the terrace, and her eyes widened. There must have been fifty people milling about the grounds. She'd imagined a small, intimate family gathering, but this was so much... more.

Children played a game of tag on the lawn, and tables and blankets were positioned to take advantage of the sea view far below. Servants bustled between the lawn and kitchens with heavy plates of food and flagons of wine, cider and lemonade.

"Mrs. Featherton," the elder Mr. Kimbrell said as he approached. "I'm some pleased you've joined us. And that you survived this one's skill at the reins," he whispered.

"I heard that Grandfather."

Anna smiled. "Thank you again, sir, for the invitation. You've a lovely home, and in the most perfect setting I think."

"I'm glad you think so. May I show you the gardens?" he asked.

―――

JORY AND TROUT CROSSED THE great hall and exited onto the terrace. He'd been relieved to learn from Parsons that Wynne's pony cart had arrived intact, and the ladies were unharmed.

He'd considered accompanying them, if only to see to their safety, but he hadn't relished the discomfort of being pressed so close to Anna on the narrow seat. Then he'd nearly suggested that she walk with him instead before he stopped himself. What she did was no concern of his, was it?

Trout abandoned him to investigate the children's game of tag, and Jory's eyes scanned the crowded lawn. Most of his cousins had arrived already, but despite their greater height and number, his eyes quickly found Anna.

She walked with his grandfather, one arm on his sleeve as she attended to whatever story he was filling her ears with. She laughed at something he said, and his grandfather ducked his head with an impish grin. Was there anyone she couldn't charm?

She wore her hair curled today, and with her soft pink dress, she looked much more like the prim and fussy Anna he'd first met by the stream five years before. Then he looked down and spied sensible half boots peeking from beneath her hem, and he smiled. Not quite the same prim lass then.

"Jory." Merryn and Gavin approached, and Merryn clapped him on the back. He winced, still not fully recovered from the hurling, and Merryn tossed him a callous grin.

"We missed you last night, cousin," Gavin said.

"I had some matters to attend to," he prevaricated.

He'd enjoyed a good sulk in his room after his encounter with Anna at the stream, and he hadn't felt fit for company afterward. Even Trout had avoided him, and that was saying something.

Friends. They were to be friends.

His heart felt lighter for having let go of his anger toward Anna, but that wasn't to say it didn't ache. It felt bruised, much like his jaw, and he wondered how long it would take to heal. Much longer than his face, he feared.

"Jory!" He turned to see Merryn's sister Bronwyn approaching with Miss Parker. He greeted her then glanced beyond to her friend.

"Miss Parker," Merryn said. "May I introduce my cousin, Mr. Jory Tremayne?" Merryn completed the introductions, and Jory bowed to Miss Parker.

She said something pleasant—he couldn't recall what, exactly—then Bronwyn turned to him. "Jory, Miss Parker has quite the green thumb. Why don't you show her the gardens?"

He'd asked for this, he reminded himself as he smiled and offered his arm to the lady. He steered them down the terrace steps and led her to see his grandmother's camellias.

There was no denying that Miss Parker was an amiable companion. She spoke intelligently on a number of topics and showed a flattering interest in anything he said. She was pleasant without being obsequious or overly flirtatious. Kind and thoughtful. Confident but not overbearing. In short, she was everything a gentleman could want in a lady.

He should have been pleased, but the heavy weight of guilt pressed on him. Guilt for betraying his heart, for betraying Anna. But that made no sense. They were *friends*, he counseled his heart. Nothing more.

His heart was stubborn, though, like Trout with a dead fish, and it refused to hear reason.

―――

WYNNE FROWNED AS SHE WATCHED Jory lead Miss Parker away. As soon as Bronwyn left them, she turned on Merryn and swatted him with her hand. He backed away, shielding himself against her assault, and she hit him once more for good measure.

"What. Are. You. Doing?" she asked with a hiss, punctuating each word with another swat of her hand.

"What?" Her cousin looked to Gavin, who merely shrugged and backed away.

"Don't look to Gavin for help," Wynne warned as she angled a glare at both of them.

"She's assaulting me," Merryn complained to Gavin. "You're a constable. Can't you do something?"

"And bring her wrath down on *my* head? I don't think so."

Wynne groaned in frustration. "Why did you introduce Jory to Miss Parker?"

"Because he asked me to," Merryn said.

Wynne's glare sharpened.

"You can't force them together, Wynnie," Gavin ventured.

"I'm not *forcing* anything," she said, and she knew a moment of satisfaction when Gavin retreated another step. "I'm just trying to help them overcome their idiocy."

Gavin snorted.

"'Tis as plain as the nose on your face that those two are meant for each other," she said. "You've seen the way he moons over her. Just look at him now. And she's no better."

They turned to gaze out over the lawn where Jory strolled with Miss Parker. The lady leaned closer to share something with him, but his eyes remained fixed on the back of Mrs. Featherton.

"Wynne," Gavin said, swallowing. "There's only so much the heart can take. Don't you think he's suffered enough? Perhaps we should let things fall where they may. What will be, will be, after all."

Wynne chewed her lip. "D'you truly think he's better off without her?"

When her cousins were silent, she said, "I

thought not." Turning to Merryn, she pushed a finger into his chest. "No more introductions."

———

ANNA WATCHED JORY ESCORT A pretty young lady about the lawn, and her stomach turned with an uncomfortable sensation she suspected was jealousy. With effort, she pulled her eyes from him and forced her attention back to Mr. Kimbrell's conversation.

"D'you play the pianoforte, Mrs. Featherton?" he asked. They'd been discussing the design of his late wife's rose garden, so the question came as a surprise, and she wondered how long her attention had been elsewhere.

"Y—Yes. Passably so," she said.

"My Evelyn played beautifully," he said.

The man's eyes shone whenever he spoke of his wife, and Anna's throat tightened at the grief that was still evident in his voice. A tendril of longing curled through her stomach, and she couldn't temper her curiosity.

"How did you meet your wife?" she asked.

He smiled, remembering. "Tain't such an unusual tale, I'm afraid. I attended the Sullivan ball, and there she was. Dressed in white silk and pearls. She was much more refined than me, and I thought she was the most beautiful creature I'd ever seen. Well above my touch, you see. But when I spoke with her, I just knew." He shrugged his shoulders. "She was the only one for me."

Anna's breath caught to hear his account, to hear the conviction in his voice. "And did she feel the same?" she asked breathlessly.

"Oh, no," he chortled. "It took her months to come 'round. I thought I would go out of my mind with waiting."

"How did you manage to convince her?"

His eyes scrunched as he considered her question. "I don't know that *I* convinced her," he said, "though it wasn't for any lack of effort on my part, I assure you. I think Evelyn just needed to stop listening to her head and start listening to her heart. She was always a ponderer, you see."

"A—a ponderer?" Anna asked.

"Aye, she pondered." He waved a hand. "Deliberated, contemplated. Which invitations to accept. What to wear. Which needlework pattern to attempt. She was the type of person who needed to talk things over with herself first. I tend to follow my heart straightaway, but Evelyn was always a few paces behind. She always said I leaped before I looked, rather than t'other way around." He chuckled then turned to her. "Which are you? A leaper or a ponderer?"

Surprised at the question, Anna frowned. She thought of all the doubts that frequently plagued her, chasing one 'round the other in her mind. Her heart and mind had forever been at odds with one another. Then she recalled all the occasions when her mother had accused her of leaping without looking, which, she now saw, must be her heart's way of putting an end to the argument.

"Mrs. Featherton?" Mr. Kimbrell asked gently.

"I—I think I must be both," she said. "Is that possible?"

"Ah," he said, patting her hand. "I knew you were a complex creature."

Complex? She could think of much better descriptors. Muddled. Confused. Addled. A gudgeon indeed.

CHAPTER EIGHTEEN

※

"Jory, I believe Grandfather is looking for you," Merryn said. "Perhaps I can escort Miss Parker to fetch a lemonade?"

"Thank you, sir," Miss Parker said, shifting her hand from Jory's sleeve to Merryn's.

Jory bowed and watched them walk toward the food tables, then he went in search of his grandfather. He found him pointing out one of his grandmother's prize roses to Anna, his head angled toward her as he regaled her with another story.

"Grandfather," he said.

"Jory, son—" Whatever he meant to say was lost as Wynne approached.

"Grandfather, your presence is requested at the children's cricket match. Jory, perhaps you can escort Anna to see the ruins? She really shouldn't miss them."

"Aye, that's a splendid idea," his grandfather

said, clapping him on the back.

Jory looked at his cousin with suspicion. If he wasn't mistaken, his cousins were going out of their way to put him in Anna's path, despite his efforts to the contrary. As he watched his grandfather walk off with Wynne, he wasn't certain the old man wasn't in on the scheme as well. *Nicely done, Wynne.*

"Shall we?" he asked Anna.

Her hand fluttered above his sleeve before she settled on his arm. "We don't have to see the ruins," she said. "I can join the others at the cricket match." Her voice trailed off as she watched his cousins walk away.

"Nonsense," he said. "Unless . . . you'd prefer to watch the cricket match?"

"No, the ruins sound lovely. Which way do we go?"

He led her to a path off the main lawn and through a tall, precisely trimmed hedge. Once they'd rounded the stables, a wide field emerged before them, and beyond that, jagged cliffs dropped swiftly to the sea.

At the edge of the cliffs, atop a jutting promontory, sat the pale ruins of an old huer's hut outlined against blue sky. The warm scents of salt and fish rose from where the spray broke on the rocks below, and he inhaled. He'd always enjoyed the serenity of the spot, and the view of the sun-sparkled sea never failed to amaze him. He was curious to see Anna's reaction.

She slowed, eyes widening, until she came to a full stop to take in the vista before them.

"Why, it's stunning!" she exclaimed, dropping his arm. She lifted her skirts and hurried down a sandy path overgrown with grass and heather, abandoning him altogether in her eagerness to reach the ruins.

A breeze lifted the ribbon of her bonnet, and he couldn't help his smile to see her so delighted. One of her curls teased her cheek, and she brushed it aside, revealing the dimple that he'd always loved. On reaching her, he crossed his arms and stared out at the sea.

"You can just see Copper Cove around that curve in the cliff, and on nights when there's a bonfire, you can see the flames from here. The cove itself will be ablaze with copper bracken by summer's end."

He swallowed, wondering if she'd still be in Newford to see it, before adding, "Grandfather often tells the tale of the first kiss he stole from Grandmother, right at this very spot."

Then he sighed. What was wrong with him? Why, for all that was holy, did he have to bring up kissing?

"Your grandmother sounds like a delightful lady,"

Anna said. "He must miss her."

"She was, and he does. I doubt he'll marry again." He thought of his grandfather and the years of loneliness ahead of him. It was not an existence he wished for himself, but unless he could move past his inconvenient infatuation with Anna, it was one that awaited him.

Then he thought of Miss Parker. Surely a life with a pleasant companion, a helpmate, would be preferable to a life alone, would it not? It was a sound argument. A rational one. If only he could convince his heart . . .

Anna looked up at the squat, crumbling building. "What was this used for?" she asked.

"'Tis an old huer's hut," he said. At her look of confusion, he explained. "The huer watches for pilchards on the sea. When he spies a shoal, he alerts the fishermen, who run for their boats and cast their nets. A new hut was built further up the coast a century or so agone, and this one has been unused ever since. Well, except as a smuggler's lookout," he added with a wiggle of his brows.

"Smugglers!" she said in an overloud whisper, and he chuckled.

"You didn't think we came by our wealth honestly, did you?" At her astonished stare, he relented. "Never worry, lass. 'Tis a common enough business around Newford—even Roddie Teague had a hand in it—but we've been straight and proper for a time now. But that isn't to say Grandfather didn't make quite a name for himself with French lace and brandy."

"Mr. Teague? And your grandfather?" she asked skeptically.

"Aye, don't let that old man fool you," he said. "He'll tell tales that will make your toes curl, although I suspect he embellishes. I used to play here as a boy, and I always imagined myself to be as fearsome as he was," he told her. "'Twas before I took up the peaceful life of an angler."

She gazed out over the expanse before them, holding a hand beneath the brim of her bonnet to shield her eyes from the sun. He leaned against the rough stone wall of the hut and watched her watching the sea.

"You grew up at Oak Hill then?" she asked, turning back to him.

"Aye. My parents died when I was but three years of age," he said, kicking a pebble and watching it skitter away.

He realized with surprise that, in all the hours they'd spent by the stream, he'd never shared much of his life with her. Nor she with him.

They'd lived in the present, enjoying the peace and companionship of two souls bound in a single moment, but they'd not whispered anything of their pasts, or their future. How was it possible to love a person so completely without knowing even the most basic landmarks of their life? He had no answer to the question, only the certainty borne of experience.

"Grandmother and Grandfather had just finished raising their own children—seven of them—and then they had to begin again with me."

"I don't think your grandfather regrets a moment of it," she said.

"No." He smiled. He was fortunate in his family.

"You said your mother was a Kimbrell?" she asked.

He nodded. "Aye. Tamsyn Kimbrell, grandfather's only daughter. My uncles each had at least five children of their own. All told, there are seven and thirty cousins. All Kimbrells except for me."

"How lovely," she said. "To have such a large and . . . fond . . . family."

"Fond," he repeated with a snort. "That's one word for it."

She laughed. "Bothersome, then?"

"Often."

"Meddlesome?"

"Frequently. And yet, always fond."

"I've a sister back in London, but we've never been close." She sighed. The breeze had picked up, and she pushed a curl from her forehead.

"Are the two of you of similar temperament?" he asked, surprised as she'd never mentioned a sister.

"Goodness, no," she said with a laugh. "Margaret is incredibly determined. She's always been quite decided on her course. She set her sights on Mr. Claxton in her first season, and then she devised a very detailed plan to achieve her goal."

"And did she? Achieve her goal, that is?"

"Of course." Anna frowned. "She was married weeks before the season ended. Margaret always achieves what she sets out to do."

"And you don't?" he asked.

"I would have to have a goal, now, in order to achieve it," she said with a twist of her lips.

"Everyone has goals. 'Tis all a matter of perspective." At her skeptical gaze, he continued. "What d'you wish to achieve here today?"

She stared at him then shrugged. "I don't have any special purpose. I merely came to enjoy the company and the fine day. See? I'm utterly devoid of ambition."

"And are you enjoying the fine day?" He hesitated then added, "And the company?"

"Yes," she said with a soft smile.

He forced down the tiny, foolish flicker of hope that flared at her words.

"There," he said firmly. "You've gone and achieved your goal then," he said. "Your ambitions are yours. Not your sister's or anyone else's. Your sister's aspirations may have been more far-reaching, but that doesn't mean yours are any less meaningful."

She stared at him for a beat, brushing another lock of hair from her cheek. "I never took you for a philosopher."

He snorted. "I'm an angler with an empty hook. I've lots of time to think."

She hesitated then said, "I've a half-sister as well. Mary. No one speaks of the relationship."

"Are you acquainted with your half-sister?"

"Yes. We were friends once."

"But no more?"

She was quiet for a moment, and he didn't think she would respond. Then she said softly, "No. Not anymore. We're estranged, though if I'm honest, it's through no fault of Mary's. I don't think she's even aware that we're sisters."

"I'm blessed with an overabundance of family," he said, "so my perspective may be flawed. But 'tis unfortunate, I think, that she doesn't know you as a sister should. Especially as you were once friends."

Anna turned and faced him more directly and smiled. "Do you know, I don't think I've been able to fully appreciate the value of family before. At least until I came to Newford. Here, everyone seems like family, regardless of blood."

"That's merely the meddlesome aspect, lass," he said, grinning.

"And the fond bit as well, I should think." She stood before him, her edges lit by the sun, skirts fluttering about her. Her eyes were soft as she gazed at him, her smile both achingly familiar and out of his reach.

She looked as pretty as a painting, her pink muslin perfectly matched to the wild heather and sea thrift growing along the path. Even in her sensible half boots, she was the loveliest lady he'd ever seen, and he clenched his fists to avoid reaching for her.

Friends, he reminded himself. That's all they were. He should offer his arm and escort her back to the lawn. Assist her to fill a plate then hand her off to one of his cousins. He pushed away from the side of the huer's hut.

"Shall we rejoin the others?"

———

ANNA HESITATED, HER HAND HOVERING above Jory's sleeve. For a tiny moment, she thought she'd seen longing in his eyes—a yearning to match her own—and her heart had skipped. But then the look was gone, and he offered his arm for her to take.

They were to be friends, she reminded herself.

Friends didn't yearn for one another. Friends didn't long to kiss one another beneath the warmth of a summer sun. Those sorts of yearnings would only make her miserable.

"How long d'you suppose you'll remain in Cornwall?" he asked as they picked their way along the path.

And that was the question, wasn't it? Although she'd been relieved to settle her debt with Wynne, her wages at The Fin and Feather weren't likely to pay her passage to Berkshire anytime soon, much less all the way back to London.

"I'm not certain," she said softly. "Until I have the means to leave, I suppose. I've written my mother to request she send our solicitor with the carriage."

She lifted her skirts slightly as he guided her around a low spot in the path, then she looked up into his face. His expression showed mild interest, nothing more. It was neither hopeful nor fearful. Certainly, it didn't match the hollow feeling she herself felt at the thought of leaving.

"You must have been disappointed to learn your mother's friend has removed to Bath."

Her lies were growing wearisome. With effort, she smoothed the frown from her face. "I didn't come to see Mrs. Steward," she said. "Although I did hope to prevail upon her hospitality."

"You didn't come to see Mrs. Steward? Then

why did you come, lass?"

She pulled in a large breath and held it, then she said, "I came to see that you were happy. I feel terrible for how I left before, and I wanted to assure myself that you were well settled."

His steps slowed until he stopped altogether, and he watched her through his lashes. "You came . . . for me?"

She nodded firmly, relieved to have at least one truth out in the open. "Yes. Although, I'd hoped to do so without"—she waved a hand at his person."

"Without me knowing you were here?"

She sighed. "Yes. And certainly without the threat of gaol."

His mouth curved up on one end. They resumed walking and, after a brief hesitation, she said, "Miss Parker is very pleasant."

She kept her gaze trained on the ground lest she misstep, but she sensed him watching her from the corner of his eye.

"Aye," he said finally. "She has much to recommend her."

She swallowed. "As do you, Jory."

His arm tensed beneath her hand, but he remained silent.

"Mrs. Featherton," Mr. Kimbrell said when they returned to the lawn. "How did you find our ruins?"

She forced a bright smile. "Sir, they were quite

enchanting, indeed."

"'Tis a good spot for kiss stealing," Mrs. Teague said. "Grandfather stole his first kiss from Grandmother at that very spot."

Anna felt a blush stain her cheeks, and Jory, she noticed, was studying the tips of his boots.

"So I did!" Mr. Kimbrell said. "My Evelyn always enjoyed the walk, and the sea wind always put roses in her cheeks, as it's done for you," he added with a smile before turning to Jory. "You and Wynne must bring Mrs. Featherton back to Oak Hill to play the pianoforte. 'Tis been an age since I've heard its sound. We'll make an evening of it."

Jory looked as surprised as Anna felt, but he merely firmed his jaw and nodded. "Of course, Grandfather. If the lady is agreeable."

"That—that would be lovely," Anna said. "Perhaps on my next half day," she added with a glance at Mrs. Teague.

"Tuesday," Mrs. Teague said, surprising Anna. "Peggy's foot is heeling nicely, and she's hoping for more wages. Mind, there's more than enough work to go around, but I can spare you for the evening."

"Excellent," Mr. Kimbrell said, rubbing his hands together. "Tuesday, then."

ANNA GRIPPED THE SIDE OF Mrs. Teague's pony cart as it careened down the path toward Newford. The sun was a large orange ball bobbing above the horizon, and shadows were lengthening with the day.

Her conversation with Jory sat heavily on her mind, but one question in particular kept echoing in her thoughts. *How long d'you suppose you'll remain in Cornwall?*

She certainly didn't wish to make a life serving ale at The Fin and Feather, but she'd come to think of her room there—her new room, of course—as home. The Teagues and Kimbrells—and yes, even Jory—as friends. She'd always had acquaintances wherever she and her mother had traveled, but never friends.

She thought of her life back in London. Of the parties and balls and routs. The morning calls and afternoon rides and walks in the park. With dismay, she realized none of the things that had comprised so much of her life before would ever be the same, even without the whiff of scandal that was bound to cling to her.

They'd never match an encouraging smile from Merryn Kimbrell, or a teasing wink from Alfie Kimbrell, or Mrs. Teague's reluctant kindnesses.

But how could that be? she wondered. How could she count them as friends when they didn't even know her name?

"Mrs. F, I believe my grandfather took quite a liking to you," Mrs. Teague said as they reached the bottom of the hill with bone-jarring haste.

"And I to him," Anna replied. Then, drawing a breath for courage, she said, "Mrs. Teague, I wonder if you could call me Anna. Or . . . Miss Pepper, if you like."

Mrs. Teague looked at her from the corner of her eye, her lips twisted wryly. "Then you must call me Wynne."

CHAPTER NINETEEN

"There be too much froth on the ale," Peggy said. "Mrs. Teague says as 'ow some froth be proper, but the gen'lemen ain't be payin' fer *excess* froth."

Anna breathed a sigh, puffing a curl from her forehead. Peggy had returned to work, and she didn't seem pleased with the quality of help that Mrs. Teague had found in her absence.

"Ye need to mop up the puddles in the 'all lest the gen'lemen slip. Mrs. Teague says as 'ow there ain't be no surer way to lose a customer than to kill 'im."

"Ye'll receive bigger tips if ye flirt a bit more. 'Aven't ye any more comely dresses? Per'aps with a bit less cloth about the bosom?"

"Ye're takin' too long to deliver the meals. Mrs. Teague says as 'ow"—Peggy scrunched her face in thought before continuing—"efficiency be the key to profit."

And now, apparently, she'd put too much froth on the ale. Anna set the mug down with a bit too much force, and the excess froth slopped over the rim. Had she truly been mourning the thought of leaving Cornwall?

She poured another ale for Mr. Alfie Kimbrell and placed it on her tray. She turned and headed toward the window table, surprised to see Peggy there ahead of her, passing around ales and whiskies.

Her eyes narrowed then nearly squinted shut as Peggy leaned over the table, allowing her more comely dress—or what there was of it—to earn her tips. The little tart, she thought, as Jory smiled up at Peggy. Didn't she have a log to dance upon somewhere?

When Peggy left the table, she marched up to the gentlemen. "I expected better of you," she said with heat. Belatedly, she realized she'd directed her words at Jory, so she turned her glare on each of the gentlemen in turn.

They stared back at her, jaws slack, before Mr. Alfie gave her a knowing wink and a grin. She huffed a sigh and left them to their perfectly frothed ales.

Some time later, as she was wiping down the bar and ruminating on her ridiculous outburst, Mr. Cadan Kimbrell entered the coffee room. When he spied her, he approached the bar before joining his cousins. She turned to him with a greeting on her lips, determined to be pleasant, but she stopped at the expression on his face.

"Mrs. Featherton," he said, reaching into his coat. "This came through the mail today. It seems your letter's been"—his lips twisted—"returned."

She reached for the letter, recognizing her own handwriting on the face of it. "Returned? What do you mean?"

"When a recipient doesn't have the means to pay the postage, letters are returned to the originating post office. I'm sorry to say this one has been returned."

Anna nodded, numb. "Thank you, Mr. Cadan," she said, not recognizing her own voice. She stared at her mother's direction as he joined his cousins at the window table.

No carriage was coming for her. No funds. But the funds were not what concerned her. She'd simply write to Mr. Gramercy directly now, certain that he, as a trusted retainer, would not disappoint her. No, the funds were not the issue.

Her mother had the means to pay the postage. The fact that she'd chosen not to spoke volumes.

Her mother had abandoned her. Left her to her fate in Cornwall.

She supposed it was no less than she deserved after the scandal she'd left her to face alone, but that didn't make the pill any easier to swallow. Never mind that less than a day before, she'd grown sad at the thought of leaving Cornwall. That was beside the point.

Weren't mothers supposed to love their children, faults and all? She sniffed and gazed out over the bustling coffee room.

Her mother's rejection burned more than she'd thought possible, and her vision blurred with her tears. Clutching the letter to her overly clad bosom, she turned and left the inn.

―――

JORY WAS STUNNED—AND NOT a little pleased—by Anna's outburst. It seemed Peggy's attentions had not gone unnoticed, and the thought brought a warmth to his stomach he'd not expected.

Anna was not entirely immune to him, it would seem. But jealousy, he reminded himself, did not equate to love.

Nevertheless, he was surprised to see her rush from the inn, a letter clutched in her hand. Trout's head came up at her departure, and she roused herself to follow.

Frowning, Jory watched Cadan approach their table. "What did you say to her?" he asked.

Cadan looked at him uncomfortably before

lowering himself to his seat. "I merely returned an unpaid letter," he said. "Post office business."

"An unpaid letter? From where?"

"I'm not at liberty to say, Jory. The lady will have to tell you."

His cousins stared first at Cadan, then as one they turned to Jory with expectant looks. Sighing, he rose from the table and followed his dog.

The day's warmth had gone with the sun, and a damp fog had begun to settle on Newford. Pulling his collar about him, Jory rounded the inn and found Anna on a low step between the building and the river. Trout crouched next to her, her canine head resting on Anna's thigh.

Anna's head was down, one arm curled about his dog, her face buried in the fur of Trout's neck. For all her dubious aromas, Trout was a good comfort.

"Anna?" he asked.

She looked up at his approach, and he caught the shimmer of tears on her cheeks.

"What's happened?" he asked.

She wiped her cheeks and indicated the letter in her hand. "My mother—she's refused my letter."

"Refused? Perhaps she simply didn't have the funds to pay the postage?"

Anna pressed her lips together and gripped Trout's fur more tightly. "She has the funds."

Jory's first thought was that Anna was hurting,

and he wished to ease her pain. His second thought was that she must have done something to earn her mother's displeasure. His first thought won.

He couldn't think of a scenario where his own family might refuse a letter from him, but if they did, he imagined the pain would be acute.

He lowered himself to sit next to her on the step, and Trout lifted her head to nuzzle him. Uncertain, he reached a hesitant arm around Anna and pulled her to him.

She breathed a shaky sigh and settled against him, her warmth filling his empty corners as the fog swirled about them. Trout settled her head back on Anna's leg, and he marveled at the dog's curative power. At her ability to sense pain.

"Jory," Anna said with a sniff. "Am I such a horrid person?"

"No, of course not," he said automatically, forgetting his own pain in the face of hers.

Was she confused? Perhaps. Indecisive, certainly. But horrid? No.

"What could you have done that was so bad?"

She hesitated, and her breathing slowed before she puffed an exhale and settled back against his shoulder. "I'm not a good person," she said with finality, and he squeezed her harder, his heart aching for her.

CHAPTER TWENTY

~~~

Tuesday arrived, and Jory wondered how he'd reached such a point. He'd every intention of courting Miss Parker, of moving past Anna. But instead, he found himself pressed against her side in Wynne's pony cart, clutching the edge lest Wynne pitch them into a ditch.

Despite her laughter, Anna's form was rigid, braced against the careening motion of the cart. He tightened his arm behind her to steady them on the narrow seat. If his hand held her a little more tightly than was seemly, it was only for the purpose of safety.

Wynne rounded the final corner to emerge onto the straight stretch before Oak Hill, and he exhaled a sigh of relief then winced as his cousin sailed over a particularly rough bump.

"Wynne!" he said sharply.

"Never fear, cousin, we've almost arrived."

Thank the good Lord.

Oak Hill rose before them, the main-level windows welcoming and aglow with candles. Parsons greeted them at the door and took coats and bonnets before escorting them to the drawing room.

Jory, who spent his nights at Oak Hill when he wasn't staying at the Feather, had always loved the home's Tudor architecture—the heavy stone and polished wood that gave an orphaned lad a sturdy sense of history. Of belonging.

Dark oak beams crossed the ceiling, and familiar portraits gazed down on the room from whitewashed walls. His grandmother's pianoforte stood proudly near a bank of floor-to-ceiling leaded windows while thick rugs in reds and blues softened the cold stone floor.

It wasn't London-fancy—it wasn't even Penhale-fancy—but his chest swelled with pride in the legacy spread before them, and he watched Anna to gauge her reaction.

If they'd eloped five years ago, this would have been her home now. Would she approve, or would she find Oak Hill too rustic for her elegant taste? Would she be blind to its charm, too accustomed to fine things to appreciate the quirky maze-like corridors and uneven walls?

Part of him insisted he didn't care, while

another, larger part of him that wouldn't be silenced yearned for her approval.

Anna greeted his grandfather with a proper curtsy then gazed about the room with an appropriate level of awe, and he relaxed.

"Mr. Kimbrell," she said to his grandfather. "I told you before that you've a wonderful home, but you must tell me about the portraits."

His grandfather dutifully walked her around the perimeter of the room, explaining the story behind each painting. When they reached the far end, Anna cocked her head to one side and asked, "Who is this lovely lady?"

They stood before a portrait of Jory's mother. It had pride of place at one end of the room, opposite an equally sized portrait of his grandmother.

"My daughter, Tamsyn," his grandfather said, and Jory was surprised to see tears form in the old man's eyes, even after all these years.

Anna hesitated, glancing at Jory, then said, "You must miss her very much."

"Every day," his grandfather said. "She was much like my Evelyn. Much like you, I suspect."

Anna blushed at his grandfather's words, and Jory's throat thickened. He cleared it and turned to see Wynne gazing at him with a smug smile. He forced his own expression to clear.

Fortunately, Parsons distracted them by

announcing supper and they all stood. Grandfather held his arm for Wynne, which left Jory to escort Anna. She placed a tentative hand on his sleeve, and he led her to the dining room.

SUPPER WAS A FESTIVE AFFAIR with just the four of them. Mr. Kimbrell regaled them with tales from his youth and stories of Wynne and Jory's escapades as children. Anna, who'd been nervous about the evening, soon found herself relaxing and looking at Jory with new eyes.

"This one," Mr. Kimbrell said with affection, motioning to a blushing Jory. "He was a proper heller. 'Tis a wonder that he's come out right. Always doing without thinking, he is, but his heart's in the proper place."

"Did you truly bring your pony into the drawing room?" Anna asked, pressing her lips together.

"The weather had turned cold," Jory insisted. "And she didn't have a proper cloak."

In all their hours spent beside the stream, they'd rarely shared details of their youth, and Anna delighted in hearing what a mischief-maker he'd been. Her affection for him, which she'd already believed to be boundless, expanded even further to see the love he and his grandfather shared.

She pictured a tiny version of him, a son or daughter with his dark gold hair and sea-blue eyes, and the sudden yearning that struck her midsection robbed her breath.

She took a sip of wine and tried to settle her thoughts, but not before she caught Wynne watching her. Pressing her lips together, Anna willed herself back to the present, away from fanciful notions.

"I can't be the only one," Jory said, turning to her. "I'm sure you must've turned your mother's hair grey a time or two yourself."

Anna thought of her most recent escapade and her flight from Greenvale, but she didn't think that tale was nearly as endearing as a pony in the drawing room.

"Well," she began, "there was a time when I longed for dark hair like Susan Brasher. She had gleaming, sable hair that drew everyone's admiration. Mama caught me in her kohl, but fortunately I'd only had time to apply it to my eyebrows." She grimaced, remembering. "Rather inexpertly, I'm afraid. I looked like a masked highwayman for days afterward."

"Oh ho!" Mr. Kimbrell said with a laugh. "Mrs. Featherton, I've no doubt you were quite the scamp like Jory."

Anna smiled, her conscience squirming at his use

of her false name. Jory knew the truth and she'd shared her name with Wynne the night of the picnic, but the rest of the family still believed the fiction she'd created. Here she sat, enjoying Mr. Kimbrell's hospitality and his food, laughing at his table, all under the cloud of the most elemental falsehood.

"Mr. Kimbrell," she said, dabbing a napkin to her lips. "I'm afraid I've another confession."

He stopped laughing and gazed at her fondly while Jory and Wynne watched curiously. She turned from them to look directly at Mr. Kimbrell.

"I traveled to Cornwall alone on the public stage." Her nose wrinkled as she recalled the journey. "But I'm unwed, you see, and I was concerned for my reputation if it were known that I'd done such a foolish thing. So"—she pulled a deep breath then plunged ahead—"I created the name Mrs. Featherton when I arrived in Newford. My name is Miss Anna Pepper, and if you're not too put out with me, I'd be honored to have you use it."

She held her breath, waiting for outrage or disappointment to darken his features. Mr. Kimbrell twisted his lips in thought then placed one hand over hers where it rested on the table.

"My dear, I knew you were a sensible lass, and I'm honored that you trust me to share your name. Know that I'll keep your secret for as long as you wish."

She blinked at him, and her eyes misted. She'd

never been accused of being sensible. The poor man must be addled, but she accepted his compliment with a smile and a weak nod.

―――

SENSIBLE? ANNA? JORY STARED AT his grandfather and wondered if the man had gone daft. He seemed lucid enough. Happy, even. He'd not seen him laugh as much in the past five years as he had this night. Not since his grandmother had passed, in fact. If his grandfather wished to believe Anna was sensible, who was Jory to correct him?

He leaned back while a servant replaced his soup bowl with a steaming lobster pie. Anna laughed at something his cousin said, and his stomach tightened to hear the sound. Light and airy, it bubbled over him, like a fizzy champagne.

She charmed his grandfather much as she charmed his cousins at The Fin and Feather. But as much as his cousins enjoyed her company in the inn's coffee room, it was clear she was meant to be in more refined surroundings. The night of the hurling and her encounter with Jago Simmons was proof enough of that. She belonged in a grand house, surrounded by grand things.

She belonged at Oak Hill. With him.

As quickly as the thought occurred, he pushed it

aside. She would never be his, and the sooner he reconciled himself to that fact, the better off he'd be.

But that didn't stop him from picturing a tiny version of Anna roaming about the halls in which he and his cousins had played. A tiny lass with blonde ringlets and bright green eyes. Fussy frocks and fitty ribbons. He imagined a prim and proper miss who refused to wear sensible shoes.

Glancing up, he found Wynne staring at him with a bemused expression, and he realized he was grinning. He bit his lip and smoothed the smile from his face before cutting into his pie.

Anna would leave Newford again, much as she had five years ago. His foolish imaginings of a tiny Anna might be her future, but they weren't his.

———

When the dessert course of stewed pears and sugared biscuits had been cleared, their party returned to the drawing room and its elegant pianoforte. Anna ran a hand along the smooth mahogany surface, surprised by how much she had missed the instrument in her mother's drawing room. She'd told Mr. Kimbrell she could play passably so, and she didn't think she'd understated her talent.

She'd learned to play because it was an expected talent for all young ladies, and if she wasn't a master, at least she wasn't dismal at it like some.

She had continued to play, though, because she found music to be a surprisingly enjoyable pastime, a relaxing way to pass an evening. An escape from herself and her own thoughts, if only for a short time.

Tonight, however, escape from her doubts remained firmly out of reach. Her nerves jangled at the thought of playing for Jory and his grandfather. What if she had, in truth, *overstated* her skill?

What if she only thought she could play but was truly abysmal?

What if it had been too long and she'd forgotten how to play?

They were too kind to tell her the truth, and she didn't think she could withstand seeing mild expressions of forbearance on their faces.

"Would you like me to turn for you?" Jory asked.

His words pulled her attention back to the room, and she swallowed and took a seat on the narrow bench.

"That would be nice, thank you." *The appearance of confidence,* she reminded herself, *far outpaces competence.*

She straightened and ran her fingers lightly over the keys, feeling the smooth weight of the ivory and testing chords and scales at various octaves. The keys were loose, the sound bright and clear, although the higher notes rang more strongly than the bass. She'd need to adjust, apply more energy to her left hand.

Satisfied, she looked up at Jory. He nodded and she began to play. She worried about her timing, and she thought her strokes might have been heavier in places than necessary, but Wynne and Mr. Kimbrell simply smiled with encouragement as she worked her way through the piece.

Jory's long fingers distracted her as he turned the pages, but they were nothing compared to what his proximity was doing to her insides. His unique scent of apples and sunshine recalled bittersweet memories, and his warmth at her back was a tangible thing as it embraced and rolled over her. Once, she thought she may have missed an entire chorus.

When she paused between pieces, Jory leaned down and spoke softly, his low voice rumbling from her ear all the way to her toes. "Stop thinking, Anna. Just play."

And so she did. After a few missteps while her mind struggled to maintain control of her fingers, she shushed it and allowed the music to guide her.

Mr. Kimbrell and Wynne disappeared from her mind, leaving her alone with Jory and the music. She absorbed his heat and let it loosen her posture.

She breathed in each note and exhaled through her fingers, and the music flowed over and through her like the sea.

When she finished, she looked up to see Mr. Kimbrell applauding and beaming while Wynne sat at his side, stunned. Anna turned to look up at Jory and inhaled sharply at the expression on his face. A mixture of joy and pride lit his features as he smiled down at her.

Pride. Directed at her. What a completely novel experience.

"That was magnificent, Miss Pepper," Mr. Kimbrell said. "Truly magnificent."

Anna's cheeks heated with the praise. No amount of polite London applause had ever warmed her so thoroughly.

"D'you know any waltzes?" he asked.

She'd come across a few waltzes in his collection of sheet music, and she nodded. "I do know a waltz or two. Would you like to hear one?"

At his agreement, Wynne stirred herself and added, "Mrs. Clifton said as how she'll call for a waltz at next week's assembly, despite Mrs. Pentreath's disliking it. Can you imagine? A waltz, in Newford!"

"I'm sure it will be lovely," Anna said, glancing at Jory.

"But the floor will be empty," Wynne said. "I

didn't wrest the assemblies away from The White Dove to have an empty floor. Hardly anyone in Newford knows how to waltz. What must she be thinking?" Wynne gazed at them in befuddlement, then something in Jory's expression must have captured her interest, for she stopped short and cocked her head. "*You* know how to waltz?" she asked, eyes wide.

"Your astonishment wounds me, cousin."

She sat straighter. "But how? When did you learn to waltz? Monsieur Auclair never taught us the waltz, no matter how many times I begged."

"A man must be allowed to have some mystery about him," Jory said.

Anna cast them both an inquiring smile. "You had dancing lessons?" she asked Wynne.

"Oh, aye. Grandfather brought in a dancing instructor . . . what, Grandfather? Eight or ten years agone it must be now. He taught all of us cousins the cotillion and the quadrille, but never the waltz."

Anna angled a measuring glance at Jory, and he had the decency to duck his head. She knew he was remembering, as she was, one particular series of dancing lessons five years before.

CHAPTER TWENTY-ONE

∞

1814 - FIVE YEARS BEFORE

Jory inspected the fly Anna had just tied off with a bit of torn linen and feathers. He was fair certain she'd been attending his instruction, but the tangled monstrosity she'd crafted defied belief. Even Trout, who'd roused herself from her favorite napping spot, eyed it skeptically.

"Lass," he said with a shake of his head as he held the fly up to the sunlight. "Nothing ever flew that looked like this. The trout will gaze upon it with astonishment and wonder what freak of nature has been unleashed upon their stream."

Anna sighed and sank back onto her heels. She idly plucked at a loose thread on their blanket, and he leaned down and gave her a kiss for her effort. When he pulled back, she gazed up at him, her eyes soft and her lips softer.

"Never fear," he said. "I'll make a proper angler of you yet."

Her nose wrinkled at that pronouncement. She might have been pleased with his kiss but certainly not his prediction. "What troubles you?" he asked.

"You've taught me to tie flies and . . . and to cast a firm line," she said. "But I've not taught you anything. You must find me perfectly useless."

He laughed. "You've given me plenty of practice in the fine art of kissing," he said, then he wiped the smile from his face as he realized she was in earnest. "What would you like to teach me, lass? To trim a bonnet? To stitch a sampler?"

She looked about them as if seeking inspiration from the trees and mud. Frowning, she turned back to him, and the uncertainty in her gaze stabbed at him.

"I'll strive to learn whatever you wish," he whispered. "What would you be doing if you'd gone to London?"

He saw the moment inspiration struck as her eyes brightened. "I'll teach you to dance," she said, and she hurried to stand.

His smile faltered, and he opened his mouth to tell her that his grandfather had brought in a dancing instructor three summers past. He and his cousins were all well versed in country dances, as well as the cotillion and the quadrille. But then he stopped himself. If she wished to instruct him, who was he to argue?

He rose to stand beside her and offered a short bow. "As you wish, lass."

Three days later, Anna stared at him in amazement. "Three days," she said. "It only took you three days to become proficient at dancing." She frowned as if this was a mark against his character. He supposed it ought to be, for his deception.

"Chin up, lass," he said. "Teach me another dance, and I promise not to do a proper job of it."

Her lips began to curve at his teasing before she pressed them together and gave him a stern look. "The waltz," she said, a light of challenge in her eyes.

"Aye?" He looked down and rubbed his thumb and forefinger along his chin. Grandfather's dancing instructor had not ventured to teach them the waltz, but he'd heard tales of it. Such an indecent dance may have been well and good for the fast society of London, but it was unlikely to land on the shores of Newford, after all.

He eyed her through his lashes. Anna stood at the edge of their blanket, hands folded primly before her, chin tilted as she awaited his agreement. He may never have a need for the steps, but if she wanted to teach him, to allow him to hold her as they twirled on the bank of the stream, he wouldn't persuade her otherwise. He wasn't an idiot.

"Very well, lass. Show me how 'tis done."

She grinned and released her grip on her hands. "First, we'll discuss the holds, then I'll teach you the steps. There are a variety of positions that are acceptable, depending upon the company. The first is called The Great Window. We begin by joining our right hands." She reached for his hand with her own smaller one and held their joined hands aloft. "Then we place our left hands on the other's elbow."

He frowned. "This doesn't feel very natural, lass. Are you sure we're doing it proper?" he asked. Indeed, there was entirely too much space between them, and he pulled her closer.

She dropped his elbow and, laughing, placed her hand on his chest to stop him. "Let me demonstrate another position then."

He dropped his hands reluctantly and waited for her instruction. Her enthusiasm for the lesson was endearing.

"For The Coronation, the lady puts her hands together like so." She held her hands together above her head. "Then you support them with your right hand and place your left on my side."

He did as she instructed and settled his hand on her hip.

She cleared her throat and said, "A little higher." He moved his hand up a fraction of an inch. "Higher . . . there." She swallowed and smiled at him.

This was better, he decided, as he watched color stain her throat. But for an indecent dance, there was still too much space between them. He drew her closer and, again, she pushed him back.

"I'll show you one more hold, then we'll go through the steps," she said, and he loved how prim her voice was despite her blush.

"For this last position, we place our left hands on the other's shoulder and our right hands about the other's waist."

She demonstrated, and he reveled in the feel of her small hand at his waist. Even through the layers of his shirt and coat, he could feel the slight pressure of her hand, each fingertip marking him.

He placed his own hand about her and felt his breathing quicken. This was much better, and he smiled.

"What is this position called, lass?"

"This is *Le Soutien Mutuel*. The Mutual Support."

"I like this one," he said, pulling her closer.

"I think you have a firm grasp on the holds," she said, laughing and pushing him back. "Perhaps we should save the steps for tomorrow. My mother will wonder what's keeping me."

The next day, he insisted on the Mutual Support.

"I'm not learning the waltz from two feet away, lass," he said as he took her hand and settled it at his waist.

Then, with very proper instruction, she walked him through the steps.

It was no wonder his grandfather's dancing instructor had not taught them the waltz. If there'd been any question before about the dance's indecency, the steps answered it. The clasping, the prolonged eye contact, the dizzying pace of the movement . . . Heaven help him. Was it any wonder it took him a week or more to master the steps?

1819 - THE PRESENT

JORY'S HEART KICKED AGAINST HIS ribs as he recalled his waltzes with Anna. He supposed his secret—his deception of five years ago—was out, and he suppressed a smile at the accusation in her eyes. But despite her displeasure with him, there was also a telltale rosiness in her cheeks that suggested she recalled their lessons as well as he did.

"You should teach your cousin," she said with an impish smile, "so she might waltz at the assembly."

He startled and stared at her. Waltz with Wynne? After the slightly improper memories he'd just recalled? Why, Wynne was practically a sister.

"What a splendid idea!" his grandfather said, sealing his fate.

"Jory, you have to teach me to waltz," Wynne added.

"I'm not sure I recall the steps," he said slowly, with one last effort to wriggle off the hook Anna had set for him.

"Oh, stuff! *You* learned, so how hard can it be?"

He glared at his cousin then turned his gaze on Anna when she said, "I'm sure you must be a very accomplished dancer."

Her innocent expression as she tucked her bottom lip behind her teeth didn't fool him, and he narrowed his eyes. She straightened and tapped a finger on her lips as if an idea had just occurred to her. "You should begin with the Mutual Support, I think."

"Aye, that sounds lovely," Wynne said.

Jory knew when he'd been defeated. "Very well," he said, "but if you step on my toes, we're finished."

His grandfather chuckled with glee and pushed a chair aside to give them more space. Anna turned back to the pianoforte and arranged her music while Jory positioned Wynne's arms on his shoulder and waist.

"Not so close, Wynne," he said as he straightened his arms to increase their distance.

"Jory, this is indecent!" she exclaimed with a delighted laugh, and he blushed. "Wherever did you have an opportunity to learn the waltz?"

He ignored her question and nodded to Anna to begin playing. She quirked her lips at him and pressed her fingers to the keys, obviously elated to be an instrument of his torture.

Wynne collapsed on the sofa some minutes later, flushed and giddy. If he'd spun her a little faster than was warranted, it was the least she deserved.

"Jory!" She held a hand to her throat and grinned at him. "I'm overdone! That was wonderful. We must hurry back so I can show Roddie." A wicked smile crossed her face. "Or you could—"

"No," he said emphatically. "No, I could not."

Wynne turned to Anna. "Thank you for playing, Anna. This was great fun. You're coming to the assembly, too, aren't you?"

"Oh, well, I—"

"Of course, you are," Wynne interrupted and answered her own question. "Peggy will be grateful to have the coffee room to herself. She and Alfie can manage without us for a bit."

"But I haven't anything to wear," Anna protested, looking down at her pink gown. Jory thought her dress was perfectly acceptable, but judging from the twist to Wynne's lips, his cousin agreed with Anna.

"Never worry," Wynne said. "We'll figure something out. We'll take up one of my own dresses if it comes to that."

Jory choked on a laugh before it could fully form. They'd have to remove half a foot or more from the length of one of Wynne's dresses, but he didn't think his cousin would appreciate the observation.

"Miss Pepper, 'twas a delight having you here tonight," his grandfather said when they moved to take their leave. "If ever you tire of waiting on my grandsons, you come stay here," he continued, taking her hand in his. "Oak Hill is much too grand for one lonely old man. We'll find you a companion fit for a lady, and you can play the pianoforte all you like. 'Tis a more proper life you're meant for."

She smiled and squeezed his hand in response, causing a blush to rise on his weathered skin.

Jory stared at his grandfather, surprised at how closely his words matched Jory's own thoughts from earlier.

The solution to his grandfather's loneliness was a simple one, and it stood before them in a pink gown. His grandfather obviously held an affection for Anna, and she for him. But he stopped himself before he could convince Anna to accept his grandfather's offer. She would leave as soon as she had the wherewithal to do so—she'd told him as much just days before—and he couldn't bear his grandfather to suffer another loss.

His reluctance had nothing whatsoever to do

with his own heart, and he forced the scowl from his face as his grandfather bowed over her hand.

When Wynne's pony cart was brought around, he took the reins from the groom and ignored Wynne's outraged sniff.

"'Tis late, Wynne, and I've no wish to tempt providence any further tonight."

"But there's a quarter moon, Jory," she protested. "Plenty of light to see by."

"Give over, Wynne. Letting me drive is the least you can do after I waltzed with you."

She huffed but moved to the other side of the cart. With Anna wedged between them, he was conscious of the heat of her shoulder, of her hip pressed against him. With every bump, every turn, he felt her, and the urge to wrap his arm about her was strong.

Quite honestly, he was surprised he wasn't the one to drive them into a ditch.

CHAPTER TWENTY-TWO

◈

TWO DAYS LATER, JORY SHOOK rain from his hat and stepped into the dressmaker's shop. A little brass bell jangled above the door as it closed, and he glanced around, relieved to see the establishment was empty.

His cousin, Morwenna Williamson, looked up from behind the counter and offered a broad smile. He studied the shop as she approached; he'd certainly never had occasion to visit her here before. He wasn't in the habit of purchasing dresses after all.

It had taken the better part of the past two days to talk himself into coming. Anna was nothing more to him than a friend, but he'd seen the longing on her face when Wynne had asked if she'd attend next week's assembly. The longing and then the disappointment when she admitted she didn't have anything to wear.

She couldn't know it was from him, but if a new

dress brought Anna joy, that wasn't such a bad thing, was it?

"Jory," Morwenna said. "How can I help you?"

He willed his blush down as he said, "I'm looking for a dress." At her raised brows, he added, "Discreetly, of course."

"Of course," she agreed. "Something for a relation, I presume. A favored aunt perhaps. Custom or ready-made?"

"Ready-made, I should think."

"And d'you have this aunt's measurements?"

What? Of course not! Morwenna waited with a curious smile while he thought. Finally, he held a hand up to his chest and said, "She's about this tall."

Morwenna nodded and made a notation in a little notebook.

"Is this aunt thin or thick?"

"Thin."

She nodded again. "And her coloring?"

That was easy. "She's fair with golden hair."

"Green eyes?"

"Aye, how did you know?"

She made another notation and sighed, saying, "Jory, I'm sorry to say you're not the first 'nephew' to acquire a dress for this particular aunt. Two of our relations have already been here afore you." She looked up and stepped back from the expression on his face, and he forced his frown to clear.

"Who?" he asked, thinking of the blue dress Anna had received shortly after her arrival. Which of his cousins was to blame?

"I'm sure you understand I can't tell you that. My customers wouldn't appreciate me sharing their business, as I'm sure you wouldn't appreciate me sharing yours."

She had a point, he conceded. He *was* relieved to know she wouldn't blather about his purchase, but he'd like to know who was buying dresses for Anna.

"Let me show you what I have that will fit the lady," she said, "if you're still interested, that is."

He nodded once, and she disappeared into the back of her shop. One by one, she brought out several dresses for his approval, but none of them were right for Anna. All were the wrong color, or the pattern was too fancy or not fancy enough.

He frowned and tugged on his lip. This had been a mistake.

"What's the occasion?" Morwenna asked. At his hesitation, she added, "I've already assured you I can be discreet, cousin."

"'Tis for next week's assembly at the Feather."

She nodded, thinking. "I have just the thing. One moment."

She disappeared once more and emerged with a silk gown the color of the summer sea beneath the ruins at Oak Hill.

He sucked in a breath. "That's the one," he said, and Morwenna smiled.

"Your aunt will be pleased," she assured him. "D'you be needing any slippers to send with it?"

Slippers? He thought of Anna's too-small pink slippers and her sensible half boots. The ivory shoes Trout had muddied at the church.

"Aye, I imagine I do. Let's see the most insensible shoes you have," he said.

Morwenna's brows lifted, then she lobbed another question at him. "And what about under-garments?" she asked.

"Un"—he cleared his throat—"under-garments?"

"Aye, Jory," she said with some exasperation. "A chemise, petticoat and the like."

Jory didn't know it was possible for a blush to burn so hotly, but he was pleased to see his cousin's cheeks had taken on a slight tint as well.

"No," he said, clearing his throat. "No under-garments." Then he had a sudden thought. "Did our other relations . . . ?"

"No, no under-garments," she assured him hastily, and he nodded, exhaling.

Some time later, his purchases had been paid for, and he'd arranged a discreet delivery to The Fin and Feather. He replaced his hat on his head, and as he turned to go, the bell over Morwenna's door rang.

Jory narrowed his eyes as Alfie stomped rain

from his boots. When his cousin looked up and spied him, an expression of guilty surprise crossed his features.

"Shopping for a new frock, cousin?" Jory asked.

Once Alfie had recovered, he grinned. "That I am. Did you find something to your liking, Jory? A nice walking dress to bring out your eyes, perhaps?"

Jory scowled and brushed past him, his shoulder bumping his cousin's a bit too firmly.

ANNA STARED AT THE PILE of open boxes on her bed, unsure how to proceed. Certainly, it was improper for anyone other than her closest family to purchase her clothing, but she'd received no fewer than four dresses in anticipation of the night's assembly. Not to mention assorted shoes, gloves and ribbons. And all of this was in addition to the blue dress she'd already received on first arriving in Newford. Her cheeks burned at the impropriety of it all, but that was not the sole cause of her distress.

A rather large part of her delighted in the silks and fine muslins arrayed before her, their beautiful colors and trims causing a tingle to chase along her arms. But another, surprisingly vocal part dreaded hurting someone, because she could only wear one dress tonight. Only one pair of shoes.

"You're certain you don't know who sent them?" she asked Wynne as they stood at the foot of Anna's bed.

"I have my suspicions," Wynne said with a grin, which was no more than she'd admitted to previously. "But I'll not speculate."

"What must the dressmaker think of me?" Anna pressed cool hands to the sides of her face to soothe the heated blush there. "To have gentlemen making such purchases for me?"

Thankfully, there'd been no under-garments in the boxes, but the gloves alone were scandalous enough, never mind the dresses.

"Don't let that concern you," Wynne said. "Morwenna is a cousin. She'll not talk out of turn."

Another cousin. Of course.

Anna chewed the corner of her lip. "What if I choose the wrong one?" she asked. Too late, she realized her question implied there was a *right* one. She couldn't deny that she wished—hoped—one of the dresses were from Jory. If such was the case, she didn't want to hurt him further by selecting the wrong dress. But if he'd *not* sent one of the boxes . . . well, that was another type of hurt altogether.

"Anna," Wynne said. "You're in the enviable position of having numerous people watching over you. Wishing for your happiness. Enjoy it. Follow your heart and know you can't go wrong."

Wynne was right. She knew it, but still, her heart pounded at the expectations placed upon it. At the thought of making a poor choice. There's no poor choice, she reminded herself. These were gifts made in friendship. Doubt fogged her brain, though, and she sagged onto the end of the bed.

"I can't go to the assembly," she whispered. "They're all so beautiful—as is the sentiment behind them—but I can't choose one. I'll remain with Peggy in the coffee room."

"Nonsense," Wynne said. She stood and lifted two of the dresses from their boxes and held them up for Anna's inspection. "Of these two, which d'you prefer?" At Anna's hesitation, she said, "Stop thinking. Just choose."

The words, so like Jory's at Oak Hill, moved her to action. She stopped thinking and pointed to the dress on the left. A beautiful gold silk.

Wynne kept the gold silk in one hand and lifted the next dress, a sprigged rose muslin. Also beautiful, but it didn't cause her heart to flutter quite like the gold silk. She pointed to the gold again.

Wynne lifted the last dress and held it next to the gold. It was breathtaking, and Anna's heart fluttered then skipped a beat. A deep blue-green silk the color of the sea, it reminded her of the waves beneath the ruins at Oak Hill. Of Jory's eyes.

Not when he was angry or laughing, but in the

tiny moments before he kissed her.

"That one," she said, smiling. Then her expression flattened as she thought of the three dresses she'd abandoned on the bed.

"Stop thinking," Wynne said again and turned her away from the pile of silk and muslin. "Now, let's talk about slippers..."

ANNA ADJUSTED THE BORROWED GLOVES on her arms and tried to calm her jumping nerves.

She always became anxious before a ball, but never like this. Normally, she worried about making a fool of herself. Saying the wrong thing, wearing the wrong thing, showing to poor advantage next to Mary Riverton. Tonight, though, she worried about hurting another if she'd picked the wrong dress. It was an altogether unfamiliar obligation, this concern for others.

A small orchestra was tuning their instruments when they entered the assembly rooms above the Feather. The master of ceremonies received them then announced their arrival to the patrons already milling about the refreshment tables.

Miss Parker was just across the room with two other young ladies. Reluctantly, Anna acknowledged that she was quite pretty in a pale green gown, and

Jory would probably dance with her. They would make a lovely couple.

"Cadan," Wynne said, and Anna turned to see Jory's cousin approaching. "I didn't expect to see you here tonight," Wynne continued. "You rarely attend the assemblies."

Anna didn't miss the speculative look Wynne cast at her from the side of her eye. Nor did she miss the slight twist of chagrin on Cadan's lips as he eyed her gown. She was both relieved and dismayed to mentally cross him off the list of cousins who might have purchased the blue-green gown.

"Cadan, a new set is starting. You must lead Mrs. Featherton out. She didn't come to stand along the wall."

Anna blushed at Wynne's gruff command, but she recovered quickly when Cadan offered his arm.

"I apologize for my cousin's poor manners," he said when they'd assumed their places. "She was raised by wolves, apparently."

Anna laughed. "She may have been," she agreed. "But at least you know where you stand with her. She's one of the most genuine people I've ever had the good fortune to meet."

"Genuine," he said. "Is that what one calls it, Mrs. Featherton?"

She laughed, and they moved into the steps of

the dance. "You truly don't have to continue calling me by that ridiculous name," she whispered when the steps brought them back together.

She'd confessed her ruse to the Kimbrell gentlemen after her evening at Oak Hill, but to a man, they all insisted on maintaining her charade. Their loyalty both confounded and warmed her heart.

"'Tis a gentleman's privilege to safeguard a lady's reputation," he replied, bringing a smile to her face.

Moments later, laughing and energized by the dance, they left the floor to find several more of Jory's cousins had arrived.

Alfie greeted her then crossed his arms and complimented her with a subtle quirk of his brow. "I'm off to relieve Roddie downstairs, but I wished to see you ladies in your finery. You look lovely, Mrs. Featherton, as I'm sure you would in *any* gown."

She smiled apologetically and marked him off her list as well. As she did Gryffyn and James some moments later.

Merryn's eyes sparkled as he approached, and her stomach did an uncomfortable turn before he spoke. "You look quite fetching tonight, Mrs. Featherton. You've a good eye for fashion—better than myself, I must confess. I've always been a sad case at choosing colors and patterns."

Anna smiled at him warmly, pleased that there

were only two gentlemen remaining. Jory and the constable. As if cued by her thoughts, the constable's voice sounded from behind her, cutting through the general noise of the assembly to reach her ears. She turned to see him approaching.

Gavin Kimbrell bowed over her hand and gave her an indecipherable smile as he said, "I have to say, you look like a maid of the sea tonight, Mrs. Featherton. That gown was meant for you, and I can almost picture you luring sailors to their deaths upon the rocks."

He gave her a meaningful wink fraught with implication, and her heart plummeted to her silver slippers. Gavin Kimbrell? Surely not. No, she refused to believe it. The man had once threatened to cast her into gaol. She forced her mouth to close as she curtsied and thanked him for the pretty compliment.

"The gown is not so fatal, I hope," she said.

"'Tis not the gown that will be the death of us," he said. "But the smile upon your face."

Anna felt a presence behind her and turned to find Jory's scowling expression aimed at the constable. She wanted to weep at his dark look, certain she'd chosen the wrong gift to wear tonight. Then he turned to her and stilled, and she knew. She'd picked the *right* one after all.

His eyes remained carefully trained on her face,

but his lips . . . His lips curved in a warm smile that zipped through her stomach to curl her toes.

Was she breathing? No, she'd stopped breathing. She forced herself to inhale then pushed the air out of her lungs slowly.

"Oh, wonderful! Roddie's arrived," Wynne said. "And just in time, love. Mrs. Clifton has only now called a waltz," she told her husband.

Anna watched Wynne and Roddie leave their group. Jory continued to stare at her, and she grew uncomfortable. Would he ask her to dance, or would he leave them? He'd probably go to find Miss Parker, and she'd be left to hold up the wall.

Her heart thumped heavily in her chest. At his silence, she felt a flush blooming on her throat. Pressing her lips, she forced her attention to return to the constable. But before she could think of something to break the uncomfortable silence that had settled on their corner of the room, Jory spoke.

"If you've this dance free, will you honor me with your hand, lass?"

―

JORY'S COLLAR WAS TIGHT AS he and Gavin entered the Feather's assembly rooms. He'd thought to use the occasion of tonight's gathering to further his acquaintance with Miss Parker, but his thoughts remained stubbornly attached to Anna.

He wondered again if she had selected his dress. What if she'd chosen one of his cousins' offerings instead? The uncertainty was shredding him to bits on the inside.

It was only a dress, he reminded himself. There was no meaning attached to it whatsoever. Whether she chose it or not didn't signify one way or the other.

And so, he entered the assembly rooms prepared to see her gowned in some pink confection or a frothy blue dress. Prepared to react normally when he encountered her in yellow satin or plum velvet.

But when his cousins parted and he saw her in the blue-green silk that he'd chosen for her, all his careful preparations fled, and warmth spread through his limbs. Say something, he commanded himself, but no words came, and his tongue remained fixed to the roof of his mouth.

Dimly, he heard Gavin complimenting her. Some driveling nonsense about her smile drawing sailors to their deaths. Jory frowned, but he thought his cousin may have had the right of it, for her beauty wasn't in the gown she wore, although she looked quite lovely in it. Her beauty was in the tentative smile she cast upon them, the faint glimmer of hope in her eyes as she stood next to Wynne.

Then Wynne left them on Roddie's arm, and he

realized the strains of a waltz were beginning. Few dancers had entered the floor—his cousin hadn't been wrong about the waltz's reception in Newford—and before Jory knew what he was about, he'd bowed his head toward Anna.

"Will you honor me with your hand, lass?"

She smiled, her dimple peeking from her cheek, and settled a hand on his sleeve as he led her out.

He didn't recall his cousins' looks of disbelief on learning he could waltz (although surely, they'd worn them) or the steps that separated him and Anna from the crowd gathered along the perimeter of the room. All of his senses were tuned to the lady on his arm. They took their places, and she lifted her left hand to his shoulder.

"*Le Soutien Mutuel,*" he whispered, and her right hand settled at his waist. Her eyes sparkled as he led her into the first turn. He inhaled deeply, and the soft scent of her hair threatened to tangle his feet.

He'd thought to move on with his life, to put Miss Anna Pepper behind him and find his happiness elsewhere. But as much as his head might wish it, his heart continued to whisper that Anna was the only one for whom his heart would ever skip.

"You're beautiful," he said, his mind incapable of anything more eloquent.

She smiled, and a blush stained her throat. "Thank you for the dress," she whispered, and his hand tightened on her waist.

"Wherever did you learn to waltz?" she asked playfully. She gazed at him through her lashes, and he realized she was *flirting* with him. Very well. He would enjoy the game, but he refused to attach any greater meaning to her words.

"'Twas an incomer lass that taught me," he said.

"An incomer, you say?"

"Aye, and a fitty one at that."

Her brow wrinkled. "Is—is fitty good?"

"Aye, lass. Fitty is very good."

She nodded once. "Well, then. She must have counted you a friend if she offered her instruction."

He concentrated on the movement of his feet rather than the feel of her beneath his hand.

"No, lass," he said with a dramatic sigh. "I believe she was merely fond of my dog. 'Twas nothing more to it than that."

She laughed, the sound trickling over him. "I've met your dog, sir, and I can say with certainty such was not the case."

"Of course, 'twas. Trout is loyal and trustworthy. A man's not likely to find a better companion."

She shook her head, rejecting his argument.

"But there can be no other explanation," he insisted. Even as he said the words, he cursed himself for casting his line where the fish were not likely to bite.

"Perhaps—" she began then stopped.

He waited as long as he could, a second or two, then he prompted her. "Aye, lass?"

"Perhaps she held you in affection."

Her words were softly whispered, but they may as well have been shouted at full volume. His heart skipped in time with the music as they turned.

"Perhaps," he agreed, refusing to allow himself to feel hope. "But that was a long time ago, lass, and I'm sure she no longer does so."

They made another full turn before she spoke again. "Perhaps you're mistaken."

And his heart—stupid, traitorous organ—jumped in his chest.

―――

ANNA KNEW WITH CERTAINTY THAT no other waltz for the rest of her days would ever compare to this dance. Jory turned her gracefully, and the crowds along the wall disappeared. She heard only the strains of the music and felt his warm touch at her side, his firm shoulder beneath her hand.

He smiled down at her, his dark gold hair curling on the ends, his eyes crinkling at the corners, and his Rs rolling in perfect, fluid cadence. Despite their differences in height, they were well matched. Perfectly suited, a voice whispered in her head.

If the heat of his gaze was anything to judge by, he was in accord, and her pulse pounded in her ears. His look was not that of one *friend* toward another. It was a look of yearning. Of one soul longing for the touch of another's.

After all the time that had passed since they'd first met, after seeing her at her worst, after her poor treatment of him . . . was it possible he still held an affection for her?

Hope bloomed in her chest, soft and warm like a spring bud unfolding.

CHAPTER TWENTY-THREE

〜∞〜

THE NEXT AFTERNOON, WYNNE APPROACHED Anna as she cleaned a spill in the coffee room. She lifted a large basked and asked, "Can you take this to the church?"

"Of course," Anna said, setting aside the mop with relief. "Is it for the vicar?"

"No, 'tis only a light repast for Jory and Merryn. Jory left for the foundry before he could break his fast, and I saw him not ten minutes past walking with Merryn to the church."

Anna swallowed and pressed down the fizzing thrill at the thought of seeing Jory. They'd not spoken any further beyond their waltz, and she was curious how he would receive her today.

Nodding at Wynne, she took the basket with one hand. Surprised by the weight of it, she quickly added her other hand to the handle and said, "I'll return shortly."

"There's no need to hurry," Wynne said airily as she returned to her office. "The next stage isn't due for another hour, and Peggy will be here by then."

Anna lugged the basket to the parish church and passed beneath the shadow of the square tower. Inside, she found Trout sprawled on the stone floor. Spying Anna, the collie jumped up and trotted to her side.

"Hallo?" Anna called, setting the basket down.

There was no response save Trout's enthusiastic hand-lick. She gave the dog an abstracted scratch behind the ear then turned to gaze about the church. It was still and cool, and the mingled scents of damp stone, wax-rubbed oak and tallow candles lay heavy in the air.

A small, shuttered window faced the chancel, set high in the stone wall just below the tower. If the gentlemen had come for the bells, they must be there, or in the tower above.

She investigated and found a set of spiral stairs near the vestry. Lifting the basket once more, she climbed until she reached a narrow stone passage that ran the length of the church.

Her footsteps were soft on the stone as she walked. Open windows allowed the sun's afternoon rays to light the floor, but not so much to warm the space, and she shivered.

At the end of the passage another short flight of

stairs led to a heavy wooden door. The hinges groaned when she pushed it open, and she found herself in a small, square chamber with narrow, wooden benches lining the walls.

Eight holes ringed the ceiling, and a heavy rope dangled from one, the end looped to avoid dragging the floor. A tight iron staircase in one corner wound up to a small trapdoor, and a shuttered window on one wall told her she'd found the room overlooking the chancel below.

She called out again, adjusting her hands on the basket. Footsteps sounded from above, and the trapdoor folded back to reveal Jory's face.

"Anna?"

She hefted the basket to show him her offering. "Wynne sent me with sustenance for you and Mr. Merryn."

"Merryn's stepped out," he said.

"Oh. Then there's more for you," she replied with a smile.

He hesitated then folded the trapdoor all the way back.

Soon his legs emerged through the opening in the ceiling, then the rest of him followed as he descended the winding stairs to join her.

"What is this room?" she asked when he reached the floor.

"'Tis the ringing chamber. Once all the bells are

rehung, the ringers will operate them from here using ropes like this one."

He took Wynne's basket and set it on one of the benches. His brows lifted as he opened it, and Anna peered over his shoulder, surprised to see roast chicken, sliced pears, cheese and raspberry tarts. Two mugs for cider. It was no wonder the basket had been so heavy.

Jory stared at the food for a moment, then he said, "Would you like to join me, lass?"

Wynne had said there was no hurry, hadn't she? And Anna was curious to see how she and Jory got on after last night's waltz. To see if something more than friendship had survived her rough handling of his heart.

"Yes," she said decisively. "That would be nice. Certainly, Wynne's sent enough food."

He laughed. "Aye, that she has. We can return down below then."

"There's no need," Anna said. "Can we not eat here in the ringing chamber?" she asked. "Or perhaps you can show me the tower."

She looked up at the trapdoor above their heads then back down to Jory. This was where he spent so much of his time, and she found herself curious to know the space. To know *him*. It might not be proper, them sharing a luncheon alone, but it was unlikely anyone would discover them up here.

"You wish to see the belfry?" he asked, surprised.

"I'd like to see what you do."

His eyebrows lifted, but after a moment's hesitation, he said, "Very well then." He took up the basket and moved to the stairs. "I'll go first, lass, then I'll help you through. Mind the stairs, though. They're steep."

She waited until he'd ascended halfway, then she began winding her own way up behind him. She looked toward him once and quickly averted her gaze when the sight of his strong legs tensing on the stairs caused a blush to ignite.

The stairs were narrow, and steep as he'd indicated, but without the basket to weigh her down she made short work of them. As she poked her head and shoulders through the opening in the ceiling, Jory reached a hand down to assist her through.

She'd come to expect the fizzing that sparked at his touch, but it still caused a shiver to ripple along her shoulders. He dropped her hand, and she turned to take in the belfry.

Dust and old wood filled the space, and a single bronze bell hung above them. Open windows on all four sides afforded a view of Newford and blue sea on one side, rolling hills and shadowed valleys on another. Intrigued, she stepped lightly to one opening and gasped when a bird flew past.

"Why, I've never been this high before," she said. "I can see Penhale from here. And look how far the sea stretches!"

Like a bolt of rippling blue satin, the sea shimmered as the sun laid a diamond-studded path from horizon to harbor.

"Aye, lass. 'Tis the highest point in this corner of the duchy. Leastways, the highest built by man."

A cart rumbled past the town green, and a lady entered Mrs. Williamson's shop at the opposite end of town. The people were miniature versions of themselves, and the belfry rose with superiority above it all, part of the town but separated by its elevation.

"It's so peaceful," she whispered as a stillness settled over the tower.

"Aye, but 'tis some cold in winter, when the wind blows through. Although the bells will sound best with a touch of frost on them."

Jory moved, and she turned to find him close behind her, arms crossed. His eyes touched her face in a gentle caress as tangible as if he'd reached for her with his hand.

She swallowed, and he stepped back.

Disappointment flooded her, and she realized how much she'd been longing for his kiss. Not only today, or since arriving in Newford, but for the past five years, she'd longed for *him*.

"Let's unpack my cousin's repast," he said.

Jory lifted a blanket from the basket and spread it on the dusty floor before returning for the food. He forked pear slices onto a small tin plate, and as she nibbled one, he explained the workings of the belfry.

"That's the only salvageable bell," he said. "Once Uncle and I finish casting the remaining bells, we'll install them alongside this one."

"How will you get the bells into the tower?" she asked. "They must be very heavy."

"Aye, the tenor alone will weigh over eleven hundred pounds. We'll remove the floorboards in the ringing chamber and the belfry then use pulleys to hoist them into the tower. Merryn's firm has the expertise needed to see it done."

Then he pointed out a complex system of wheels and pulleys that would allow the bells to swing in full circles when rung. "The sound is loudest when the bells are rung face up," he said. "But volume doesn't signify if the bells aren't tuned properly."

She detected pride in his voice and smiled to hear the enthusiasm he felt for his craft. She recalled Wynne's words the day of the Oak Hill picnic. *When he feels something, he feels it strongly, and his conviction is formidable.*

He'd felt that way about her once, and she'd thrown it away. How could she have been so careless with such a treasure? By her inaction, her indecision, she'd forsaken this man. She could have had a lifetime of his gentle love, if only she'd had faith and believed in him. Trusted his love for her. Was it too late?

"THE TUNER'S SKILL IS IN knowing which part of the bell to adjust to achieve the desired result. A shave here, an adjustment there to coax the perfect tone from the bronze. 'Tis a precise craft. Sound is a very mathematical phenomenon."

Jory listened to himself drone on about bells and clappers while Anna watched him with a polite smile. Surely, she must be regretting her interest on hearing his overly detailed explanations.

He'd never had this problem five years ago. Five years ago, he'd not worried overly much about her impression of him. He'd been so certain of his own feelings, it had only made sense that she felt the same. But now . . . If only he knew how to read her as well as the bronze heft of a bell . . . if only she responded to him in mathematical certainties.

Why had she come? Granted, Wynne had sent food—enough for him and Merryn and the rest of his cousins, in fact. The blanket was a nice touch. Wynne wouldn't have given his or Merryn's comfort a second thought, so he could only assume she meant for Anna to enjoy the food with him. But why had Anna asked to see the belfry?

He thought of their dance the previous evening, and the hope that had flared in his chest at her words. *Perhaps she held you in affection.*

What did she mean by "affection"? Certainly, his grandmother had held him in affection. And his mother, he presumed, while she lived. Wynne held him in affection, but that didn't mean they were in love with one another. Was that all Anna meant? Did she care for him like a cousin or a sister?

He suppressed a groan. What man wished the love of his heart to look on him like a brother?

He stopped blathering about the bells and looked at her. She smiled around a slice of pear, a bead of juice gathering at the corner of her mouth. He stopped breathing, and she swallowed.

"Jory," she whispered. She sat close enough that he could see the different shades of green in her eyes—like the underside of a canopy of trees backlit by the summer sun.

"Aye, lass?"

Uncertainty clouded her eyes for the merest of moments, then she leaned forward and touched her lips to his. His eyes widened. She tasted of pears and cider, and before Jory could give it too much thought, he closed his eyes and returned her kiss.

This kiss was not like any they'd shared before. This kiss had simmered for years, on fires banked by yearning and regret. He threaded his hands through the hair at her nape and breathed her in, reveling in the scent that was uniquely Anna. In the soft curve of her lips, the cool taste of pears and the velvety smoothness of her skin beneath his thumbs.

He nearly wept to hold her again. Her fingers were feather light on his skin as she held his face, but they left every inch parched and burning. Alive, like he hadn't felt in five long years.

But her affection, her desire to kiss him didn't mean she wished to have and hold him 'til death did them part, did it? The reminder was like a cold splash in the stream on a summer's day. He began to pull back, but she tightened her hands and held him to her.

Perhaps one more taste . . .

Finally, with reluctance, his pulled his lips from hers and nuzzled the hair at her temple as he tried to catch his runaway heart.

"You should go, Anna," he said with equal parts amazement and befuddlement for his own stupidity. "Tain't proper, you being here like this."

―――

TAIN'T PROPER? HE WORRIED ABOUT propriety *now*, after all their solitary afternoons, all their kisses by the stream five years ago? Anna pulled herself from the loose circle of his arms, and he let her go. She rubbed her hands along her own arms, chafing them to warm the sudden chill there.

Her lips tingled, bruised where his had been, and she lifted one hand to soothe them. The rough pads of his fingers had scorched her skin, and she imagined she could feel them still.

His eyes were dark, stormy seas, unfathomable as he gazed at her, and his chest rose and fell in a strong rhythm. Her fingers had left his hair rumpled.

He watched her, eyes hesitant as he waited for her to do something. Say something.

"Jory," she whispered, but what did one say in a situation such as this? There were no words to convey the depth of feeling that flowed through her.

Below, the door of the church closed with a thump. Seconds later, boots rang on the stone steps, distant but coming closer, ascending to the ringing chamber.

"Merryn's returned," Jory said.

Anna gazed at the scene around them—the blanket and the cider. The raspberry tarts. It had all the appearances of... of an assignation. A fiery blush erupted, and she hurried to stand.

Jory rose as she dusted her hands and shook out her skirts. "Merryn's discreet," he said. "He won't say anything."

Anna cocked a disbelieving brow at him.

"Well, other than to my cousins. And Roddie," Jory added. "But they won't talk."

"I know," Anna said in a harsh whisper. "But what will they *think*?" She held her hands to her cheeks, willing her blush down, but it only burned hotter.

Jory pulled her hands down gently. "I'll distract him and send him on his way," he said. "Wait here."

He hesitated as he stared into her eyes, then he leaned down and pressed another kiss to her lips before dropping through the trapdoor. It closed behind him just as the door to the ringing chamber opened.

The gentlemen's muffled voices could be heard below. Anna stilled to listen, but she couldn't make out their words over the rapid thumping of her own heart, so she crouched low on the blanket.

"Have you seen Anna?" Merryn asked, his voice a low rumble. "Cadan saw her walking this way with a luncheon basket. I'm famished. I bet Wynne sent some of her raspberry tarts."

A pause. Then, "Aye, Anna came by the church."

Anna rolled her eyes. Jory was not particularly good at deception, it would seem. He'd give her away for certain.

"And?"

"And she's gone. You just missed her."

A moment passed and Anna imagined Merryn's frown at missing out on Wynne's raspberry tarts.

"You made a fitty pair at last night's assembly," he said, and Anna's brows lifted even as she leaned closer to the floor.

"I'm not sure what you mean."

"Just ask the lady to marry you and be done with it. 'Tis clear you're besotted."

There was a pause—an uncomfortably long pause—then Jory said, "I should check on Trout."

Anna clenched a fist. Could he not provide a proper response to a very sensible comment from his cousin?

"Fine," Merryn said. Did she detect a sigh at the end of his agreement? She could sympathize with his frustration. "But I need one more measurement from the belfry," he finished.

What? The belfry?

"Tell me what's needed, and I'll get it for you," Jory said. Anna closed her eyes and shook her head.

"'Tis no matter. I won't be but a moment." Footsteps sounded below and Anna pictured Merryn walking toward the spiral staircase.

She jumped from the blanket and searched for a hiding place. The belfry was a small, square room, and unless she could crawl up into the bell itself, there was no place in which to conceal herself. Her heart thudded beneath her muslin as the sound of boots on iron reached her.

Confidence, she reminded herself.

She straightened from her crouch on the blanket and brushed at her skirts with one hand as the trapdoor swung back.

Merryn's head poked through the opening, and he looked at her with surprise before a large grin split his face.

Anna forced a smile to her own face and reached for a raspberry tart. "Just go," she whispered as she handed it to him.

His grin stayed in place as he took the tart. He saluted her with it before backing down the steps and letting the door close.

CHAPTER TWENTY-FOUR

JORY WATCHED AS ANNA SET her tray on the edge of the table and handed the *Times* to James before passing mugs of ale around.

Just ask the lady to marry you and be done with it.

Merryn's words from the previous afternoon resounded in his mind. Again. He hated this indecision. It was a wholly new experience for him. Five years ago, he'd let his heart lead and hadn't given his head a second thought. But now, his head would not quiet, and it was driving him mad.

But was Merryn right? Should he just lay his heart bare once more and ask her to marry him? The thought caused a heavy constriction to seize his throat. He'd have to be daft to consider it.

No man went to the gallows twice.

His cousins groaned as Alfie held his hand out for the society page, and Jory pulled his attention back to the table. James cast Alfie a sideways grimace but complied with a bemused shake of his head.

"What?" Alfie said. "I merely wish to know if there have been any developments on the matter of Lady K's disastrous ball."

Anna's lips twitched as she straightened. "And are there any new reports?" she asked.

He skimmed the page. "No, but here's a fascinating bit on Lord L, who was recently seen in close company with a Lady L, though not *his* Lady L." Alfie winced at the poor man's troubles before continuing.

"Oh, and here's more on our poor Lord G." He cleared his throat and began to read with an air of importance. "'This author has learned that the colorful Lord G has fled over hill and vale to York on the heels of his recent abandonment at the altar.' Who goes to York?" Alfie asked. When his cousins only grumbled their agreement, he continued reading.

"'But whether his flight is to nurse a broken heart or his empty coffers is anyone's guess. Whispers amongst the servants suggest the salty Miss P, sad to say, has absconded to Cornwall of all places. One can only wonder how many hearts the spicy lady will lay bare there.' What d'you think of that?" Alfie asked the table at large as he leaned back. "You can't tell me you're not eager to learn more, especially since the lady's come to Cornwall.

Guard your hearts, lads."

Jory stared at Alfie, disbelieving the words his cousin had read. He felt the blood drain from his face, and a cold clamminess seized the back of his neck. His heart thumped heavily as the ocean roared in his ears, drowning out the sounds around him.

It couldn't be, he thought, searching his cousins' faces and the coffee room for another answer, but there was no denying the truth.

The "salty Miss P" could be none other than Anna Pepper. And she'd done it *again*.

She'd stilled next to him, her tray balanced on the edge of the table. Alfie's wide grin promptly fell when he looked on the two of them.

Jory's lungs burned, and he realized he'd not been breathing. He swallowed then drew a shuddering inhale and held it. Pushing back from the table, he stood and walked away.

He needed to leave. Leave his cousins' looks of dawning realization. Leave Anna. Leave his own skin if he could but manage it.

He walked past Wynne and ignored her concerned expression. Trout trotted after him with anxious steps. He pushed through the inn door into sunshine that was at odds with the seething chaos inside him. Distantly, he thought the day should have been less cheerful and more sympathetic—grey and mizzly, at the very least.

Around him, the bustle of the inn's stable yard continued, unaffected by the tightness in his chest. He dodged a porter carrying a trunk and replaced his hat on his head with careful deliberation. Placing one foot in front of the other, he walked.

For the last five years, he'd thought himself alone in his pain. The poor soul jilted by Miss Anna Pepper. A dubious honor, to be sure, but one that had been his and his alone. And now, to learn that he'd just been another fool among fools . . .

How could he have been so wrong about her? About them? Then, as he was now. He'd been so certain that she was the only one for him, but it was clear his heart couldn't be trusted. It had been clear that night five years ago, if only he'd bothered to heed the warnings of his mind.

The church lay ahead at the end of the high street, the path to the stream paces beyond that. Trout whined at his side and licked his hand. He left her at the front of the church and climbed the stairs, his footfalls echoing in the long hall to the ringing chamber. Finally, he wound up the spiral staircase to the belfry.

A shaft of sunlight pooled on the wooden floor, and he moved toward its feeble warmth. The church's lone bell hung still and silent, and memories from the last time he'd been in the belfry pummeled him. Had it only been yesterday?

He recalled the blanket, spread on the floor beneath where he now stood. Anna's pear-and-cider kiss. The smooth warmth of her skin. The pull of her smile. Hands on his hips, he hung his head.

Anna stared at Jory's retreating figure. She hadn't moved from the window table. She *couldn't* move. The look on his face, pale and stripped of emotion, had paralyzed her.

She'd never meant to hurt him—not five years ago and not now—but it seemed that was all she was capable of doing.

Returning to Cornwall had been a mistake. She should have left well enough alone. Why couldn't she have silenced her doubts and simply married Greenvale?

Like Jory's grandfather, Anna had often been accused of leaping without thinking. How many times had her mother bemoaned that very fact? If she'd only done that with Greenvale, she wouldn't be here now. Jory wouldn't be hurting now.

But the thought of marrying Greenvale left a queasy, greasy feeling in her stomach, even more than it had before she'd returned to Cornwall.

She gazed at the gentlemen's faces directed her way, shock and pity mingled with concern.

"Go," Gryffyn whispered, breaking through her stupor.

With a jerk of her head, she turned toward him.

"Go," he said again in a louder voice. He stood and took the tray from her numb hands.

Alfie watched her with a wretched expression of remorse. "I'm proper sorry," he said.

Anna smiled wanly. "You're not to blame," she assured him. "I'm afraid the fault lies solely with me." She smoothed a shaking hand over her waist and watched the hallway where Jory had left. Gryffyn was right. She needed to go to him. Explain, if such a thing were possible. She couldn't imagine what he must be thinking.

She turned and left, muslin swirling about her ankles in her haste. She spied Jory entering the church some distance ahead, and lifting her skirts, she hurried her steps.

Trout licked her hand when she arrived, confusion clouding her dark brown eyes.

Anna called out. The church was silent and empty in response, but then, she'd not expected him to answer.

She went to the stairs near the vestry and strode along the hall to the ringing chamber, her half boots soft whispers on the stone. The ringing chamber, too, was empty, so she climbed the spiral staircase and pushed on the trapdoor. It gave easily and she peeked through the opening. Jory stood in a shaft of sunlight, boots spaced apart on the wooden floor as he faced away from her.

She pushed the door open all the way, and it fell back with a thud and a puff of dust. Still, he didn't move. She climbed through the opening and brushed her hands off.

"Jory?" she whispered.

He was silent for a beat, and she thought he wouldn't respond, then his manners took over.

"Anna."

She swallowed, uncertain how to proceed, especially as she still faced his back. She recalled how they'd sat in this same space only a day before as he explained the workings of the bells. Remembered the heat of his kiss as it had spread through her veins, pushing her blood along like a warm current breaking up ice floes. Yearning washed over her again, followed by the heavy weight of loss.

She took a step toward him and placed a hand on his shoulder. He stiffened then turned to face her, and she let her hand fall. His blue eyes were cold and dry as he gazed at her.

"You promised yourself to another man," he said, "and you left him too." It was a statement rather than a question, but she responded.

"Yes." She gripped her hands tightly to keep

from reaching for him again. "I couldn't—"

He narrowed his gaze. "How many?"

"What?"

"How many,"—he gritted his teeth—"have you left?"

"Three," she whispered. "Counting you."

His eyes widened and he took a step back, coming up on the stone wall of the tower. He shook his head at her in disbelief. She could hardly believe it herself, but she wouldn't lie to him. She resisted the urge to look away from the accusation on his face and held her gaze steady.

"Are you so inconstant then in your affections? D'you value your heart so cheaply that you give it so carelessly?"

She couldn't fault his anger, his tone of indictment. He was hurting, and she was the cause of his pain, after all. Then she considered his question. She thought of all their afternoons by the stream five years before when she'd been so... Well, she'd just *been*. That was all. She'd been *Anna*, nothing more, nothing less. Not a disappointing daughter or a foolish gudgeon or a wealthy heiress. Not an unwed lady with a married woman's name.

She'd been her true self, and only with him. She'd never felt so *right* in the years before or since.

The irony of this moment was cruel, indeed. Her heart chose now to assert itself, overruling her head, and the doubts swirled to a stop on one undeniable truth: She loved Jory Tremayne. Like one of his beloved bells, the realization rang clear in her heart, the sound pure and rich. How had she not heard it before?

"No," she whispered, tears clogging her throat. "I've never given my heart to anyone but you."

―――

JORY STARED AT HER, UNABLE to believe his ears. She'd promised herself to *three* men and had left each of them.

He wasn't the only one. He wasn't even one of two. Three were a string. He was one in a *string* of fools. Had he been the first, he wondered, or had she already begun leaving suitors scattered behind her like crumbs when he'd found her by the stream?

No. He didn't wish to know.

Anger surged like a wave on the beach, and he waited for it to recede. He inhaled and closed his eyes, rubbed his forehead with one hand.

"Jory," she said. "Please believe I never meant to hurt you. Whatever you think of me, please know that. I only desire your happiness. Tell me how to make this better," she begged.

He scoffed and turned from her. "I wish . . ." He didn't know what he wished. He didn't know what he thought, what he felt anymore. He'd always been so certain of his emotions, but now they were in a proper tangle.

"What? What do you wish, Jory?"

He'd thought he could be her friend. He'd hoped to put the past behind him and move on from her, but he found he could not.

Then, foolishly, he'd thought she might still harbor an affection for him. He'd thought there might still be a chance for them to find happiness together.

But now, what did he wish?

He wished he'd never met her.

He wished his heart wasn't so pathetic, following in her wake as Trout followed him.

He wished it was more obedient to his mind's desires, but as long as she remained in Newford, his heart would never be his own.

"I wish . . . I wish you'd go. Leave Newford and leave me in peace."

Even as he said the words, he knew they wouldn't free his heart. For when she went, as she surely would, she'd take it with her again. Silence settled on the belfry, heavy and still. Without looking up, he waited until, finally, he heard the soft thud of the trapdoor closing.

Eventually, he collected his dog and his dignity and began walking. He stopped at his cousin's bank and was relieved to find James had returned from the Feather.

"You wish me to deliver a draft to Miss Pepper?" his cousin asked.

Jory nodded and rubbed a hand over his eyes. "Discreetly, of course," he said.

James steepled his fingers over his desk and leaned forward. "Tell me one thing, Jory. I gather you're not married to the lady—"

"Married? Are you daft? Of course not! She's just jilted some poor lord in London, or did you miss that part?"

"No, I thought you weren't, and I told Wynne as much." James shifted uncomfortably. "But are you honor-bound to marry her for any reason? 'Tis not our way to abandon ladies—"

"Abandon *her*?" Jory scoffed. "You have it backwards, cousin. And what, precisely, does Wynne have to do with it?" he asked, although he suspected he knew the nature of her role in his affairs, if not the extent of it.

James waved a hand then leaned back in his chair. "Why can't you deliver the draft yourself?" he asked. "And why so much?"

"Can you see it done or not?" Jory asked, his patience wearing thin. The sooner he could rid himself of Anna, the better, but she couldn't leave Newford until she had the means to do so. He turned toward the window in his cousin's office and rubbed a fist on his chest to ease the angry burning that flared every time he thought of her.

He turned back to find James staring at him, trying to bore directly into his brain to read his thoughts. Jory crossed his arms and waited. Finally, his cousin sighed and nodded. "I'll see it done," he assured him.

As Jory approached the path leading to the stream, he hesitated. Fishing had always provided a respite for him, the stream a restful place of peace and serenity, but he couldn't go there today. Anger surged anew at the realization, and he continued walking. Had she taken his stream from him as well?

He entered Oak Hill through the servants' entrance and climbed the stairs to his room. He couldn't bring himself to return to the Feather. Not tonight. He fell atop his bed, not bothering to remove his boots. At Trout's plaintive gaze, he relented and allowed her on the counterpane next to him. She stretched, her head resting on his shoulder, and sighed, echoing his own resignation.

The clock on the mantle chimed the hour, and the sky outside his window began to darken. Trout shifted and moved her head from his shoulder to his chest and gazed at him with sorrowful eyes. He stroked her head, rubbing his thumb along the smooth place between her brows until her eyes began to droop.

Much later, Jory asked, "What are we to do, Trout?"

On hearing her name, the collie's ears twitched and she grinned, panting foul breath in his face. He pushed her away and rolled from the bed.

CHAPTER TWENTY-FIVE

※

ANNA RETURNED TO THE FIN and Feather and entered through the empty stable yard. Wynne looked up when she arrived, her brows raised in silent question, and Anna shook her head.

The Kimbrell gentlemen had left, and the coffee room was noticeably quieter without their presence. Belatedly, Anna realized she still wore her apron. She'd left in such a hurry she'd not taken the time to remove it.

"I kept yer tips from the Kimbrell gen'lemen," Peggy said with a look that dared argument.

"Fine," Anna said.

"Ye can't run off like that. I 'ad to finish servin' 'em, and I with me own customers as well," Peggy added defensively.

"Take them," Anna agreed. Her eyes burned, and she blinked to clear them. She eyed the stairs and thought of escaping to the privacy of her room and throwing herself across the bed. A bout of self-indulgent tears was warranted right about now, but truth be told, she'd grown tired of running.

Instead, she took a clean linen and wiped a table, busying herself with the mundane task while she held the tears at bay. When she'd risen that morning, she'd been hopeful, brimming with optimism, still fizzing from the kiss she'd shared with Jory. Now she felt raw, her insides twisting and wringing themselves into knots.

Jory wished her to leave Newford, and truly, she couldn't fault him. She'd brought him nothing but misery, after all, and her heart ached with the knowledge. But where could she go without funds? And more importantly, *how* could she leave, knowing she'd probably never see him again? How could she bear a life without Jory in it?

Despite her best intentions, a tear escaped. She sniffed and wiped her cheek.

"Miss Pepper," a voice said softly from behind her. She turned to find James watching her with sympathy, twisting his hat.

"Did you forget something?" she asked, forcing a smile.

He ignored her question. "Are you well?" he asked instead.

The words prompted new tears to pool in her

eyes, and she blinked them away, nodding. "Yes," she said, although she was certain the watery quality of her voice was unconvincing.

He pulled a slip of paper from inside his coat and grimaced before extending it to her. "Jory wished me to give you this," he said.

In hindsight, his low tone, combined with his refusal to meet her eyes, should have warned her. But instead, her heart skipped at the mere mention of Jory's name. She took the paper then frowned.

"A bank draft?"

"Aye."

"But what am I to—" She stopped as realization hit her. Jory was giving her the means to leave. He truly wished her to go. She'd heard him speak the words, but now, seeing a *bank draft*, his desire became all the clearer. She inhaled, but the breath shuddered in her chest.

James peered at her from beneath his lashes, his jaw tight. "I don't know what's passed between you," he said.

"I've hurt him," Anna said, angrily wiping her cheek. "Time and time again."

"D'you love him?" he asked.

"More than anything."

"Did you intend to hurt him?"

"No!" Her voice rose with the heat of her denial. "But intent—or lack thereof—doesn't reverse the damage. Whether I meant to drop the crock or not, it's still broken."

"Lack of intent doesn't mend the crock, you're right, but it helps to know there was no malice in the act."

"I'm not sure Jory will see the distinction."

James nodded, thinking. "My cousin is nothing if not stubborn," he said. "He can nurse a grudge better than anyone, especially if his pride's involved. But I've also seen the way he looks at you, and if that's not love . . . Well, there's no hope for the rest of us then."

Anna frowned at him. What he was saying couldn't possibly be true. He'd not heard Jory's desperate plea for her to leave. He'd not seen the look on his cousin's face as he confronted her with her past fiancés.

"Jory had a governess until he was nine," James continued, and Anna's frown deepened at the abrupt change in subject. "By that age, the rest of us had moved on to tutors, but Grandmother was in ill health even back then. Miss Miller was more like a mother to Jory than a retainer, and I think Grandfather was reluctant to separate them."

"Surely, Mr. Kimbrell was well-intentioned to keep her on. What happened?" she asked.

"Gavin, who's of an age with Jory, had left his governess the year before. When Jory defeated him at—well, I don't even recall what the challenge was now. But when Jory defeated him, Gavin responded in the way boys have done since the beginning of time. With scorn and ridicule. He chided Jory for still having a governess, in front of quite a few of our friends. Jory didn't speak to him for weeks, and I believe he told Grandfather he was too old for a governess. Miss Miller left soon after," he added with a rueful twist of his lips.

Anna's heart twisted at the image of a young Jory, sacrificing a beloved governess for the sake of his pride, but she failed to see the lesson she was meant to learn.

"Thank you for telling me the story," Anna said. "But I don't see how this is relevant to the situation today. Gavin's offense was a minor one. If Jory didn't forgive easily then, he certainly won't do so now."

"The point is, Jory will sooner cut off his leg than remove a splinter from his toe. You must convince him otherwise."

Anna looked at the bank draft as she absorbed his words. For much of her life there'd been too many doubts blowing through her mind like crisp leaves caught in a brisk autumn wind. She'd been unable to see through the swirling chaos, but now, the wind had settled.

She loved Jory, and if his cousin was to be

believed, he loved her. Wasn't everything else irrelevant?

Anna stared at the bank draft for a moment more before returning it to James, and he smiled.

JORY WISHED NOTHING MORE THAN to remain in his room, curled next to his dog, but his grandfather would learn soon enough that he'd returned to Oak Hill. He'd not hurt him by missing supper, and so he washed and descended the stairs.

The meal was a noisy affair, as several of his relations had ridden to Oak Hill to dine, as they often did. Thankfully, none of the group from the Feather were present. Jory didn't think he could bear their pitying glances.

Merryn's sister had come, however, and she'd brought Miss Parker. Jory pushed his heavy heart aside like an unwanted pea on his plate and focused on the conversation around him. He was operating on the hope that if he ignored his misery long enough, it would go away. So far, that was proving to be a flawed theory.

Miss Parker sat to his right, a constant reminder of his earlier—often neglected—intentions to forget Anna and move forward. But every time he looked at the lady . . . or spoke with her . . . or even thought of pursuing a friendship with her... a sharp stabbing sensation pierced him near his heart. When she turned to speak with one of his aunts, Jory sighed with relief and lifted his wine. When he looked up, Uncle Alfred caught his eye.

"I'm away to Bideford tomorrow," his uncle said, lifting a fork and eyeing his full plate.

This was the first Jory had heard of his uncle's travel plans, and his brows lifted. "I'm surprised you'd leave now with the new order we've had from St. Ives."

"Aye, it can't be helped. The delivery is due at the port by week's end, and Mr. Paxton's unable to make it on account of his wife's lying-in."

His uncle tucked into his fish pie, and Jory considered his words. With a heavy cart laden with ships' bells, the ride to Bideford would take two days. A journey there and back could easily stretch to four or five days. Or more.

"I'll go, Uncle," he said. Aye, time away from Newford was what he needed to gain some perspective. Perhaps Anna would have gone by the time he returned.

Uncle Alfred gazed at him, lips pressed in thought, before he relented. "Very well, if you wish to go. Meet me at the foundry at sunrise and I'll go through the order with you."

Jory excused himself early, explaining he had an

early morning of travel ahead of him. If his relations stared at him a little intently, he chose to ignore it. He couldn't, however, ignore his grandfather, who cornered him in the hall near the stairs.

"You have the look of a man fleeing the excise men, Jory."

"I'm not 'fleeing'," he said. "I'm merely retiring so I can rise early. I've a long day's journey on the morrow."

"Aye. You've an early day of fleeing ahead of you." At Jory's frowning silence, his grandfather tugged his lip for a moment, and Jory thought he might be able to make his escape. Then his grandfather lowered his voice and leaned closer.

"I saw you return home that night all those years agone, son. I know she's broken your heart before. But can you not see the love she has for you? 'Tis there, shining in her eyes, just as it was in my Evelyn's for me. If you go now, I can't help but think you'll regret it. Not just for this day, but for the rest of your days."

Jory looked down, hands on his hips. His grandfather's words echoed his own fears, but he didn't know how to proceed. How to continue risking his heart time and again, only to have it savaged.

He thought again of the other two gentlemen Anna had left, and his resolve sharpened on the edge of his anger.

"You don't know what she's done," he said.

"Is it your heart that's hurting or your pride?"

"Must it be one or the other?" Jory asked. "Can it not be both?"

"Your heart can be mended so long as you both live. The other, son, 'tis just foolishness. I don't wish to see you hurting when happiness is within your reach."

Jory stared at his grandfather. His words caused a fleeting spark of hope to fire inside him, like a firefly's glow on a dark night. But before the spark could be fanned into flame, his anger rose to extinguish it and he nodded curtly.

"Good night, Grandfather."

———

JORY ROSE BEFORE THE SUN and folded clothing into a canvas bag. After breaking his fast with hot coffee and sausages, he gathered his dog and departed for the foundry.

His uncle was already there when he arrived, and together they loaded and stacked wooden crates onto the back of his uncle's cart.

"Thank you for making the delivery," Alfred said as he slid one last crate into place.

Jory nodded, eager to put Newford behind him,

if only for a week.

"I won't pretend I haven't heard what happened at the Feather," his uncle said. "About your young lady and her troubles in London, that is. Understandably, you're upset, but are you sure you wish to go to Bideford? Ought you stay and set things aright?"

With jerky movements, Jory tightened the ropes securing the crates. When he straightened, he sighed.

"There's nothing more to be said, Uncle. Nothing to set aright."

Alfred pressed his lips together then nodded and stepped back as Jory climbed onto the seat. Jory called for Trout, who vaulted into the cart and settled next to him, eager for adventure.

He flicked the reins and drove on. As he passed the Feather, Jory kept his gaze trained ahead. He refused to think about Anna, or her reaction to the bank draft his cousin would have delivered by now. He pulled his hat lower to shade his eyes against the rising sun as Newford's high street fell away behind him.

Jory traveled away from the sea, away from the gentle estuary and bobbing fishing boats and rolling hills. As he moved inland, mines dotted the landscape, the stone towers of their engine houses dark slashes on the horizon.

He passed through St. Gluvias and Truro. The sun rose high as he climbed the steep hill out of Bodmin to the desolate moor beyond, where granite tors and the occasional shepherd's hut dotted the broad expanse. The plateau was silent save the rattle of the cart's wheels and the slow clopping of the horse's hooves on the packed road. It suited his mood perfectly.

When he reached Launceston on the far side of the moor, rolling, green pastures yielded to lavender hills in the distance. He passed the Chapple Gate toll house and slowed his pace.

The delivery wasn't due in Bideford until the end of the week, and he was in no hurry to return to Newford.

ANNA REMAINED AWAKE UNTIL THE early hours of the morning, listening at her door for Jory's return to the Feather.

With each creak of the inn's wide, wooden stairs, she peeked outside, only to sag with disappointment on finding one of the maids or another of the inn's guests.

The black sky was easing to indigo when she finally sank onto the bed and gave in to sleep. After a fitful hour, she rose, her eyes itchy and red. She dressed and stabbed pins into her hair, heedless of her puffy appearance, and hurried from the room.

"Wynne," she said as she approached the office.

Wynne looked up and narrowed her eyes at Anna's appearance. "Are you well? You're looking some whisht," she said.

Anna waved the words aside. "Have you seen Jory?" she asked.

Wynne's lips twisted, the silence heavy as she gazed at Anna. Finally, she said, "He's gone to Bideford. I heard it from Gavin, who had it from Uncle Alfred this morning."

"Bideford? Where on earth is that?"

"Devon," Wynne said.

"Devon?" Anna closed her eyes to hear herself parroting Wynne like a simpleton. She inhaled then asked, "When do you think he'll return?" How could she convince Jory not to cut off his leg if he was in Devon?

"A sennight, perhaps. He's to make a delivery to the port there. I gather it was an unexpected change of plans." Wynne's voice trailed off as she realized the implication of her words.

Anna had driven him from his home then. It was one more transgression to add to her growing list.

Her shoulders sagged until she recalled James's encouraging words from the previous day. Very well. She would wait.

She took a broom from the corner of Wynne's office and began sweeping the entry. When the floor was clean, she straightened the chairs in the private parlor.

Once they were arranged to her satisfaction, she retrieved a linen and began wiping the tables in the coffee room. Never mind that they'd been well cleaned the night before. Certainly, an extra scrubbing couldn't hurt.

―――

ON THE SECOND DAY OF his journey, Jory crossed the Tamar into Devon, and the route turned more northerly. The excitement of the adventure had worn off for Trout, and she stretched and snored at his feet.

Jory's anger evaporated on the wind, leaving him dried and spent. He missed his anger. It had been firm and supportive, holding him upright. Without it, he sagged beneath the weight of his own thoughts.

I've never given my heart to anyone but you. Anna's words wouldn't be silenced. He'd been too angry in the belfry to heed them, but now they echoed in his mind, no matter how he tried to convince himself of their insignificance.

Five years before, he'd pulled her along on the

tide of his own certainty, admitting his love for her and proposing an elopement. Now he recalled her question by the stream mere weeks ago. *How could you have loved me?* While he'd been sure of their course, she had clearly doubted his affections. And now, he found himself questioning hers.

For a man given to certainty, the very *uncertainty* of his thoughts was overwhelming. How did she bear it? With an awareness that grew stronger with each mile, her hesitation began to make sense.

Slowly, he realized her leaving five years before had been an inevitable consequence of her doubts, no matter how much he might wish otherwise. But in making his escape to Bideford, was he not guilty of the same?

What a pair they made. Was it any wonder his cousins were so amused?

Then he thought of their kiss in the belfry. *She'd* kissed *him*, rather than the other way 'round. Had she grown more certain of her feelings then?

But the larger question—the only question that mattered—was whether he was willing to risk his future happiness for the sake of his pride.

His grandfather's words were clarion clear in his mind, and the answer came to him, sure and firm: No. His pride was nothing to the possibility of a life with Anna.

But he'd told her to leave Newford. Had

instructed his cousin to provide her with the means to do so. Was it too late?

He flicked the reins, suddenly eager to complete his delivery and return home.

CHAPTER TWENTY-SIX

~~~~

OVER THE NEXT THREE DAYS, Anna watched the street beyond the inn for any sign of Jory's return, and her breath caught every time a shadow darkened the entry. Her nerves buzzed with an edgy combination of anticipation and dread, and her stomach rejected any notion of food.

To distract herself, she penned a letter to Mary Riverton, of all people. Well, four letters, to be precise. The first three landed in her fireplace grate to catch on the low flame and curl to ash. But the fourth . . . the fourth was short and to the point.

Anna wrote of how she missed their friendship and would be honored to resume their correspondence, although she understood if Mary preferred to keep her distance given Anna's recent scandal. Her knowledge about Mary's father she kept to herself. If her old friend was receptive to her overture, perhaps there would come a time to share what she knew. But for now, the act of reaching out and letting go of her anger, and the possibility of reconnecting with her friend, left her shoulders lighter.

In her anticipation for Jory's return, she lost count of the number of times she botched the Kimbrell gentlemen's orders, passing coffee to Merryn and ale to the constable, or forgetting James's newspaper. But the gentlemen merely rearranged their mugs and smiled—or in the case of Alfie, winked—while Peggy rolled her eyes at Anna's ineptitude.

They'd given up all pretense of calling her Mrs. Featherton, and it was a relief to be Miss Pepper once again.

Thankfully, none of the gentlemen asked about the report in the *Times*—about the colorful Lord G or her flight to Cornwall. That was a tale she'd not care to share any more than necessary. And certainly, the details in the *Times* sufficiently conveyed the salient points.

She refilled Gryffyn's whisky and carried it to him, glancing again toward the entry as the door opened to reveal the darkening street beyond. Then her eyes widened, and her breath stopped.

None other than the colorful Lord G himself ducked and stepped through the inn's low portal. He frowned as he glanced about the inn then, followed by Anna's maid and Mr. Gramercy, Greenvale advanced toward the coffee room.

Anna recalled the whisky in her hand and set it before Gryffyn with a thump before approaching the new arrivals.

Greenvale stopped short on seeing her, and Meg and Mr. Gramercy shuffled behind him. After a pregnant pause, Anna offered a belated curtsy.

He frowned when she rose. "What the devil are you wearing?" he asked.

It was not the first question she'd expected from him. "An apron," she said, holding the ruffled garment from her skirts.

Mr. Gramercy emerged from behind Greenvale's shoulder with a polite bow. "Miss Pepper, I received your letter, and I've come to lend my assistance. With your maid's help, I've brought your things."

She nodded in greeting. After a brief hesitation, she asked, "And how does my mother fare?"

Red stained his cheeks at the question, and he swallowed before responding. "Your mother has journeyed to the Continent. I believe she's in Italy at present." Belatedly, he added, "She sends her regards, of course."

Anna stared at him a moment longer before turning to the maid. "And Meg. How is your gentleman? Will, was it?"

Meg's brows climbed toward her hairline at

being addressed directly, and she blushed as she dipped into a curtsy. "He's well, miss. Thank you for asking."

"Anna, why don't you take your guests into the private parlor?" Wynne suggested from her elbow, reminding Anna that she and Greenvale stood in full view of the coffee room. She felt the heat of the Kimbrell gentlemen's stares behind her, and her heart pounded uncomfortably in her chest.

She was a coward and as such, she'd hoped to avoid a confrontation with Greenvale. But now that he was here, she supposed she ought to get it over with. It certainly wouldn't do for Jory to return and find her entertaining a former fiancé. She untied her apron and hung it on a peg behind the bar then led the way to the inn's private parlor.

Her legs shook, and she sank onto the nearest chair before they failed her entirely. Meg took up a position in a corner of the room and made a thorough study of the stitching on her sleeve while Mr. Gramercy shuffled a thin leather case from one hand to the other, clearly wishing he were anywhere else.

And Greenvale . . . Greenvale removed his gloves and flicked them with a snap against one palm while she waited for him to speak. Perhaps she should begin? Yes, she supposed it was the obligation of the jilter rather than the jiltee. One would think she'd have the jilting business down by now.

"Lord Greenvale," she said. "Allow me to—"

He cut her off with a haughty look as he clasped his hands behind him. "Save your explanations," he said, turning to the window. "I've no interest in hearing them. If we leave now, we can reach York by Tuesday. We'll put it about that you were called away unexpectedly to tend a sick friend. Once we're wed, that should settle the wagging tongues."

"Once we're . . ." Anna couldn't believe what she was hearing. Was he suggesting they proceed with the wedding? She opened her mouth then closed it again with a snap. Finally, she said, "Lord Greenvale, why on earth do you still wish to marry me?"

His eyes were hard as he stared at her. "Your reputation is in shreds. No one in London will receive you now. Marriage is your only option if you've any wish to salvage your good standing."

"Which again, begs the question: why do you still wish to marry me?" She enunciated slowly, curious as to why this man would desire to have anything to do with her after her treatment of him. "Certainly, you can have no great affection for me."

Greenvale pinched the bridge of his nose and paced before the window.

"Which leaves my dowry," Anna said. She'd suspected it from the beginning as he'd never professed any tender regard for her, but she was surprised at how easily she was able to acknowledge the truth. She felt neither sadness nor anger at his mercenary desires. Only relief to speak openly of them.

"Yes," he said, surprising her with his honesty. He stopped pacing and sat heavily across from her.

"Why?" she asked. "Do you have gambling debts? A mistress or two?"

He lifted his head and stared at her. She thought he'd refuse to answer, then he sighed. "My father took on considerable debts before he passed. I went to York to seek an extension of the largest of them, but it's been denied." He paused to rub his forehead with one hand. "If I don't return to settle it, I'm ruined and my mother and sisters destitute."

Anna straightened. Greenvale had sisters? And a mother? She'd always assumed he'd sprung fully grown from whichever cabbage patch produced imperious lords.

"You have sisters?" she asked.

He nodded. "Three. One still in the school room."

"And your mother?"

"Heartsick over my father's actions." He leaned back and crossed his arms over his chest.

"How much is the debt?" she asked.

"I don't think—"

"How much?" she pressed.

"Four thousand."

"And will satisfying that debt save your mother and sisters from a life of penury?"

He nodded slowly then said, "It will go a long way to doing just that. I have investments that are beginning to show promise, but they'll never have a chance to succeed if this debt is called."

Anna considered his words while the small mantle clock ticked in the silence. "Mr. Gramercy," she said without breaking eye contact with Greenvale.

"Yes, Miss Pepper?" Gramercy asked.

"Am I contractually obligated to marry Lord Greenvale?"

"No, although—"

"And is my aunt's inheritance mine to direct?"

"You're of age and as yet, unwed, Miss Pepper, so . . . yes. But—"

"Very well, then." She straightened. "Lord Greenvale, I'll not marry you. To do so would only make us both miserable, and to be honest, my heart isn't mine to give. Indeed, it hasn't been for quite some time."

His brows narrowed into a steep V at her words. He drew a breath and prepared to speak, no doubt to remind her of her ruined reputation again, but she held up a hand to forestall his words.

"I'm sorry for the trouble I've caused," she

continued, wincing at the understatement. "I never should have agreed to marry you, and for that, I offer you my most sincere apology. It was poorly done of me. But I must beg you to release me from my promise. Indeed, I would consider it a tremendous kindness on your part, and in exchange, I will settle your debt."

Greenvale stared at her. "You wish to settle my debt?"

"Yes, my heart will rest easier to know I've helped set things right for your mother and sisters. And for you. I did you an ill turn, after all. And perhaps this will give you time to find a bride who will truly make you happy."

He looked skeptical at that last bit, then he recovered, arguing, "But I can't accept your charity. It wouldn't be honorable."

"And holding me to a marriage I've no wish for... would be? My lord, you must allow me to make amends in this manner. It's hardly charity since we were betrothed after all, and it would be ungentlemanly of you to refuse. Think of it as a loan if you must, but I'll not expect repayment."

Her words were met with stunned silence. Anna rolled her shoulders, surprised at how much lighter they felt. First, her letter to Mary Riverton and now resolving matters with Greenvale. For all her avoidance of difficult things, she'd never realized how much better she'd feel for doing them.

Finally, Greenvale offered a hesitant nod of agreement.

"Mr. Gramercy," she said, and the solicitor approached. "Tomorrow, we'll visit the bank, and I will introduce you to Mr. James Kimbrell. He can assist with the"—she waved a hand airily to indicate bankerly things—"details. But for now, let's secure rooms for you."

———

ANNA DIDN'T MISS THE SUSPICIOUS look Wynne cast the incomers as they approached her desk. She waited quietly while Wynne jotted their names in the inn's register, but when Wynne turned to retrieve keys from the wall, Anna stopped her.

"*Not* room eight, I should think," she said.

Wynne halted, her hand hovering above the keys. With an annoyed twist of her lips, she selected a key from another row.

"Here you are, Lord Greenvale. Room three for you, and room six for Mr. Gramercy. Miss Pepper, I'll have a cot sent up for your maid."

Anna nodded and hid her smile, delighted at Wynne's loyalty.

She'd not had a true friend since Mary Riverton, but since coming to Cornwall, she'd felt a part of something. She felt like she *belonged*. As unfamiliar as the sensation was, she was curious how she'd got on before without it.

"Your trunks have already been taken up," Wynne added, and Anna's pleasurable thoughts were diverted to the clothing—and shoes!—that had accompanied Gramercy.

When she and Meg entered her room, Meg immediately opened her trunks and went to the wardrobe to begin unpacking. She stopped short on seeing the gowns already filling the space.

"Oh, miss, this one is lovely!" she cooed, taking down the blue-green dress and running a hand over the smooth silk.

Anna couldn't contain her broad smile, nor prevent the pleasurable flip of her stomach as she gazed at the dress. Then her smile faltered as she thought again of Jory's face as she'd stood before him in the belfry. What if he couldn't be brought around? What if her love wasn't enough?

Meg lowered the dress and looked at her with a question in her eyes.

"It's lovely," Anna agreed. "Quite the most beautiful gown I've ever seen."

Meg replaced the dress in the wardrobe and returned to the trunks. Anna shook off her doubts and asked, "Is your Will any closer to securing your hand in marriage?"

Meg blushed. "Yes, Miss Pepper. He says we can be married as soon as . . ." Her voice trailed off.

"As soon as you return from Cornwall."

"Yes, miss."

"Then why on earth are you here? You should have stayed in London," Anna said.

"Mr. Gramercy thought as how you'd need a maid to make things proper-like. And besides, who will curl your hair?" she asked as she removed a pair of curling tongs from the trunk.

"Curl my—Meg, you must return to Will. My hair will bear up," she said.

Good heavens, what was she saying? Her heart skipped a beat, and she was surprised to find her hair was not the cause. While she appreciated a perfect bouncing tress as much as the next lady, excitement over Meg's pending nuptials—over the love she shared with her Will—was causing the organ's rapid pace.

She eyed the wealth of muslin and silk filling her trunks with unexpected hesitation. So many dresses that she'd been desperate to acquire if only to make Mary Riverton envious. But none were as precious as the rainbow of assembly gowns hanging in her wardrobe.

"Meg," she said eagerly. "We must see you properly clad for your wedding."

CHAPTER TWENTY-SEVEN

~~~~~~

JORY COMPLETED HIS DELIVERY ALONG the bustling quay in Bideford, then he and Trout climbed back onto the cart.

He hesitated outside The King's Arms, then again before The Red Lion, his empty stomach arguing for ale and a stargazey pie or roasted beef. But as much as his stomach complained, it couldn't drown out the sound of his own thoughts urging him to return to Newford post-haste.

He flicked the reins, and the horse broke into a trot along the western bank of the River Torridge, the town's arched Long Bridge receding behind them.

He retraced their journey, driving south and crossing the Tamar back into Cornwall. The horse threw a shoe in Launceston, and he was forced to stop and await the farrier. By the time the horse was re-shod, darkness had fallen, and he resigned himself to a night spent at The Bell Inn.

He left Trout in the stables—against her whining objection—and found a small table in a corner of the inn's coffee room. It wasn't long before a friendly barmaid approached with an ale and a grin.

"Be ye passin' through or stayin' a bit?" she asked. She was tall and curvy, with midnight hair and eyes framed with thick, dark lashes. In other words, she was nothing like Anna. But her presence as she set the ale before him made him think of Anna nonetheless, and he wondered what she was doing. If she'd left Newford or was at this moment bringing ale to his cousins.

"Just passing through," he said.

"Ye be wantin' comp'ny after yer meal?" she asked.

"No," he said. "Just the ale and beef, please."

Her lips twisted with disappointment before she flounced away with a twist of her hips.

The barmaid's flirtation recalled the night of the hurling, and Anna's encounter with Jago Simmons and the disrespectful southern team. His fist tightened, and he was torn between wishing she was still in Newford and wishing her far from the Feather. He knew his cousins would care for her, but he couldn't ease the urgency to be home. To assure himself she was well.

Later, with his belly full and the horse rested, he

changed his mind about a room and collected Trout from the stables. She bounced on seeing him, as if he'd been gone a sennight rather than an hour. Within minutes, they were on the road again, traveling across the rough moorland by the light of a brilliant full moon.

The moor, stark and raw by day's light, possessed an eerie beauty in the dark of night. A thick, hazy swath of stars split the sky, and if he weren't so anxious to reach Newford, he might have enjoyed the sharp shadows and chalky highlights the moon cast upon the ink-black tors. But as it was, all he could think on was Anna.

He rested the horse again on the far side of the moor and tried to nap in the back of the cart, Trout curled into his side. Her soft snores whistled in his ear while the sounds of night echoed around them.

He waited for sleep that didn't come while he plotted and strategized what he'd do if Anna had left Newford. He'd have to go after her, as he should have done five years before. It was that simple.

Why had he told her to leave, again? He couldn't imagine a lifetime without her. He'd just have to make her see it as well.

An orange halo rimmed the horizon as he crested the hill above Truro, the sun mere inches from breaching the line between night and day.

Some hours later, the familiar clusters of white cottages dotting the edge of the sea greeted him, and he entered the top of Newford's high street. He spied his cousin outside the bank and pulled the cart to the side.

"James," he greeted as he looped the reins around one hand.

His cousin looked up then approached the cart, resting his forearm on the wooden edge.

"You've returned," he said.

Was that censure in his cousin's tone? If so, Jory counted it no less than he deserved for haring off to Bideford. "Is—is it done then?" he asked.

"Did I give her the draft, d'you mean?"

"Aye." Jory swallowed. Of course, James had done as he'd asked. His cousins were nothing if not dependable.

"I gave her the draft," James said. "It was precisely what you asked of me, after all." He pressed his lips and stared at Jory, accusation in his eyes.

Jory eyed the reins looped around his hand and clenched his fist more tightly, watching the leather tighten. It was done then. She'd left. Again.

"The lady returned the draft, though," James said, watching him.

Jory stilled, then his heart skipped to hear his cousin's words. He looked up. "She did?"

"Aye."

Warmth started in his chest and spread to his fingertips. She'd returned the draft. She hadn't left then. But why was James casting such a hard stare in his direction?

"D'you remember when we were lads and Gavin teased you about having a governess?"

Jory frowned at his cousin's change of topic. What did Miss Miller have to do with anything? "Aye," he said slowly.

"You were daft then, and you're daft now," his cousin said, apropos of nothing. "The lady's solicitor arrived from London. It seems she has her own funds and has no need for yours."

Jory's heart thumped heavily, the blood slowing in his veins, and the warmth of moments ago left him. He sensed his cousin wasn't finished, though.

"And," his cousin said, confirming his thoughts, "he's brought a fitty gentleman with him. I met them this morning. The man has the look of a fiancé about him."

"What are you saying?" Jory asked.

"I don't think I could be any clearer, Jory. Your lady's intended has arrived. Lord Greenvale. You'd best act quickly."

The blood that had moments ago slowed now rushed through Jory's ears. *Your lady's intended has arrived.*

She'd jilted the man once before. Did this

Greenvale think she'd change her mind? *Would* she change her mind?

Jory stared at James, and Trout shifted and whined at his side. His cousin lifted his brows, waiting. Frowning, Jory loosened the reins from his fist then flicked them against the horse's back. The cart lurched into motion, and James stepped back with a smile.

CHAPTER TWENTY-EIGHT

JORY PULLED THE CART INTO the stable yard at The Fin and Feather to find four horses hitched to a glossy black carriage. He frowned at the gold crest painted on the door, at the velvet curtains covering glassed windows.

He quickly set the brake on the cart then handed the reins to one of Mr. Malvern's ostlers and climbed down.

A gentleman exited the inn and approached the coach. Attired in buff trousers, a precisely tailored coat and beaver hat, this could be none other than Anna's fitty Lord Greenvale. He spied Jory and hesitated, no doubt put off by the scowl facing him.

A motion at the carriage window caught Jory's attention, and he turned to see a flash of pink beyond the curtain before it settled back into place.

Anna. She was leaving with Greenvale.

His tongue felt thick in his mouth, and time

slowed around him. He'd asked her to leave. Anna was only doing as he'd requested, his brain insisted.

His heart, however, refused to believe it. She wouldn't leave. Not with Greenvale. Not after the kiss they'd shared in the belfry. Not after the emotion he'd felt in her touch. But his heart, he reminded himself, had been wrong about her before.

He stared at the carriage, recalling the day five years before when he'd stood silent in the trees outside Penhale and watched her leave.

Not this time.

He reached the carriage before a surprised Greenvale and pulled the door open.

"Here now," Greenvale said from behind him as Jory peered into the coach. An older gentleman stared back, eyes wide, and a maid squeaked from her seat next to the window. A maid wearing a pink dress. They watched him uncertainly, waiting.

His head now satisfied with what his heart had been telling him, Jory nodded briefly. "My apologies," he said.

Greenvale frowned as Jory withdrew from the coach. Jory waited while the man climbed in, then he firmly closed the door and motioned to the coachman. With relief, he watched the conveyance lumber out of the stable yard, narrowly clearing the arched entry.

"Jory," Anna whispered from behind him.

JORY TURNED TO FACE HER, and Anna didn't think she'd ever seen anything as dear as his face. Golden whiskers roughened his cheeks, and his eyes were red from his travels. But his was a face she'd never tire of seeing, especially if he continued to gaze at her as he was now.

"Anna." His whisper was rough, and it scraped her spine with a shiver. "You didn't leave."

"No." Was he pleased? She rather thought he might be.

A horn blared, announcing the arrival of the stagecoach, and they both jumped. Anna reached for Jory's hand and pulled him toward the inn. She wound through the entry, past Wynne's grinning face, holding his hand firmly in hers.

At the coffee room, Peggy approached. "Jory," she said with a flirtatious smile and entirely too much familiarity. "Can I get ye an ale?"

Anna tugged on his hand and glared at Peggy.

"No, thank you, Peggy," he said with a chuckle, and Anna tugged harder.

They passed the window table where several of his cousins were gathered. Anna's face heated as they stared silently at her leading their cousin through the inn. When they reached the private parlor, Anna peeked inside, relieved to find it empty. She pulled him in and closed the door.

Now that she faced him, she was uncertain where to begin. She twisted her hands together while he waited. Opened her mouth then closed it again.

"Anna," he said, taking one of her hands and rubbing his thumb across the top. "Stop thinking. Say what's in your heart."

His words with his gentle, rolling Rs, soothed her riotous thoughts much as his thumb soothed the restlessness in her hands.

"I love you, Jory Tremayne."

His thumb stilled at her blunt confession, but he didn't interrupt.

"I think I always have," she said. "Ever since our first encounter by the stream. My heart knew the truth long before my head did. I tried to find happiness apart from you, but each time, my heart and my head were at war with one another. My head told me to marry Signor Rossi"—she paused at the frown on his face then forged on—"but my heart wouldn't let me. Then my head told me to marry Greenvale"—Jory's frown deepened—"but again, my heart wouldn't permit it. If only I had listened to my heart five years ago, then we wouldn't be where we are today."

He stared at her, silent, his hand warm on hers.

"Now would be a good time to say something," she said.

"And where are we today, Anna? What is it you wish?" His thumb resumed its slow motion across the top of her hand.

She hesitated then plunged ahead. "I wish to know if you still hold an affection for me. I wish to know if you can ever forgive me. And I wish to know if—" she stopped, her cheeks growing warm again.

"Aye, lass?"

"I wish to know if you'll marry me."

———

Jory's hand stilled on Anna's, and blood thundered in his ears. Had he heard her properly? Her delicate brows angled in worry as she gazed up at him. Judging by her anxious expectation, he thought perhaps he *had* heard correctly. But just to be certain . . .

"You wish to wed?" he asked.

She nodded.

Then, to clarify, he said, "You wish to wed *me*?"

Her lips thinned in irritation, but she nodded again.

"Then, aye. To all of your questions. I still hold an affection for you. I never stopped loving you, despite my best efforts. And there's nothing to forgive, lass. I rushed you when you weren't ready to love. My own love for you was so loud, I didn't stop to listen, to see if you were in the same place. And aye, I'll marry ye—thank you for asking."

Her smile, which had started when he began speaking, widened even further, and he lifted his hand to rub his thumb over her dimple.

"But now that I have you on my hook, I'll not give you a chance to escape," he warned, dropping his hand to hold both of hers.

"I'm not going anywhere," she assured him earnestly.

"Still, I'll not take the chance." Keeping his eyes on hers, he raised his voice slightly and called out, "Come in, gentlemen."

Not a beat passed before the door opened on his cousins' eager faces. He delighted in the blush that stained Anna's neck when she realized the private parlor wasn't as private as one might reasonably assume.

"They saw you dragging me about like Trout with a bone. You had to know they'd not let their curiosity go unanswered," he whispered.

She swallowed and nodded, fighting a smile.

He raised his voice so his cousins could hear and repeated, "So aye, lass, I'll marry you. We'll do a proper job of it later, but for now, I need you to say the words."

"What do you mean?" she asked.

"Here, before witnesses, say the words, Anna. 'I, Anna Pepper, take thee . . .'"

Her eyes widened, then she smiled. "I, Anna Pepper, take thee, Jory Tremayne . . ."

EPILOGUE

HURLING DAY, ONE YEAR LATER

"Look!" Wynne said, pointing. "Roddie's won!" Anna and Wynne craned their necks to watch the raucous crowd of gentlemen approaching from the end of the street. And indeed, there was Mr. Teague atop the shoulders of his teammates. Anna scanned the crowd and quickly found Jory, Trout trotting along beside him.

"Hurry," Wynne said. "Let's go below to meet them." She raced off, her rounded belly lending her a slight wobble as she left Anna behind.

Anna moved to follow at a much slower pace, her own girth having grown much beyond what she would have believed possible. Indeed, she feared her width was about to outpace her height, but Jory didn't seem to mind.

She reached the entrance to the inn and found Wynne bouncing on her toes. Presently, the crowd of celebrating gentlemen reached them, and Jory headed directly toward her. She smiled in response to his grin then covered a gasp with both hands when she spied an angry scrape on one cheek. One of his sleeves was torn, his knuckles were bruised, and green stains marred his trousers where he'd been flattened into the grass by the opposing team.

He reached her and without a word of greeting swooped down to capture her lips beneath his. She gripped his shirt in both hands, reveling in his heat.

He stroked her cheeks with his thumbs as his lips moved over hers, and she breathed him in, marveling yet again that he was hers. That soon they'd be a family of three. Tears threatened, and she squeezed her eyes tight. Eventually, he pulled his lips from hers, and the hot July air was a cool balm to her skin.

"I thought kisses were for the winner," she said, pulling a leaf from his hair when she could find her voice.

He touched his forehead to hers and whispered, "Who says I haven't won?" His cousins joined him then, and Jory pulled away.

"Anna," Alfie said with a wink. "You look more lovely every day. Any sign of . . ?" His voice trailed off and he waved a hand in the direction of her belly.

"No, Alfie," she said with a smile. "You'll have to wait a bit longer to settle your bet."

"Don't forget I'm counting on a lass," he said. "You won't let me down, will you?"

Jory cuffed his cousin on the back of the head, and Anna laughed. "I'll try my best," she said. "But don't expect any news for a while yet. This baby needs to wait at least another week. We wouldn't want to miss the bell dedication."

She smiled up at Jory. He and Merryn were nearly finished installing the new church bells, and a dedication ceremony was planned for the following week. It was expected to be a festive event, with a grand picnic on the town green to celebrate the first time in fifty years that all eight bells would ring.

"And your mother wouldn't wish to miss the birth," Jory added.

Anna's smile faltered. Shortly after she and Jory had exchanged their vows—the ones in the parish church, not his cousin's inn—her mother had written of her own nuptials.

Anna had been surprised as she'd not expected her mother to remarry after her father's passing. Her surprise, however, was nothing compared to the shock of learning her mother had married none other than Signor Rossi, a man ten years her junior.

But thoughts of her mother's marriage weren't what caused her smile to fade now.

She gazed about her, at the life she'd built in Cornwall, and her mother's imagined criticisms rang loudly in her head. Certainly, the life she'd found was not the polished existence her mother had intended for her, but it was the life of her heart, and she couldn't bear to subject it to her mother's disapproval.

Then she recalled the letter she'd just received from Mary Riverton. They'd been corresponding for the past year, and Mary promised to visit at the end of the London season. Anna's smile firmed on the thought of seeing her friend again.

THAT EVENING, ANNA WAS SURPRISED to receive another letter from Italy. Her mother wrote that she wouldn't make the journey to Cornwall for her grandchild's birth after all, her social obligations in Italy being what they were. It seemed Signor Rossi's business interests required careful nurturing of his connections. Anna handed the letter to Jory and exhaled slowly.

Jory read the short missive then said, "I'm sorry, lass. You must be disappointed."

Anna closed her eyes briefly to concentrate on what she was feeling. "Disappointed," she repeated, testing the emotion. "Mildly so. Resigned, yes. But mostly . . . relieved." She opened her eyes.

Jory gazed at her in confusion. He'd never met her mother, and he couldn't quite understand why a lady wouldn't desire her mother's counsel during her lying-in.

"I wish my mother happiness in her new life," Anna explained, rolling her shoulders. "I've accepted that while she may *nurture* Signor Rossi's social connections, she has never been, nor will she ever be, a nurturing mother. It's simply not her way. But I've found family here." She lifted his hand and kissed his bruised knuckles. "I have everything I need."

THE FINAL BELL HAD BEEN hoisted into position and the last of the pulleys removed from the bell tower. Merryn's firm had rebuilt the belfry floor, but Jory hadn't been able to forget the luncheon he'd shared with Anna on the previous floor's dusty planks.

Merryn had quirked an eyebrow at him when he'd requested the old floorboards, then his cousin's gaze had cleared when Jory asked him to recommend a carpenter. Preferably one skilled in crafting benches. He couldn't have his wife and child sitting on the cold bank of the stream when winter came.

"I have to say," Merryn began, "I'm excited to hear the full peal."

"'Twill be magnificent," Jory said, looking up and mentally caressing the smooth bronze curve of the tenor bell. It had taken quite some time to perfect the bell's pitch, but he was pleased.

"'Tis hard to say which babe you're most enamored of," Merryn said, following his gaze. "The one that's yet to come, or that one."

Jory frowned at him. "Clearly the one that's yet to come."

Merryn held up his hands in surrender. "I know, but 'tis an enjoyable pastime to tweak you, cousin."

"You'll have your time, never fear. You'll find a lass of your own that makes your eyes cross and curdles your stomach like pilchards that have gone off." Jory smiled at the thought, eager to do his own tweaking.

Merryn laughed. "Don't be daft, cousin. No lady will have me, and besides, what man in his right mind would wish for such a fate?"

"No man wishes for it, cousin, but mark me. 'Twill be worth the pain for the right lass."

OAK HILL, ONE WEEK LATER

"D'YOU WISH ME TO BAR your husband from the room?" Wynne asked on a whisper.

Anna laughed at the image of Wynne forcibly ejecting Jory from her side. They were well matched in force of will, but she thought Jory might best his cousin in sheer strength.

"Not yet," she said before inhaling on another pain. "He's merely anxious." She looked to where he paced before the fireplace. At her glance—indeed, at the slightest movement—he hurried to her side.

"Tain't proper," Wynne said with a frown.

"Give over, Wynne," Jory said, brushing his cousin's concerns aside. "I'm certain you'll want Roddie beside you when your time comes."

"There are some things that should remain a mystery," Wynne said, waving a hand over Anna's belly beneath the linen. "And this is one of them."

"Jory," Anna said, forestalling any further discussion. "Are you sure you don't want to go to the dedication ceremony? You really shouldn't miss it after you've worked so hard to complete the bells."

He looked affronted that she would ask. "My child's about to arrive, and you ask if I'd rather be elsewhere?"

"No," she said. "What was I thinking?" She placed a hand on his whisker-roughened cheek. He lifted his own hand and covered hers, his palm warm on her cool fingers.

"And I'd never leave you," he whispered. "Are you sure you don't want me to tell Wynne to go?" She laughed then winced on a pain.

Two hours later, their daughter arrived—healthy, red and wrinkled—to the sound of her father's bells ringing a full peal over Newford and the surrounding valley.

THE END

Want more of Wynne and Roddie's story?
Subscribe and receive a FREE copy of
Discovering Wynne at
https://www.klynsmithauthor.com/
books/discovering-wynne

Don't miss the next in the Hearts of Cornwall series. Gryffyn meets his match in Matching Miss Moon.

BOOKS BY K. LYN SMITH

Something Wonderful
The Astronomer's Obsession
The Footman's Tale (A Sweet Regency Short Story)*
The Artist's Redemption
The Physician's Dilemma

Hearts of Cornwall
Discovering Wynne (Prequel)*
Jilting Jory
Matching Miss Moon

Holiday Tales
Star of Wonder

* Subscribe at klynsmithauthor.com
to receive these and other free bonuses!

ABOUT THE AUTHOR

K. Lyn Smith lives in Birmingham, Alabama with her real-life swoony hero. When she's not reading or writing, you can find her with family, traveling and watching period dramas. And space documentaries. Weird, right?

Visit www.klynsmithauthor.com, where you can subscribe for new release updates and access to exclusive bonus content.

Made in the USA
Columbia, SC
23 March 2023